LOST IN THE WOODS

An Urban Fantasy Fairy Tale

DEBORAH WILDE

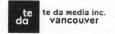

te da media inc.
vancouver

Book Cover Design by Croco Designs

Issued in print and electronic formats.

ISBN: 978-1-998888-13-9 (EPUB)

ISBN: 978-1-998888-14-6 (paperback)

Chapter 1

Einstein said that insanity was "doing the same thing over and over again and expecting different results." Having my entire professional career dictated by the scientific method, with its controlled constants and carefully adjusted variables, I was no stranger to that way of thinking. I was as likely to re-run an experiment the exact same way and expect my outcome to change as I was to click my heels together three times and say "There's no place like Perrault" to achieve my desired hypothesis.

That said, perhaps it was better to be slightly insane.

Or perhaps I already was, because here I sat, Ubering through the Toronto streets during a record snowfall to accuse my former lab colleague, Dr. Carol Shaw, of sabotage. This was the same woman who, more often than not, had at least one writing implement tucked into her frizzy hair and forgotten about, and was famous for her long-standing record of most wall crashes in our chair races down Perrault Biotech's hallowed corridors.

The idea that she'd screwed with my scientific research by inserting wolf DNA into my rapid regeneration burn serum on behalf of a shadowy venture capital group called

Golden Radial was, in the words of the great Vizzini in *The Princess Bride*, inconceivable.

Yet, despite that, the immunologist was the likeliest suspect. Carol had proximity to my lab to steal the vial with my serum, doctor it, and return it. She also had the genetic know-how to splice wolf stem cells together with my heat shock protein. She wasn't a Weaver, but she was still a level four Hothead, a fire elemental with decades of experience studying the combination of magic and science.

So here I was, paying surge pricing to confront the world's most baffling villain.

We were halfway across town now, and my impatience at our slow progress was choking me, but at least each rollover of the Uber's odometer brought me one click closer to answers.

I looked out the window, clocking more familiar landmarks. Carol had hosted a BBQ for the staff last summer, and I'd fallen in love with her home in the central Toronto neighborhood known as Cabbagetown. The area had a small village feel to it, the homes mostly semi-detached Victorians or charming brick row housing. It looked like something out of a period film.

Kids sledded in Riverdale Park West, shaking off flakes as they trudged up the hill dragging bright plastic sleighs, while snow on the roofs and eaves of jewel-like townhomes sat like icing on gingerbread houses.

The driver dropped me off in front of Carol's place, and I crunched through the unshoveled walkway, my breath coming out in white puffs and my nose already going numb.

Extracting answers without arousing her suspicions would be tricky, but once I did? I touched my chai pendant for good luck. Moving forward with my life and my work depended on this meeting.

I rapped on the front door, the knock keeping time with my heart pounding against my ribs.

Carol cracked it open, keeping the security chain on, her eyes growing more owlish behind her round spectacles. "Raisa? Goodness, what brings you here in this storm?" She tucked a curl behind her ear, exposing an orange crayon snagged in her locks like a fish in a net.

I repressed a relieved grin. The conclusions that led me here had to be wrong, but maybe she could point me down a better path.

"Sorry to drop in on you. I phoned yesterday but there was no answer." I kept my voice casual and light, but with a hint of urgency underneath. My posture was relaxed, and I propped one hip out, mirroring what I could see of my colleague's stance to create rapport. I'd researched the hell out of the science of lying last night. "I know it's kind of abrupt, but I've got a job interview Monday and I've been really worried about it. I was hoping I could get your thoughts in person. Career advice."

This was a lie, a pretty massive one. There'd been few places willing to even interview me when Perrault Biotech's reputation was so tainted. And by tainted I meant that Dr. Richard Woodsman, our lab director, had blown up the place and corrupted specific backup data—including mine —which was stored off-site, on the night the cops barged in to arrest him for money laundering. After that, it was hard to list the lab on my résumé without getting a lot of pointed questions about my ethics.

"You came out in the worst storm we've had all season," Carol repeated, brow furrowed, "to ask me career advice?"

"Yes," I said with what I hoped was youthful vigor. "I wanted your insights."

Carol shooed me into her foyer, closing the door against the harsh wind. "But your burn research! You were always so passionate about that. Why would you make a career shift?"

"After everything that went down, I don't have much of a choice." I sighed heavily.

Twelve years ago, when I was seventeen, I'd promised my identical twin sister, Robyn, to "make history." I'd thrown myself into that vow, honing my magic and earning a PhD in chemical genetics, where I began my research into rapid regeneration.

I'd dubbed the serum I was working on Red Carpet, both because I imagined it unfurling through the body like a red carpet, but also because rolling out the red carpet was to give someone a special treatment. I wanted my formula to make burn victims feel like rock stars, recovering like ballers, a far cry from the slow, painful teeter back and forth between okay and very not okay. I didn't want anyone else to hurt like Robyn had, for the hospital to assure some other family that this really was the best they could do.

Nothing could bring my best friend and wombmate back. I knew that. Was this my way of imbuing her death with meaning? You didn't need a psych degree to answer that. But I'd like to think that she'd be proud that she still got to make a difference in the world, long after she left it.

Carol locked the door. "It would be a shame to abandon all that work."

Frowning, I toed off a boot. Why? Because she believed in my serum or because she had a vested interest in it after she added the stem cells?

"What else can I do?" I placed my boots on the tray, snow already melting off their soles. "All my data is gone, and no one is interested in taking on work that was started at Perrault."

"Did you have any physical samples you could analyze to re-create the data so you don't have to switch your focus?"

Sure, if I'd pinned Gideon Stern down and stolen his blood after I first injected him when the serum was live in his veins or taken numerous tissue and bone marrow samples later to obtain a clear picture of what had been done to my research.

4

However, Carol didn't know about Gideon. More importantly, Golden Radial had no idea he was the living embodiment of their ambitions, and I intended to keep it that way.

I stuffed my scarf and gloves in my jacket pockets. "There was one sample, but it was destroyed in the fire."

"That's such a shame." She clucked her tongue and shook her head. With her frizzy hair, she resembled a distressed baby chick.

"Tell me about it."

Carol led me into the living room. Oh, goody. She had a dog. The animal was asleep on one of the two sofas. It was large and sandy-colored, with a sad, saggy face.

I eyed it warily. I didn't like big dogs at the best of times, but especially not when I'd gained entry under false pretenses. Amazingly, there wasn't a trace of dog hair on the carpet. Carol probably had to spend half her life vacuuming up after that beast—and the other half dusting the dozens of fake tropical plants in brass stands. Wow. That was quite the commitment to plastic florals.

I took the chair farthest away from the dog and closest to the front door, ready and willing to flee into the snow in my socks if it kept me from being drooled on should the pet awaken.

After I declined Carol's offer of hot chocolate, she perched on the edge of the smaller couch. "Are you looking to go into HIV research?"

"Not exactly." I folded my hands in my lap. If she was innocent, I had to keep my questions vague enough that she wouldn't have concrete information should anyone interrogate her. That would keep Carol safe if she wasn't Golden Radial's minion, and me safe if she was. "I always felt a kinship between our areas of expertise. I tried to instantly alleviate pain and suffering from burns, and you were looking at one-shot immunology treatments to overcome

HIV. Both of us are trying to establish fast pathways to massive life-changing healing."

I waited for her face to light up with the look of someone about to go into excruciating detail about their project. An expression I may have worn a time or two (or always, whenever anyone was unwise enough to ask about it), but Carol just smiled. It was pleasant, but it wasn't the unhinged obsessive grin I was used to seeing from my colleagues when invited to launch into the minutiae of their work.

"Are you interested in working with stem cells?" she said.

I suppressed a shiver. I'd worked with modified heat proteins, and Carol's research involved a lot more than stem cells, so why jump to that question? "There are exciting new possibilities in that area, but the background reading I'd have to do to even begin to explore them would be immense. It'd be a very different concentration than what I've focused on so far."

"Stem cell research is such a good fit with your Weaver magic," she enthused.

Her face radiated with the fervent gleam I'd expected earlier, and my heart sank. Carol wasn't passionate about her own work; she was passionate about enticing me to do Golden Radial's bidding. There was no two ways about this. Looks like this didn't lie.

A wave of nausea rolled over me. "Could I use your bathroom?" I said faintly.

"Of course. Down the hall, second door on the left."

I got out of there without throwing up. Once at the bathroom sink, I splashed cold water on my face and blotted it off with a towel while I stared at my reflection in the mirror.

The last time I'd seen my mentor, Woody had given me a flash drive with my data and his notes on wolf DNA. He'd experimented with it to enhance human characteristics including strength, speed, heightened senses, and, for the final shot in the werewolf-creating cocktail, enhanced muscle mass.

His research had been top secret, undertaken at the behest of a venture capital firm called Golden Radial, over years and a series of tiny asks—all for the good of humanity of course—that had ended with Woody laundering money for them and nuking the lab.

Dig into Golden Radial and they were as advertised.

Would a reputable venture capital firm provide funding for medical research? Sure. It wasn't weird for them to have invested in Perrault Biotech when patents could yield big dividends.

Would a reputable firm have directed said research into the illegal creation of supernatural beings in private trials in Switzerland where the records were tightly sealed?

Not in a million years.

That's why despite pressure from Golden Radial to further his research, Woody had, instead, tried to destroy all the data in spectacular fashion.

Sadly, the officer in charge of the money laundering investigation, Inspector Gideon Stern, had almost died in the lab fire that Woody set. I'd used the single physical manifestation of my serum to save him, but whoops! I'd turned him into the world's first wolf shifter. Though that was very hush-hush and not going on my résumé.

Who said the sciences weren't exciting?

I replaced the towel on the bar.

Despite Carol being a powerful fire elemental, I'd assessed the risks before I came over and determined I had nothing to fear. The weeks following the lab's destruction had been a wild ride to find Woody and a backup of my data so I could fulfill a deathbed promise to my twin.

However, with each passing day since I'd retrieved my research, I grew more confident that the fiction of it being destroyed in the fire held firm. I didn't feel like dangerous people were watching me anymore.

As for Carol herself, not only was she forty pounds lighter than me, but she was also the type of person who took spiders outside rather than step on them. I was even surprised she had such a big dog. She'd probably faint if it ever brought her a dead animal or anything, but knowing her, her pet had probably been a senior animal who'd lived years at the shelter. She was just that kind of person.

Apparently, she was also the kind of person to betray a colleague.

I pinched my cheeks to get some color into them and returned to the living room, prepared to obtain a detailed analysis of what she'd done to my serum and the name of who had given the order, before hailing another hilariously overpriced Uber.

Except the living room wasn't as I remembered it.

I did a double take.

There was no longer a dog on the sofa.

I blinked. Once. Twice.

The plants were on the ground, their stands overturned and the meticulously dusted pots smashed to smithereens. Blood dripped onto the coffee table and down the skirt of the sofa, plopping in cruelly cheerful drops on the ground.

Carol's lifeless eyes stared back at me, her body exactly where the dog had been. Her tan sweater was slashed to ribbons and splattered in blood like a paint-by-numbers picture with only one color. The violence of the scene was shocking.

Personal.

A distant logical slice of my brain whirred through my fog of horror. She couldn't have been killed while I was in the bathroom, could she? No. This wouldn't have happened in silence or in the couple of minutes I was in there.

I stuffed my fist in my mouth to stifle a scream. If Carol

had been dead this entire time, then who had I been talking to?

Was the killer still here, hiding and watching me?

I spun around on leaden legs, my shoulders tight and high, expecting the killer's breath to tickle the back of my neck and their fingers to ghost across my back, but the room was empty.

Boots thudded up the front stairs. "Police!" The cops banged on the door demanding entrance.

Thank God. I just had to make it to the front door, and I'd be safe.

Unless they were in on it? I froze, my heart slamming against my ribs. I hadn't told anyone I was coming over.

I had to get out of here. Get somewhere safe and call for help.

The front door shuddered with the sound of a body thudding against it.

I grabbed my boots and jacket, planning to run out the back door.

Little did I know that instead of listening to Einstein, I should have been taking advice from the world's foremost traveler and survivor of many a dark path: Doctor Who.

The door crashed open, wood splinters flying, and a female cop raced inside with her gun pointed at me. "On your knees!"

Geronimo.

Chapter 2

Two days earlier with nary a dead body in sight...

Red and green Christmas lights strung along the ledges of the tower across the street shone in through Dr. Nakahara's office window, festively tinting the rush of falling snowflakes. The scientist had warmed up the bland space in this university hospital building with a richly colored landscape by a local Toronto artist, while her celebrated career as a microbiologist and immunologist was evident in her crowded bookshelves and framed awards.

Even though she wasn't Nefesh like me, a person who possessed magic, the Mundane cancer research expert had worked with the intersection of magic and science in her field for decades. My hope was that she would put Red Carpet under the auspices of her well-funded and well-documented research and away from anyone seeking to continue perverting my serum's uses and create more wolf shifters.

Not that I could tell her that part.

She'd been excited to help me, however, she'd insisted on determining the serum's viability before she got approval or publicly mentioned it.

That made sense, and I had my own reasons for agreeing

to keep it secret a bit longer, namely our safety. Golden Radial could not get wind of our talks before our position was bulletproof. Literally.

However, *a bit longer* was not supposed to mean two months since the Marrakesh debacle, with endless conversations about the viability of my rapid regeneration serum while we ran and re-ran my digital simulation. One without wolf stem cells coded into it, since even if I had the know-how to add the sequence digitally, the point was to make a furry-free version of the serum work.

I should have taken up knitting before spending all this unpaid time sitting in the office watching the screen, and made myself some new footwear. I knit magic into people, how hard could a pair of socks be?

For those of us working with magic and science, clinical trials on people were forbidden until the digital results could be flawlessly replicated, at which point they were scrutinized and approved by a special governing body. I'd have given my left kidney to present my work to them because my entire interaction with Dr. Nakahara, while not exactly an exercise in Einstein's insanity, was coming pretty damn close.

I swiveled my chair from side to side, calculating the odds of Dr. Nakahara jumping out of her ergonomic marvel at the end of this latest simulation and yell, "Eureka! It worked!"

They were not in my favor.

She scratched a hand through her short silver hair, the glow from the large monitor on her desk casting a bluish tint over her dark copper skin. "I congratulate you, Dr. Monte-fiore, I really do. You've achieved the perfect balance of Weaver magic and science with your Hsp60 heat shock protein. Your serum heals all burn-related wounds, whether in the internal organs, muscles, or bone. You'd spare people the trauma of multiple skin-grafting surgeries, even lung damage or death from smoke inhalation. All this would happen in mere minutes without surgical intervention. It's astounding. However..."

"No one wants a burn treatment, no matter how miraculous, if the trade-off is rapid terminal cancer," I said quietly.

She tapped a key and Pumpkin Spice, my virtual 3D lab subject, stopped spinning, reduced to nothing more than a dark outline.

Watching my baby hang lifeless against a black void made my throat grow thick and my chest tighten. I'd gone through hell to rescue Pumpkin Spice.

My shoulders slumped. I'd spent years refining this serum to be administered on-site. The tumors that the serum induced in the digital simulations were the final stumbling block, yet I'd been certain that Dr. Nakahara would have a solution to take my work to the next important stage.

"Maybe if the tumors showed up in a single spot in the body," she said, "we could, with time, find a way to combat their sudden and explosive growth. But this cancer is unpredictable and doesn't present in the same manner twice."

If we'd run the same experiment, gotten the same results, and expected something to be different, we'd be the insane ones, but this was worse because no matter what variable we changed up, the end was the same: yay! No burn injuries, but boo! Spontaneous lethal tumors.

I gnawed on the inside of my cheek. "There's no way to nuke the turbo cancer, is there?"

"Is that the technical term?" One side of Dr. Nakahara's mouth quirked up as she pointed with a 2B pencil at the screen. "But to answer your question, there isn't. The issue is encoded into the heart of your serum. Since it magically knits into the body at a cellular level, you can't expect cells to regenerate at the amplified speed required for the burn injuries, while *not* exhibiting an out-of-control cellular division."

"Is using another protein as a damping switch to attack the cancerous tumors totally off the table?"

"Unfortunately, yes," she said. "It was an inspired idea, but I've examined it from every angle and coded all the best protein candidates into your formula." Her statement gave me hope because she wouldn't have put all that time and work into this if she didn't think something would come of it. "There's nothing that will work fast enough to whack-a-mole the tumors out of existence."

Well, that dashed that.

"That's the technical term, is it?" Despite my defeated posture, I gave her a wry smile. Okay, I was down, but not out. Time for my Hail Mary pass—or whatever the Jewish equivalent was. A chai score? I scratched my chin, hoping my next idea sounded off-the-cuff and not carefully rehearsed. "What if we took an entirely different route?"

Dr. Nakahara sat back in her chair and crossed one denim-clad leg over the other, gesturing for me to continue.

"Use induced pluripotent stem cells to create a vaccine. Approach the problem of the tumors from a preventative rather than a reactive basis. Vaccines are the new frontier in cancer research."

Dr. Nakahara shook her head. "There's room to make new ideas work, yes, but most people, even at a very desperate time in their lives, aren't willing to take that kind of a risk. They want more certainty in their treatments. As a result, there's less interest in funding those cures."

I held up a hand. "Hear me out. Please. Studies done over a hundred years ago reported that transplanted tumors were rejected in animals immunized with embryonic tissue. The vaccine in those tissues allowed for cellular immunity against transplantable and carcinogen-induced tumors."

"That was a controlled experiment with a specific type of transplanted tumor. Your serum induces multiple cancers in multiple sites of the body. It's a far more complex problem."

"I know, but carcinogens increase the risk of cancer," I said, "because they damage cellular metabolism or damage DNA in cells. Right?"

"Correct."

"Consider my serum a carcinogen and tell me if it's possible to tackle the tumors it produces with induced pluripotent stem cells that were enhanced in the lab for a boosted immune system. A vaccine with a short-term intense impact that would be injected right before the burn-healing serum."

The wolf DNA added to my serum had exceptional regenerative abilities thanks to its stem cells. It had been powerful enough to counteract the cancers brought on by my original formula.

Too bad it turned the one person I'd given it to into the world's first healthy wolf shifter. Golden Radial had, up to that point, managed to produce only mangled hybrids, but I'd pulled off the real thing. A perfect specimen.

I'd be proud of that except for the fact that Gideon Stern was a tool. A cancer-free tool, mind you, but Stern didn't exactly look on the bright side when it came to occasionally becoming a wolf.

I had to stop these tumors from occurring *without* creating another wolf shifter, hence the idea I'd been tossing around: amp the immune system on a short-term basis. Just long enough for the serum to heal the patient without inducing tumors.

Dr. Nakahara pursed her lips in thought.

I touched my chai pendant.

Science was at the point where we could take a simple gene from an animal and graft it into a human. For example, we could take the gene that made jellyfish glow and give ourselves a cool party trick under black lights. However, anything more complex involved entire systems with multiple cells addressing various functions. Graft all those into us and our system would attack and kill them.

Unless…

They had a magic delivery system knitting them in at top speed at the cellular level.

That's where my serum came in. After years of trial and error, I'd landed on an edited protein derived from the Hsp60 gene as the best partner for my magic. Proteins were incredible large complex molecules that did the heavy lifting in cells. Without them, our tissues and organs wouldn't have structure, function, or the ability to regulate.

I magically knit the heat protein into the fabric of the affected cells to achieve accelerated wound healing throughout the body—in the digital model at least. I had no doubt the serum would work on a person. I just had to crack this final, admittedly huge, tumor-shaped obstacle.

"Theoretically, it's possible." Dr. Nakahara jolted me out of my thoughts.

"Okay." I sat up a bit straighter.

Her office landline rang, and she reached for the receiver. "Sorry. One moment. Hello?"

I turned away to give her some privacy, schooling my frustrated grimace into a placid smile.

Humans had two types of stem cells, embryonic and adult. Embryonic ones were naturally pluripotent, meaning they could become any kind of cell: liver, blood, brain, etc. Their versatility made them perfect for repairing and regenerating damaged organs and diseased tissues, but their source, embryos, made the ethics of using these cells a hotly debated topic.

Adult stem cells weren't pluripotent, so an adult stem cell from, for example, blood vessels, would regenerate only the same kind of cells. However, they could be modified, reprogrammed in a lab, to become pluripotent.

The trouble was, I didn't know if the stem cells that had

been added to Gideon's dose of my serum were embryonic or adult. Had they been modified to become pluripotent or were they specific adult stem cells with only one regeneration outcome? Had a scientific process or a magic one been used?

It wasn't like stem cells could be dumped into the physical serum either.

Woody didn't even know the stem cells had been added successfully to my serum until I told him about it. Had *he* intended to place the wolf stem cells into the sole physical sample of my cure at some point? All he'd said was that he would never have handed it over to the bad guys, which I believed. He wouldn't have blown up the lab that he'd sacrificed his entire life for if he meant to give Golden Radial my work and carry on.

Would he have added them at some point to satisfy his scientific curiosity and *then* destroy all traces?

He claimed not, but the jury was still out.

Regardless, I was convinced of his innocence in this matter. He wasn't the one who doctored my sample. When the cops showed up that night to arrest him for money laundering, Woody wasn't at the lab, but he wasn't far away either.

My friend and the lab's office manager, Ella Fortose, told me that Woody had read the texts she'd sent him about the police arriving with a warrant. He could have easily returned, gotten into my lab, and stolen the vial with my physical serum; instead, he'd burned it all down.

I suppressed a shiver. Woody could protest that he'd been careful, but the fact remained that it was a miracle no one had been killed.

However, it's not like there were tons of people on the short list. Perrault Biotech wasn't a huge corporation.

One of my colleagues knew how to use wolf stem cells to prevent the tumors. Once I, too, had that knowledge, I'd extrapolate a way to create the short-term immune system booster, pair it up with the serum, then Bob's your uncle.

No burns, no cancer, and, best of all, no more wolf shifters.

So, who had doctored my work?

Dr. Nakahara hung up the receiver. "A rescheduled budget meeting. The good times never end. But to get back to your idea."

"Yes. I was thinking about how there are mammals like whales, elephants, even bats who are cancer resistant. If we used their stem cells—"

"Dr. Montefiore." She shook her head, her tone impatient but not unkind. "You have the kind of mind that I'd love to have on my team, and this is worth pursuing. I would love to see an on-site application for burn wounds, and removing the need for painful grafting surgeries and the loss of life due to smoke inhalation would be revolutionary."

I held back my excitement like riot police running crowd control. "But…?"

"I simply don't have the resources to go down this road. It would have been one thing to bring your burn serum into official channels, if we solved the problem of the tumor growth, since the serum itself is already viable and ready for clinical trials, but what you're proposing might take decades. If it's ever achievable at all."

My dream felt as impossible to achieve as traversing the entire board of Snakes and Ladders in a single turn. I'd been so certain of my path for so long, an open book with a single narrative of fulfilling my promise to my sister.

Now I kept dangerous secrets from friends, colleagues, and the world at large about shifters, and the one person I longed to speak to refused to have anything to do with me because I'd ruined his life.

I took a deep breath and sat up. All it took was one answer to set me back on the right road to keeping my promise. "I firmly believe that my mastery and understanding of Weaver magic, along with my chemical genetics background, is exactly what's needed to team up with the immunologists here and create an intense immune system amplification," I said. "One that would not only work in conjunction with my serum to prevent lethal tumors but have huge ramifications for the future of cancer research."

Dr. Nakahara leaned back in her chair and stared up at the ceiling, the seconds crawling by at a glacial pace.

"I was the only one to bring a rapid regeneration serum into existence for burn victims," I said insistently, "and I'm certain that I can do the same for this particular shot."

Provided I found that damn scientist who'd inserted the wolf DNA and got some answers. I notched my chin up a bit more. One thing at a time.

"My thinking has gotten too inside the box lately." She exhaled, looking at her pockmarked lab ceiling tiles and fluorescent lights. Something quirked at the edge of her mouth, then she nodded. "It's time to shake things up again."

My heart fluttered in my throat like a butterfly had taken up residence in my esophagus. Which sounded poetic and uplifting until you remembered that human hearts are the size of our fists. I was choking on anticipation. "You mean…?"

"You start Thursday, January 4."

Today was December 21. I had two weeks to find the scientist and get answers, but I'd do it. I might not achieve my dream of being in human clinical trials by thirty, but my work was still moving forward. I was still honoring Robyn.

Dr. Nakahara unmounted my flash drive and handed it over. I'd been careful during all our meetings to make sure I retained the only copy of my information. "We'll announce your position after the holidays," she said.

"No mention of the serum though, right?"

Luckily, she took my terse tone of voice for disappointment, and not unease.

Dr. Nakahara patted my arm. "Not yet. Best not to tip our hand before all the official paperwork clears." She winked at me. "Once we have your background checks complete and your paperwork all submitted, it'll be too hard to get rid of you. Trust me."

This was actually happening. My cheeks tingled with a hot flush and my eyes prickled with tears. Dr. Nakahara had my back. Both me and my work would be in good hands with her.

Make history, Red. The voice I heard wasn't my sister's, but Gideon's raspy growl. I shook it off. It didn't matter who said it. I was, indeed, going to make history.

Dr. Nakahara stood up and extended a hand. "Welcome to the team."

I shook it with a smile that I didn't have to fake. "I can't wait."

Chapter 3

"Don't give up your day job." Ella gamely swallowed her bite of lemon biscotto, setting the misshapen treat on the unchipped plate that was reserved for guests.

"Especially when I just got mine yesterday."

I was still getting used to this version of my friend, a sixty-something who wore jeans and sweaters (still somehow more elegant than any I owned), instead of ironed silk blouses and tasteful skirts. Despite our age difference, the two of us had clicked, and during our time as colleagues, we'd gone for lunch on a semi-regular basis. I'd also visited her in the hospital when she was healing from the injuries that she'd received the night of the fire.

I poked the cookie on my saucer. The ribbon of raw dough really made the burned edges pop. "That said, I won't audition for *The Great Canadian Baking Show* in my spare time."

My nonna's recipe had seemed easy enough to follow when my cousin, Levi Montefiore, texted it to me. I wasn't sure how I'd gone so wrong, and I wouldn't be responding to his requests for photos of how they turned out until I'd visited an Italian bakery and artfully plated their product.

Golden boy did everything well, including bake. Levi wouldn't gloat, *necessarily*, but why give him the ammo? Baking was basically chemistry. Chemistry was a science. How was I supposed to know that my favorite thing would betray me so epically?

Ella pushed a polished lock of dark brown hair behind her ear and picked up her steaming mug of tea, cradling it between her hands. Damn, her cuticles looked so soft and supple.

I folded my jagged, cracked disasters into my palms and out of view.

"I'm thrilled about your new job." She blew on the tea. "And statistically, the chances of working at two labs that explode are infinitesimal, so it bodes well for job security."

"Your optimism is wasted in retirement." I spooned my tea bag out of my mug and dumped it with a splat next to the inedible biscotto. "You should take up life coaching."

The radiant heater in my living room made banging noises as it turned on. Since heat rose, my fifth-floor apartment was usually warm without having to often use my heater, even with thin windows, but it had been colder than usual this December here in Toronto. In addition to the snowfall, we'd had freezing rain and daytime temperatures inching into the minus teens Celsius.

Ella shuddered. "No, thank you. I'm done mothering people to help them get shit done. Present company excepted."

"Nice save," I said wryly.

She winked at me.

When I returned to Toronto after my visit to Vancouver to see Levi, Ella and I tried to arrange a coffee date, but this was the first time she'd been free, given her busy retirement schedule. It was nice to just hang out.

"Did you book that Caribbean cruise yet?" I said.

"Just working out the details with my friend. What

about you? Did you talk to your mom about moving in with her or is that off the table now that you're employed?"

"I could, but that would mean more time for her to hound me about working in her security firm. Like I spent all those years getting my PhD to weave wards for shady rich people and soulless corporations."

"Sadly, help often comes with strings," Ella said. "Especially with mothers."

I saluted her with my mug. "I'd rather lie down in the middle of the 401 and let eighteen-wheelers crush the life out of me than live with Mom."

"Dr. Raisa Montefiore," Ella teased, "always with a plan."

Like now. I felt guilty inviting my friend here under the false pretenses of celebrating my hire, but I couldn't be honest with her. The people who'd been looking for Woody after the lab explosion had magic and guns.

I rubbed the goose bumps that broke out over my arms. If Gideon hadn't taken the bullet intended for me...

Yeah, well, Gideon Stern, injured ex-cop, erstwhile partner, and reluctant wolf shifter, had also abandoned me that night in Morocco.

It was pretty easy for him to ghost me, since he'd holed up in Hedon, the magical alternate reality ruled by the Queen of Hearts and Moran, her decapitation-happy second-in-command.

I'd sent Gideon one text about a month ago. It's not like Moran had any authority over me, and for all his bluster over the Black Heart Rule, Ash had assured me that a simple direct message from here on earth wouldn't violate it.

Seconds later, I received a message from an unknown number. There were no words, just an image of a heart and a scepter: the Queen's personal logo.

I hadn't gotten truly close to anyone since my sister's death. Hell, my Red Carpet serum, my life's work and the single physical embodiment of my deathbed promise to my twin, lived in Gideon's blood. How was I supposed to let all that go?

I'd typed two choice words in response, then deleted it all with an angry sigh.

Since then, I'd heard through the grapevine that Gideon had healed nicely, but that was the extent of the updates. Whether he was still in Hedon or off doing business here on earth for the Queen remained a mystery, but I doubted she'd released him from their bargain where he'd offered his police experience and shifter abilities in exchange for her permission to search for Woody in her realm.

Focus, Raisa. I unclenched my jaw and, returning fully to the present, sipped my grocery store brand—and frankly far below mediocre—orange pekoe. No fancy name brands until I turned my financial situation around. My bank account was down to single digits and the unemployment benefits I'd finally been approved for barely covered rent and ramen.

I studied Ella speculatively through my lashes. I'd met with Dr. Nakahara yesterday. If Ella could help me with this one hurdle, I'd have the rest of the winter break to analyze the wolf stem cells.

"There's a caveat to this job." I balanced my mug on my knee. "With my research gone, I'm switching my area of focus."

"You're giving up your promise to Robyn?" Ella leaned forward, her brow creased with worry.

I nodded, hoping she read my blush as shame that I'd failed my sister and not that I was lying about the demise of my life's work. Half lie. White lie?

"Is there really no way to re-create your data?" she said.

"I could replicate the magic process, but the chemical formula was refined so many times over the years and was so complex and specific that I can't conjure it out of memory. Believe me, I've tried." Was a full-body sigh too much? Too

23

late. "I plan to stay in the broader field of chemical genetics because I'm not masochistic enough to throw away a PhD that I'm still paying off, but the thought of starting fresh with the serum after all that's happened is disheartening." My voice cracked on that last word.

"That's understandable." She patted my hand, her movement making my 1970s secondhand floral couch creak.

"Plus, it wasn't an option. Dr. Nakahara's focus is cancer research. It's okay. There are other ways for me to benefit humanity. We tossed around some ideas, and I was drawn to preventing muscle loss in cancer patients."

Ella frowned. "Since when are you interested in muscle mass?"

"The bigger, the better, baby." I leered at her theatrically and she snickered. "But seriously, my preschool teacher died from muscular dystrophy. Robyn and I adored her, and Woody conducted research into enhancing muscle mass. It wouldn't be an illogical next step."

For years, Woody provided data for Golden Radial–funded experimental trials in Switzerland. On the surface, both Woody's research on muscle mass (not a secret) and these trials to cure muscular dystrophy (private but not secret) were important, given that a key symptom of the disease was progressive muscle weakness.

Yeah, well, surface was all it was. Those conducting the trials had taken desperate people seeking medical help for a debilitating disease and turned them into mangled and deformed (obviously very secret) wolf shifter prototypes.

Those who'd survived, that is.

I suppressed a shudder at the memory of the poor man stuck in a monstrous human-wolf halfway state who'd attacked us in Morocco. I pray he'd been the last of this kind.

"Why would you want to follow in Woody's footsteps?"

I blinked at Ella's harsh tone.

"It's his fault you lost your data." She brushed her hand over her ankle that had been operated on. "And I can now predict when it's going to rain."

"Woody believed in me," I said hotly. "He believed in all of us."

"He broke the law and disappeared, leaving me as the one the police focused on for the money laundering when I had no idea…" A muscle ticked in her jaw. "Forgive me if I don't share your belief in his character."

"I get it." I rubbed my hand over my chin. "But I'm trying to put the pieces of my life back together and I have to start somewhere."

"Well, don't start with him. He's vanished and any muscle mass research he was involved in wrapped up before I came aboard." Ella had started at the lab less than three years ago, only six or so months before I had, and while Woody remained in hiding, as far as I knew, he was safe.

Needles fell off the replacement cactus which sat on my crooked IKEA bookshelf. I rose, swept them up with my hand, and deposited them into the small trash can by my desk with a scowl. How did I keep killing desert plants? "It's still an interesting field."

"I appreciate that you're grieving the loss of your research and your promise to Robyn, but this is your chance for a clean break from everything related to Perrault Biotech. Why not find an entirely new focus?" She shook her head sadly. "You can't keep trying to fix the world because of people you've lost. It's not healthy."

"Maybe not, but humor me. Please? Were any of the other scientists at Perrault involved in similar research? They might have some advice, and as the newbie on this team, I'd appreciate any words of wisdom."

She was silent for a long time.

I stared through the lacy pattern of ice on the outside of my single-pane window to the gloomy Toronto afternoon, glad that I didn't have to brave the cold and slush. Though that would mean I had a life instead of chasing dreams where I had to lie to friends and put off giving Levi an answer about moving to Vancouver to be closer to him.

Huh. I guess with my new job I had a concrete reason to tell him that wasn't happening. I rubbed the wistful ache in my chest.

It's okay. I'd still fly out for his wedding on Valentine's Day. I'd been surprised they'd chosen that date, but the Canadian press was all over the idea of the handsome House Head getting married on the day devoted to corporate manufactured love.

Though they didn't exactly phrase it that way.

The wedding promised to be a lavish affair with hundreds of guests, including House leaders from around the world and even some celebrities. It felt totally out of character, especially for Ash, but Levi had an image to maintain, and she accepted that.

"Alexei," Ella said.

"Huh? Sorry. I zoned out. What about him?"

"When I started, he was at the tail end of a study on muscle hypertrophy."

My heart sank. "He's not a geneticist."

Even if the wolf stem cells hadn't been altered before being added to Red Carpet, whichever scientist was involved required the expertise to graft the DNA both correctly and relatively quickly. Not only was the gene-splicing equipment popular, there was only a single physical sample of the serum and a limited quantity of wolf DNA so the person had only one shot.

Alexei didn't have the know-how.

Ella stood up and stretched. "Sorry, kiddo. That's all I've got."

I told her I'd deal with the mugs and walked her to the door, waiting as she bundled up to brave the weather.

"Wait." She rummaged in her bag and pulled out her phone. "Help me with one clue."

I crossed my arms. "Since I won't get Oreos or a title if I solve it, what's in it for me?"

Ella was famous at the lab for her cookie rewards when any employee correctly solved a cryptic crossword clue. There had been fierce competition to be the Helper Brain of the month and get our picture pinned to the corkboard in the lunchroom.

My heart twinged. Those days were gone for good.

She laughed. "You'll always be my favorite Helper Brain, but your reward will now be me still speaking to you after that abomination of a cookie you pawned off on me."

"Fair. Hit me."

She showed me the clue. *Al and Mo get into rows.* Two words. Eight and five letters.

The trick with Ella's beloved cryptics was to not get sucked in by the obvious. "Rows" could mean fighting, but it could also mean a line of things. However, two people did not constitute a row of individuals. I rolled my eyes. "Al and Mo. Aluminum and molybdenum. Periodic table."

"Look at that," Ella said, typing it in. "It fits."

"Which you knew all along." I wagged a finger at her. "That was a pity clue."

"A cheer-up 'because you're smart and you've got this' clue."

"I like that better."

We hugged.

"Enjoy your downtime before the new job starts," she said. "Maybe we can do New Year's brunch."

"Yes, please." I shut the door and tidied up, debating whether I had the energy to phone Alexei now. He was a nice enough man, but he droned on and was about as exciting as racking pipette tips.

I sighed. I couldn't afford to dismiss any source of information, and the sooner I had all the data on these stem cells, the better.

I grabbed my laptop and dug up the PDF of the Perrault Biotech employee contact sheet, hoping that his info was still current. It was, but unfortunately, Alexei wasn't much help because he'd been studying muscle mass through the lens of exercise.

I learned everything about that lens over the next ten minutes during his vigorous monologue. I glazed over around the three-minute mark—somewhere between blood flow restriction and diabetes—but no matter how I tried to extricate myself, including breaking a glass and scolding an imaginary cat for projectile vomiting, Alexei wouldn't shut up.

I threw myself on the sofa, resigned to this as penance for lying to Ella when he said something that made me sit up. "Repeat that?"

"Heat can damage cells. See, what happens is—"

"I'm well aware of the effects of heat on cells, Alexei," I said tersely. "I'm a chemical geneticist who literally weaves infrared and red light into cells, remember?" Even light that I couldn't see with the naked eye I could sense. I could manipulate light with a higher Kelvin count, like blue light or sunlight as well, but handling the wide spectrum was tougher for me. I was more apt to lose control. "What did you say about heat shock proteins?"

"Don't you work with them?" he said doubtfully.

I expelled a long, slow breath. "Yes, but why was Carol working with them in your trial?" Not only was Dr. Carol Shaw a fire elemental and an immunologist researching ways to boost the body's immune system to combat HIV, but her lab had also been next door to mine. "She's an HIV expert."

"True," Alexei said, "that's what she's dedicated most of her career to, but back when Woody and I were first discussing this study, he proposed bringing in a number of colleagues to widen its vision. More brains were better than one. That type of thing. Woody insisted there was a lot of merit in studying muscle mass." I'll bet he did, especially with Golden Radial pulling the strings. "Carol investigated the correlation between muscle mass and the immune system in conjunction with my hypotrophy work." Alexei paused as if weighing whether or not to break a confidence. "Her mother had MS, you see."

A lot of people confused multiple sclerosis and muscular dystrophy, even though they were very different diseases and attacked the body in different ways. However, they had some similar symptoms, including atrophied muscles.

I white-knuckled the phone. Who's to say Golden Radial hadn't conducted trials for MS with the research Woody—or another of their fundees—had provided? Legit trials, even? If Carol believed that the rapid regeneration properties in my serum held a cure for the disease that afflicted her mom, she'd stay one hundred percent loyal to Golden Radial and whatever bullshit they'd fed her to mess with it in the first place.

I smacked the cushions. "Stai scherzando!"

Alexei coughed. "Excuse me?"

"I've got to go. Thanks so much for your help." I rushed through the goodbye so he couldn't wax rhapsodic about compound exercises again and hung up.

My call to Carol went directly to voice mail, and I didn't leave a message, since the best offensive was a sneaky one. It was better to show up and determine her guilt firsthand rather than give her time to prepare a lie, so I got up bright and early the next day to confront her at home.

The snow was coming down hard on Saturday morning, and not trusting my shitty snow tires, I bundled up, pulled on my winter boots, and called an Uber.

The best thing about being unemployed, beyond cutting down the need to do laundry and riding the constant anxious buzz of watching my meager savings wither away, was that it gave me time to think. As a PhD student, I'd been an elite in the sport before. Now I'd reached Olympic medalist levels of achievement.

Between wondering where Woody had ended up after his mic-drop goodbye in Marrakesh, and creating various plans—some more bloodthirsty than others—about what I'd do to Gideon Stern should we meet again, I was blessed with a veritable plethora of things to brood about.

My favorite subject by far, however, involved how the hell my serum had been corrupted. There hadn't been a large window of opportunity. The physical sample had existed for only about ten days before the night from hell.

I waited in the lobby of my building, peering out through the fogged-up glass door for my ride.

Woody and I had been certain that no one outside the two of us was aware of the physical sample, but that wasn't true. My assistant, Julian, was, and he was friendly enough with Carol that if she'd come into my office while he was checking on the vial, he wouldn't have hidden it from her. Why should he? He wouldn't have gone into detail about the project, but she was familiar with the broad strokes of my work, just as I was with hers.

Carol had been away on vacation when the cops showed up with their warrants and Woody destroyed the lab. At the time, I'd considered it a blessing; now I wondered if she'd deliberately removed herself from the scene.

I checked the model and license of the car that pulled up, then hurried out into the snow and bitingly cold wind, racing for the warmth of the vehicle.

If Carol was responsible, either she hadn't left town and had added the wolf DNA sometime during those ten days, or she had left town and taken care of it beforehand. That part didn't matter.

What did matter was that she knew Julian and I were

prepping to run something past Woody. After months of revisions, we'd been frantically adjusting the coding on the damping switch that we hoped would stop the tumors. Should it work and the serum remain tumor-free, Woody would consent to me contacting Dr. Nakahara, who'd help make the successful tumor-suppressing protein cell a reality.

Woody finally consented to the meeting on that fateful day and had gone off for one of his doctor-sanctioned walks for his blood pressure. I'd spent a couple hours trying to track the cancer scientist down before Ella raced in with news of the warrant and the money laundering.

I hadn't discussed Dr. Nakahara with Carol, but if she was working for Golden Radial, they might have had that information, because someone high up in that group had a solid science background that they weren't disclosing.

Someone I doubted was listed on the company profiles on the website.

Golden Radial's cover was so tight that not even Levi, as Head of House Pacifica, which governed Canada's largest geographic magic community, or Ash, an accomplished private investigator, had been able to crack it.

But Carol might be the crowbar we needed.

All of which brought me to this moment. The Uber pulled up to Carol's house, and I knocked on the door.

Chapter 4

***Present day in Dr. Carol Shaw's foyer with cops and
nowhere to run...***

"On your knees!" The female officer glanced into the
living room at Carol's body, then back to me, her lips
pressed into a thin line, her jaw set, and her eyes hard.

I dropped to the ground, barely feeling my shins whack
the tiles. Whatever the officer said next was lost to the
thumping of my heart, and I couldn't get my throat to work
properly to swallow.

The barrel of the gun seemed to expand and distort to a
cartoonishly grotesque size.

"Planning on going somewhere in a hurry?" the cop said,
nodding at the boots and jacket I held.

Another officer joined us, his fingers crackling with elec-
tricity. He edged along the wall into the living room.
"Clear."

The female cop stayed with me while her partner
checked the main floor and the upstairs.

He returned, shaking his head. "No one's here, and the
back door is chained from the inside."

Their stares lasered in on me.

"Where's the murder weapon?" the male officer said.

"Mu-murder?" I gave a shrill laugh. "I didn't kill anyone."

"This woman stabbed *herself* multiple times?"

"She was like this when I got here. She was like this the whole time." At their twin looks of disgust, I backpedaled. "I mean, I didn't sit around watching a corpse." Except I had. I gagged hard. "There was a dog."

"No evidence of pet bowls or animal hair," the man said.

"That's because it wasn't really here. It was Carol the entire time." I went to scrub a hand over my face, because with every word I was digging my own grave deeper, but the female officer's hand tightened on the gun. I dropped my arm to my side. "Rigor mortis has set in across her entire body, which means she's been dead for more than two hours. I only got here twenty minutes ago. You can check my Uber record."

I'd made some spending money during university a few times playing a patient for the Faculty of Medicine. Their students had to diagnose and appropriately respond based on the issue that the "patient" presented to them. One time I'd been a corpse. I'd learned all kinds of cool things.

"Unless you killed her earlier and came back," the female cop said.

"And pay surge pricing twice?" I joked. It landed like a lead balloon.

"We'll see." The man picked up my purse from the post at the bottom of the banister and fished out my wallet. "Depending on time of death and your alibi."

Cold seeped up through my damp jeans and my teeth were chattering.

"Raisa Montefiore." He frowned at my driver's license. "You any relation to Levi Montefiore at House Pacifica?"

"He's my cousin," I said dully.

"Fuck," he muttered.

"That doesn't matter," the other cop said. "She won't get away with this just because she's related to some big shot." She holstered the gun, pulled out a set of handcuffs, and strode quickly toward me. She seized my wrists and snapped on nulling cuffs, looking me straight in the eye with a clear warning. *Don't try anything funny.*

I'm not sure what she expected with my hands bound and my magic flatlined.

"Raisa Montefiore, you're under arrest for the murder of Carol Shaw," she said.

I certainly hadn't killed Carol. But someone had.

And they wanted me to take the fall.

Chapter 5

The officers led me to the car, rattling off my rights under the Canadian Charter of Rights and Freedoms, but their words blurred together.

I wasn't crazy. I hadn't imagined that dog or talking to Carol, which meant someone had imagined it for me.

A talented Illusionist had altered my reality. They must have fled when the cops arrived, otherwise, why not Houdini up evidence of a dog to make my story even less believable?

I rubbed the skin under the cuffs. Had they murdered Carol, or was the Illusionist (the proper term for a Houdini), yet another pawn sent in after the fact? And why murder the scientist at all? Had she refused to continue helping Golden Radial or was she simply a loose end that needed to be tied up?

The ride to the precinct was a noxious blur, the faint odor of sweat and aftershave mixing with a hint of tobacco and the oil from the cruiser. It was also silent. So silent.

I started babbling, filling the air with anything that popped into my head, as much to wake myself from this nightmare as protest my innocence. "I'm the last person who'd murder someone. I came to see my former coworker for job advice. *In the sciences.* Killing her would be more of a mobster résumé builder. I mean, I've seen the movies and I could never put a horse head in someone's bed."

The male officer glared at me through the partition, and I shut up for the rest of the drive.

Endless viewings of *Law & Order* had not prepared me for Canadian murder charges. I descended into a Kafkaesque blur of being brought from the cruiser into the station and locked up— still cuffed and without my powers—in an interrogation room. I should have felt something, right? The cuffs digging into my wrists, or the sweat trailing between my shoulder blades, but I didn't.

I didn't feel anything at all.

The worst part, though, was that I couldn't stop replaying the moment I saw Carol's bloodied corpse. I was barely able to rouse myself from my stupor to demand a phone call.

The cops had confiscated my cell phone when they did a cursory search of my bag and person. I didn't know the names of any lawyers, much less have the money to hire them, but it wouldn't have mattered if I did.

Cold logic had pierced my shocked haze, allowing me to put the pieces together.

Either Alexei had ratted me out, or, more likely, when I called Carol, one of our phones was bugged and it set off an alarm somewhere up a chain. Someone must also have been tracking my movements because whomever was behind this had helpfully tipped off the cops. How else would the police have shown up at that precise moment?

Spending years buried in a lab didn't leave me with a lot of time to collect enemies who had the manpower and reach to pull off something like this, ergo, Golden Radial was behind it. That meant an ordinary lawyer would be useless in foiling any plot to shut me up for good.

Like Golden Radial had done to Carol.

A tendril of rage took root, turning into a bud, then a tree, then a whole freaking forest. These psychopaths had killed my colleague and magically illusioned her as a fucking dog. Had the Houdini gotten some twisted thrill pretending to be her? Had the killer, if it wasn't the Illusionist, held the knife they'd stabbed Carol with while I was offered hot chocolate? Did they hold it by my neck, ready to drive the point into my jugular if their plans went sideways?

Should I get myself alone with them, I wouldn't require my magic to exact vengeance. I itched to tear that individual apart, see their eyes bulge and feel their heartbeat slip away as I dismantled them down to their tiniest atom.

When I was finally granted my call, I used it judiciously and phoned the one person with the power to assist me. Screw Golden Radial if they thought they had me trapped and helpless. I wasn't alone. My hand tightened on the land-line receiver. Unless they meant for me to bring him into this?

Levi answered, and maybe it was selfish of me, but I couldn't be sorry I'd called him. Besides, it was one thing for Golden Radial to strike at me, and quite another to take aim at the head of a magic community.

My cousin's warm greeting turned to a fraught silence while I relayed the events leading to my murder charge, and then to a dangerous promise that he'd take care of it. The old me would have begged him to be circumspect and not do anything that could jeopardize my serum going into human clinical trials and my promise to Robyn being fulfilled.

But I couldn't find that version of myself.

My sister had told me to "make history," and I'd internalized that to mean producing a rapid regeneration burn serum.

Maybe making history meant taking down the puppet master at Golden Radial. I hadn't developed my serum to become famous. So what if the general public never learned of Golden Radial's agenda or that I was the one to thwart it? I'd know that in stopping them, I left the world better than I found it. I'd have saved countless others from pain and misery, which was all I ever wanted anyway.

Whoever was calling the shots had ended the career of my mentor, Dr. Richard Woodsman, one of the finest people and most brilliant minds in his field. That person put my promise to my dying twin in jeopardy and perverted my life's work. They caused me to ruin Gideon Stern's life instead of save it.

Now they'd brutally murdered Carol for her role in this tragedy. She'd deserved my anger—not a brutal end.

However, the person in the shadows at Golden Radial didn't care about human life. Whether this was all about profit or scientific curiosity, they were a monster and they had to be stopped.

Woody had been right to try, but it had been too little too late.

"Get me out of here as soon as possible," I said evenly to Levi, my anger snuggled around me like a favorite blanket. "Then we're going to destroy this motherfucker."

He laughed darkly. "It'll be my pleasure. Hold tight, Red."

The line went dead.

I no longer flinched at the nickname everyone had used when Robyn was still alive, though only Levi had the right to use it now.

I was led back to the interrogation room to wait. Golden Radial hadn't meant for me to take the fall. They could have easily planted evidence definitively linking me to the murder were that the case. This was a warning. Perhaps it was also an exploration to see how much I knew and what data I still possessed. I ran and re-ran through my conversation with

Carol's imposter. Nothing implied my knowledge of wolf shifters or that I still had my research.

I drummed my fingers on the table. The phone call to Levi had literally been my get-out-of-jail-free card. My one chance to walk away for good.

But where would that leave me? Abandoning my promise? Burying myself in research that was banal enough not to ever catch their interest? I had no doubt they'd be watching me for some time to come.

I rested my forehead against the table. In my mind's eye, Carol's face was replaced by Dr. Nakahara's. How could I take this job?

How could I not?

It wasn't just about my serum, though for twelve years, Red Carpet had been my passion and my solace, my path out of the darkness, and I wasn't going to stray from it now.

Carol was gone, though, and with her went any answers about the integration of the wolf stem cells into my serum. Without that information I no longer had a starting point for the immune system booster. I wanted to scream and kick things over, but everything was bolted tight.

I was cuffed and locked up, yet I refused to be beaten. I was part of Dr. Nakahara's team now, and one way or another, my serum would become viable. I'd make sure of it.

But until I brought down the person behind this, I'd never get my life back.

My involvement with Golden Radial was already decades long, though I didn't know that until recently. The trials they conducted, which initially produced those crude shifter prototypes, were the same ones that my preschool teacher, Miss Toby, was invited to participate in.

The price of her entry ticket? Handing over twin sisters in her care to an Eastern European woman who'd experimented on them. Yeah, recovering that buried memory had been near the top of the suck-ass hit list of events since the night of the fire.

My gut said the Eastern European woman who'd experimented on Robyn and me as toddlers was the key to everything: Miss Toby going into that demented trial, Woody being pressured to work on wolf shifters, my serum being fucked with, the B&E of my apartment after the lab burned down, and now Carol's murder.

My tormentor wasn't another puppet. No, judging from the evidence I'd accumulated (which was a surprisingly large amount, considering how stealthy Golden Radial was), she was the one pulling the strings.

I couldn't keep referring to her in such opaque terms. She was the Eastern European woman who had haunted my and my twin's dreams. She was the Big Bad, my personal nemesis.

Then lightning struck.

When Robyn and I were kids, Mom gave us a set of books with fairy tales from around the world. One of my sister's favorites was about the old witch, Baba Yaga, who ate people. That part freaked me out, but I loved that she lived in the forest in a hut perched on top of chicken legs that could stand up and turn around.

I imagined braining this Eastern European woman with a chicken bone. I doth pronounce thee, Baba Yaga.

She was the spider at the center of a web that had been drawing me closer for years. It wasn't even the good kind of web where I'd get some positive press in those sticky strands like "some pig" and the classic "terrific."

However, she wasn't going to wrap me tighter and tighter until she devoured me. Not so long as I had breath in my body, because old Raisa was gone, scattered like ash.

I wasn't reborn like a phoenix in a glorious blaze of fire. No, this new self was forged in the same darkness that had led me to this moment.

Smart. Logical. Laser-focused. I embraced my best quali-
ties. Any emotion that didn't serve my goal got jettisoned
like trash. I had less than two weeks to find Baba Yaga and
still start my job, at which point I'd have to do the background check. With Baba Yaga out of my life, Levi could
make the fake arrest go away, and all would be well.

The cops decided they'd been holding off long enough
and walked into the room to question me, but Levi had
made good on his word. Janna Favreau, a blonde lawyer
with a sharklike smile, entered, declared that she worked for
House Ontario, was now my counsel, and told me not to say
a word.

I was registered with that House as Nefesh in accordance
with federal law. Legal aid was one of the trade-offs for
complying with legally documenting my magic and paying
taxes toward House resources, protection, and education.

The last was important because it ensured that all
students in countries where magic was legal studied Nefesh
history. Here in Canada, it happened in grade eight social
studies. Ten men supposedly descended from each of the
Lost Tribes of Israel banded together in the 1600s as devout
believers of Kabbalah, an ancient Jewish mystical approach
to studying the Torah.

Their ultimate aim was to achieve the fifth and highest
plane of the soul, Yechida, by bringing magic into the world,
rather than spend years studying to get there. Let me tell you
as someone with years of academia under her belt, I was
both unsurprised things did not go as planned with this
shortcut, and also empathetic to the lure of cutting to the
chase and knowing stuff already.

While the ten men did acquire magic, they also released
it into the world at large, leading to many other people
suddenly possessing extraordinary powers. Those abilities
didn't embody the Kabbalistic principle of Yechida either,
but that of Nefesh, the entry level, animal part of the soul,

steeped in impulses, basic human drives, and pleasure principles.

We Nefesh were born with our powers, one type per person. Well, all except for Ash, but she was quite the exception.

I was a Weaver, thus I couldn't also be a Hothead, someone with fire magic. Every type of Nefesh had only generalized, blobby abilities at birth. When I was three, I was able to create a light shield that didn't do much, which was good since I had no control at that point.

Our talents were honed during childhood and rooted in psychological primal drives, though I suspected nurture had as much to do as nature. What type of Weaver might I have been if I hadn't undergone experiments as a toddler?

I'd never know.

After hearing my story, including that a Houdini was involved either as the killer themselves or as an accessory, and that Carol was also Nefesh, my lawyer informed the police that this was a sensitive case involving House security. Therefore, House Ontario was invoking their legal right to bring it under House auspices to investigate.

Why hadn't I called House Ontario when I was arrested? Why waste my one phone call on the receptionist at the counsel office when I could directly phone the Head of another House and get things happening faster?

Finally, and most important for me, since there was no murder weapon, my prints were not on the body, nor was there blood on my clothes, or any other actual proof to hold me as a suspect, Janna demanded my immediate release.

She was a total boss in her power suit and statements uttered with one hundred percent certainty that they would be obeyed. I liked her immensely.

I was discharged by the same cops who'd arrested me. It was the most deliciously satisfying part of my day. True, that wasn't saying much, but I took any win I could at this point.

"Must be nice to have friends in high places," the male officer sneered.

I met his gaze coldly and held out my hand for my personal belongings. "Pray you never find out just how high."

Janna drove me home in her Lexus. She explained that given I was moving to Vancouver—Levi, you presumptive fucker, we really needed to have that talk—House Pacifica had petitioned and received permission from House Ontario to investigate.

"I had no idea Houses could transfer internal investigations," I said.

She pulled up to the curb outside my apartment. "It's rare, but I pushed for it."

"Why?"

"You and Carol Shaw are both tied to Perrault Biotech, a lab that was destroyed as a result of arson," Janna said.

I didn't like where this was going, but Levi trusted my well-being to Janna, so I'd put my faith in her as well. I raked a hand through my short blond hair, sending my pixie cut into spikes. "Neither of us were complicit in that."

"You misunderstand. When Levi called me today and I heard that once again that lab was connected to all this?" She shook her head. "My gut is telling me that there is much more to this than meets the eye, and whatever it is, is rotten. I don't believe that House Ontario has the capacity to see the full scope of this, but your cousin is good at that." She glanced sideways at me. "I heard some of what your uncle was involved in and how Levi brought him to justice."

"Involved in" was the understatement of the century. Levi's dad, my zio Isaac, had been part of an evil global hydra called Chariot. Ash and Levi searched long and hard for any Chariot connection to my predicament, but they hadn't found anything. That was almost worse because it was like I'd landed in some bizarro-world version of an *Oprah* studio audience. *You get an evil nemesis! And you get an evil nemesis!*

"I'm hoping…" Janna fiddled with the strap of her gold watch, looking flustered for the first time in our brief acquaintance. "My ex-fiancé was investigating Perrault Biotech and he's disappeared."

My jaw hit the ground. There was no way Janna meant Gideon. "That's awful. What's his name?"

Don't say Gideon Stern. Don't say Gideon Stern.

"Gideon Stern."

This powerhouse was the fiancée who'd wanted to get back together? The woman he hadn't told about becoming a shifter? I'd imagined her to be high maintenance, not high awesomeness.

"How long has he been missing?" *Come on, be ghosting Janna for longer than me.* I'm not proud to say my fingers were crossed.

"He texted me a couple weeks ago," she admitted.

"Oh, he did, did he?" I snapped. I hope he got fleas.

Janna shot me a strange look. "Did I overstep?"

"No. What? No." I gave a tinkly laugh. It sounded as fake as it was, so I caught myself and snorted sharply instead. Kill me. "Did he tell you anything?"

"Nothing truthful. I don't buy his explanations for leaving town suddenly and opening a private security firm with a hush-hush clientele. Gid loved being a police officer. I'm worried something's happened to him."

"What outcome are you hoping for, Janna?" My stomach ached.

"Can you ask Levi to find Gid? If he's gone into hiding because of whatever is going on, or trying to keep me safe?" She shrugged helplessly. "I want to speak to him face-to-face. He owes me that much. Can you help me get him that message?"

She'd gotten me out of jail. Of course I could get a message to her ex. I was a polite Canadian.

The smile of agreement I gave her cracked my face, and I had to clear my throat to make sure my "Certainly" sounded human and not like an animal's growl, a warning that came out of the dark and that only a fool would fail to heed.

"Thank you," she said. "Now, you have my card in case you need anything. Even once you've moved to Vancouver, feel free to call me."

"I'm not moving, but yeah, I will." I opened the passenger door.

"And Raisa?" She leaned over with a rustle of fabric and the faint whiff of perfume topped with notes of oranges and lilies, fiddling with a nonexistent ring on her left hand before resting it on the steering wheel. "Ask Levi to call me the *second* he's spoken to Gideon."

"Of course." I closed the car door without slamming it, and walked, not stomped, up the front walk and into my building. Really nailing adulting.

Once inside, I sank onto the light blue sofa in the lobby and buried my face in my hands, my thoughts all tangled up. I could pass this off to Levi. His fiancée, Ash, was allowed into Hedon, and though the Queen of Hearts had forbidden her and Levi from involving themselves in anything concerning Gideon and myself, this was about Janna, not me.

Even Her Majesty wouldn't deny Ash telling Gideon to contact his ex. I didn't think. Regardless, it wouldn't be my problem, and I'd have kept my word to Janna.

I grabbed one of the sofa cushions and smacked it against the couch. "Porca fucking miseria! Why did I have to like his ex? Why did I have to meet her at all?"

At the wary look from the startled postman coming out of the mail room, I smoothed the cushion back into place.

My momentary relapse was over, and my smart, logical, and laser-focused self was back in control.

I headed up to my apartment.

The police wouldn't find whoever had ordered Carol's murder. Ash and Levi might, but I refused to sit around and hide while they tracked that person down. This involved my life, my work, my sister, my coworker—and my new job that I was starting in less than two weeks, come hell or high water.

That said, unless Gideon planned to hide his shifter status forever, it was as much in his interest to locate and stop Baba Yaga as it was in mine, because she'd sniff him out eventually.

I slipped inside my place and locked the door behind me using the extra security dead bolts I'd installed. They felt distressingly inadequate, like a child posting stuffed animals as sentries against the very real monster under their bed.

Once I'd removed my outdoor winter gear, I headed into the kitchen to make myself a cup of tea to warm up. I filled a mug with water and stuck it in the microwave, formulating my new plan: obtain a token to Hedon and get the Queen's permission to speak to Gideon.

There were three kinds of tokens that got you into that magic alternate reality: gold, bronze, and basic. The gold VIP token allowed unlimited visits between here and that realm. Anyone who possessed one could also jump between locations here on earth, so long as they touched down in Hedon as a brief stopover between destinations.

I ate a couple of tablespoons of peanut butter directly from the jar, then the microwave beeped. I added the tea bag, milk, and honey to the boiling water in my mug and padded into the living room.

There was no psychological cost to using a gold token, at least not for the holders. Moran, Ash, and Gideon were exempt, but any plus-one (aka me) they brought along for the ride was subjected to the Queen of Hearts peering into their memories.

My love of knowledge had nothing on hers.

If I got a bronze token, the second way into Hedon, I'd also relive one of my memories for the Queen. Each of those coins provided only a single one-way trip, but at least the user could specify their destination.

Sinking onto my couch, I tucked my feet underneath me and sipped my tea, hissing as the liquid burned the top of my mouth. I doubted that I'd be able to find a bronze token. Before Ash became friends with the Queen, not even Levi had access to them.

Basic entry-level token it was. Once I had my ticket in, I'd find the fixed portal from Toronto into Hedon. I shuddered to think which memory the Queen would make me relive this time, but there was no way around it.

I didn't plan to approach Gideon until I'd spoken with the Queen of Hearts. The restraining order against me was to stay away from Gideon; it didn't ban me from entering Hedon altogether. Her Royal Highness either didn't think I'd take it upon myself to find a way in, or she meant to be entertained by me doing precisely that. Both were equal possibilities.

However, in the event that Her Majesty interpreted the situation differently, by leaving Levi and Ash in the dark, they'd be spared her wrath.

The other big plus to keeping my plans to myself was that I'd be spared pitying glances, or worse, questions from the nosy duo about my feelings around Janna and seeing Gideon again. (None, thanks for asking.)

I tentatively tasted the tea again, gagged at my liberal use of honey, then shrugged and took another sip.

Once I got to Hedon, I'd convince the Queen to let me deliver Janna's message personally. Assuming I received royal permission to visit Gideon, how would I phrase my request for assistance? Asking nicely wouldn't get me anywhere, nor would punching Stern in his fat face—a move I'd considered when he failed to send me one simple text stating he was alive and healthy, and inquiring after my own well-being. Sadly, he was protected by the Black Heart Rule and any assault on his person ended with the attacker being entombed in stone, alive and aware for eternity.

There was only one way forward: disarm him with a charm offensive. I'd also be able to assess Gideon's recovery after he'd taken a bullet for me, then deliver Janna's message.

What Gideon did or did not do concerning his ex was none of my business. His silence these last couple of months was a clear indicator that any friendship we'd developed was purely one-way. It stung, but I was a grown-up.

I just hoped that Gideon didn't shoot the messenger. I frowned, tapping a finger against the ceramic mug. Or thanked her, scattering dust balls in his haste to run off and call Janna.

However, should he wish to repay me for my time and energy—and he big-time should—he could help me find Baba Yaga.

Thanks to his years of training and experience as a police officer, he was my best hope of finding her in the shortest amount of time.

Luckily, we weren't starting from scratch. I'd gotten a couple pieces of useful information from Woody. His sparse notes on Golden Radial had yielded the name of his contact in that organization: a Mundane called Jeremy Wade. This was a relatively common name, and my cursory internet search when I got back from Marrakesh yielded a lot of results. Only one, though, had a photo matching the silver-haired man who'd followed me before I headed off to Morocco to track Woody down.

There was a single mention of Jeremy being legal counsel for the group, but I hadn't dug deeper in case they had a way to log searches. He'd given me the chills in my brief glimpse of him, and I didn't want to ever see him again.

Instead, I'd kept my head down and focused on my discussions with Dr. Nakahara, since I didn't want to poke the hornet's nest.

Silly me. The hornets had been buzzing around me this entire time.

No more playing possum. I may have been a woman, a scientist, and a Canadian, but from now on, I'd fight back as dirty as I had to.

After all, there was no point playing by the rules when my enemies weren't going to.

With Carol's murder, it would be foolish to reach out directly to Jeremy. However, the more I knew about him, the safer I'd be. I fired off a text to Ash and Levi asking them to look into him. Carefully.

My other clue was Lausanne, a name Woody had overheard from Jeremy. Other than it being a city in Switzerland, the country where the muscular dystrophy trials were held, it hadn't meant anything to either of us.

First things first: find a token to a magic world, convince its deadly ruler to walk back a previous decree, then lure a grumpy shifter who didn't want to speak to me into helping me locate the monster from my childhood who had no qualms about killing people.

I mean, it wasn't ideal, but what plan ever was?

Chapter 6

The beef patties at A Wan Irie Likkle Place were even better than I remembered. I swallowed the first bite of spicy meat and buttery flaky pastry with a moan, my eyes rolling back in my head.

Sadly, Birdie, the owner of the takeout joint, did not share my expression of bliss. He watched me warily from behind the pastry case. It was hard to believe that this scrawny Jewish dude with dark red hair, freckles covering his pasty white skin, and the heaviest Jamaican accent I'd ever heard was descended from Jewish pirates of the Caribbean, but he *was* clicking a pair of metal tongs in an ominous fashion. Maybe he'd deploy them like a cutlass, leaping across the glass counter to attack in time with the dancehall music pumping out of the speakers mounted in the corner of the ceiling.

"Like I said." I licked a crumb off my lip. "I'm here of my own volition. No one sent me, but you're the only person in Toronto I know who's gone into Hedon. How do I get a token and where's the fixed location? Also, two more patties, please."

"Don't be messing with that place." He grabbed another

couple of the beefy delights—in my head I snickered like a twelve-year-old-boy—and slid them into a white paper bag. "It's no good."

I took the bag, waiting for him to ring up the purchase. "Trust me, I know, but I have no choice and I'd rather not ask around and draw attention to myself."

He passed me the point-of-sale terminal and I tapped my card against it. "There's no guarantee you'll get a token first time around, and if you fail, they'll want their pound of flesh."

I sighed. "I don't really have any spare cash to bribe—"

Birdie tugged up his sleeve, revealing a nasty set of raised white scars crisscrossed along his forearm.

I dropped the patty I was about to polish off back in the bag, appetite gone. "Oh," I said faintly. "You meant a real pound. Of course you did."

As much as I suddenly adored every bit of flesh on my body, I couldn't walk away. My life and my work wouldn't be safe until I found Baba Yaga, and for that I needed Gideon's cop skills.

"I'm willing to take the risk," I said.

Birdie sighed, gave me an address, and sent me off with two sun-shaped tarts called Gizzada. On the house. They were a parting gift where parting meant, "You'll be dead soon, enjoy these coconut treats."

I should have worn a dark cloak with a hood for this clandestine journey instead of a puffy winter coat, but fuck traditional questing fashion, it was freezing out. I pulled my pink toque with its jaunty pom-pom low over my brow and ears, wrapped my fuzzy scarf snuggly around me from my neck to my nose, and set off into the icicle-laden outdoors.

Keeping my head down and my pace quick, I ducked into the closest subway station, and scarfed down my takeout during the short journey, trading the Little Jamaica neighborhood where Birdie's store was located for one filled with dodgy corner stores.

When I emerged, the sky had flatted into a gray soup and cold rain was falling. A brisk walk led me to a café sandwiched between a run-down bakery and a pharmacy that looked like it got its drugs from boxes that had fallen out the back of a white panel van.

The humble coffee shop was an oasis of cheer on this gloomy narrow street. A sign above the door read "Brewhaha" in curly yellow letters, the word surrounded by kittens blowing kisses.

Anything that cutesy had to be evil. I rubbed my sleeves. I was totally going to lose a pound of flesh. Hopefully they'd let me pick which pound.

Resigned, I pushed inside to the smell of freshly brewed coffee. The shop was cozy and inviting, one wall dominated by a field of painted sunflowers with mismatched armchairs and couches scattered throughout the space. Bookshelves held dog-eared paperbacks while cats, from ceramic likenesses to knitted figurines, covered every flat surface. They were fat, thin, blue, floral, dozing, frolicking, peeking out of teacups, wearing hats, and even a selection of plastic disembodied cat heads hung as wall decorations.

"Welcome to Brewhaha," an employee said in a dead voice from behind the counter. This was no blond cherub cheerfully greeting customers, unless the cherub had fallen from the heavens, got his septum pierced, and bought stock in black hair dye. In his late teens, he wore a black jacket and vest, topped with a high white cravat.

Dude looked like his surroundings caused him physical pain. I didn't blame him because not only was he forced to wear a name tag with Edgar (yeah right, you Poe wannabe) written in the same curly yellow font as the sign outside, a fluffy white kitten was in mid-gambol over the letters.

On the wall behind Edgar was a large colorful chalkboard featuring drinks with punny drink names like I Love You a Latte and Livin' La Vida Mocha.

What had this poor guy done to deserve such purgatory?

"I'll have an I'm Brewtiful to go with a double shot of espresso." I perused the menu. "And a token to Hedon," I added in a mumble, my cheeks growing pink.

Edgar squinted at me then turned around, staring at the chalkboard with a scowl—as if the weight of his burden working here wasn't enough, of course some other dumb-named item had been added without anyone telling him. "You mean an order of He Done Me Oolong?"

Was this a code for the token?

"Yes," I said meaningfully, praying I didn't end up double-fisting artisan beverages.

He picked up two boxes of tea. "Green or black?"

"Neither!" I placed my hands flat on the counter, glanced over my shoulder to make sure we were alone, and leaned in. "No tea. Give me a token to Hedon."

"I can only sell you the items on the menu. You want your original coffee order of Brewtiful then? What size?" Edgar tapped the display cups next to the cash register. He didn't look like he had any skin in the Hedon game.

Could Birdie have screwed me over? Sure. That was par for the course whenever Hedon was involved.

I sighed, resigning myself to my fate. You won for now, Gideon. "A small, please."

Edgar spooned richly scented ground espresso into the portafilter, clanged it into place, and hit the button to dispense my drink.

I impatiently tapped my winter boot against the scuffed floor. Maybe the jolt of caffeine would help me figure out where to find a token?

He slid a travel sleeve on the takeout cup and rang up my purchase.

Despite my disappointment, I tipped him well. This café

was punishment enough. There was no need to be a shitty customer just because he couldn't help me. "Thanks."

"No problem."

I grabbed my drink, but as I turned to leave, Edgar smirked. Faintly—like I was his mother and wasn't supposed to see it, even though he was so clever and totally wanted me to know.

My hand tightened on the cup hard enough to make the lid pop off. *Try to play me for a fool, would you?* I could outthink, outplay, and definitely out-attitude this little schmuck with one hand tied behind my back. "Is the Queen of Hearts hiring her minions from the kiddie pool now?"

Edgar's smirk slipped—just for a fraction of a second. "No idea what you're talking about."

Gotcha, you little liar. Warmth surged in my chest. I was not conceding defeat by slinking out that door.

Facing him with a cold smile, I nodded at the small plastic cat figurine on top of the largest display mug. It stood on its hind legs, a vicious scowl on its face, and all ten claws extended. "Unless you want me to shove that cat somewhere extremely painful, you'll hand over a token. Now. Got it?"

"You're nuts, lady," he said, but it would have been much more convincing if he hadn't been grinning from ear to ear, eyes warming in challenge.

It was one thing to do his job and prevent randos from getting a token, but this little emo bastard did not get to nail me with the crazy card. Was there a Hedon-employed squadron of misanthropic adolescents around the city, getting dopamine hits via mild gaslighting?

My phone rang, but I ignored it. It was probably a bot telemarketer.

I didn't want to threaten Edgar with my magic on the slight chance that he was Mundane, plus, it was best to conserve my energy for Hedon, so I grabbed the plastic cat.

"You've got three seconds to hand over a token or kitty is getting a new home."

"Threats will get you nowhere."

I squared my shoulders. "Oh, I'm more than happy to escalate from threats, believe me. I've had a hell of a week."

He huffed a laugh, then his entire body began to shake, the tremors spreading out from his feet and through the floor.

Stacks of mugs on saucers rattled.

I stumbled sideways, grabbing on to the counter to steady myself. What the unholy *fuck* had I just walked into?

My foe stood there with a tranquil expression on his face. No, that wasn't right. He was smiling, wide and bright, and in that moment, I saw past the black hair dye, the goth clothing, and the piercings to the child he once was.

A psychotic little monster who enjoyed deploying his rare Bombshell magic.

Not all monsters operated from the shadows. Some worked under bright lights in aggressively quaint cafés in the metro Toronto area. I sucked in a breath. If he unleashed his powers, he'd have his pick of my pound of flesh, because I'd be scattered in chunks in the wreckage. All righty. This particular one could serve as a warning to others.

The phone rang again. *Not now, robocaller.*

Pale orange magic bloomed over my hands, the warmth sinking into me like it was a cat giving a contented purr. I made gimme motions with my fingers, gathering the light to me in a long twist. If I choked him out—just enough to make the tremors stop, *I* wasn't a monster—we could have a civilized conversation about customer service.

And if that didn't work—

The bulbs blew, popping one by one.

I screamed and covered my head from falling glass. *Testa di cazzo!* I hadn't done that.

With no electric light in here and an overcast day

outside, I chose every Weaver's favorite backup plan: get the fuck out.

The lock on the door clicked into place, kiboshing that hope pretty damn quick, and a ground tremor knocked me sideways.

A chair slid backward and smashed into my hip. I swore but I also got an idea. I snatched up the chair, sprinted to the counter, and flung it at Edgar.

He sidestepped it as calmly as if he was Neo, post-Matrix awakening, able to experience time in slow motion.

The cell went off for a third time, marking roughly the fifteenth ring. Someone was desperate to get hold of me and I doubt they wanted to discuss my phone plan.

I fumbled for my cell with shaking hands, practically dropping it in my haste to answer. I hit speakerphone then stuffed it into my bra with the top sticking out, without checking the screen. "Hello?"

Cracks appeared in the ceiling and cat figures rained to the ground in hails of black and calico. Some were surprisingly sturdy and just bounced, but others shattered in aggressive feline fragments. Talk about food safety issues.

I had to stop this kid before the shock waves blew me and this place apart.

Meanwhile, Ella was yelling something on the phone, but I processed her words as only a distressed stream of sound.

Wait. Ella? My heart skidded around in my chest like it was sliding on thin ice. Had Golden Radial come after her for pointing me to Alexei, who'd led me to Carol? "What's wrong?!"

The ground surged up, sending tables and chairs lurching and crashing like ships in a storm.

I protected myself as best I could, which still meant about seven hits to some very susceptible body parts.

"Carol's dead!" Ella cried.

"Oh." My shoulders relaxed; at least it wasn't a new problem. What a fucked-up baseline. "That's unfortunate."

I grabbed another chair and, hopping over the wide cracks spreading across the floor, stumbled behind the counter.

"Unfortunate?! Raisa, someone's been murdered!" Ella shrieked as I dodged a pile of crocheted ginger cat stuffies. "And somehow you were arrested for her death?"

A chunk of ceiling smashed down behind me, catching me on the heel.

My snow boots saved me from that particular injury, but I lost my hold and dropped the chair on my other foot.

Edgar opened his mouth and snapped his face upward in a silent scream. His skin undulated over his body in small waves, but despite all that, he bobbed on his toes like a kid excited to get on their favorite scary ride.

My stomach contorted into an unbreakable knot, and I gripped the top of the chair hard enough to turn my fingers white. "No," I whispered.

"No shit, Raisa," Ella said. "I know you didn't kill her, but what happened?!"

I had to stop Edgar. Holding the chair, I took two more steps, the rumbling ground vibrating up through my feet.

"Raisa!"

I tripped over a jagged piece of floor that exploded upward in my path. "I'm okay." Barely hearing my lie over my pounding heart, I reached for the phone, which had fallen out of its boob holder and onto the ground—and froze.

Edgar was doing these full-body rolls, making him look a bit like a cat himself, albeit one on the verge of yakking up the world's nastiest hairball.

This wasn't some sexy choreography the emo shit had learned. No, these moves spanned from his feet all the way up to and including his facial features. Even his hair stood

57

on end. He was getting ready to blow, and when he did, I'd be dead.

But not Edgar. As a Bombshell, he could detonate as many times as he pleased (or as many as the structural integrity of this café allowed) and be fine. I, however, would not. And it wouldn't matter that he worked for the Queen and not Golden Radial, because at the end of the day, the largest piece of me anyone would be able to find probably wouldn't be larger than your average beaker.

I was sick and tired of being thwarted in every single fucking thing I did. Couldn't the universe cut me a break?

Magic surrounded me in a pale orange haze. Not because I could use my powers, but because the rage swelling to fill every inch of me had pushed it out to make room.

The sight of Edgar's skin rising up and down like stormy waves made me want to puke, but there was no way I was taking my eyes off him.

He gave a slow lizard blink and smiled. It stretched painfully wide. "I told you not to threaten me. I'm totally going to get a promotion for this."

"We'll see about that." I swung the chair into Edgar's chest with all my strength, connecting with a deep grunt.

He was slammed backward against the counter.

The very foundation trembled and the corner of the ceiling caved in.

Ella was screaming at me over the phone, but as she was neither in imminent danger of combusting (Edgar), being combusted (me, the café, the two unbothered cat statuettes remaining), or getting murdered (Carol, RIP), I decided she could wait.

I grabbed a glass bottle of Irish cream–flavored syrup and bashed it into Edgar's skull.

The front windows blew out; his head remained intact. Sticky amber liquid flowed down the side of his face, but none of the glass shards cut him. Fanculo! He had some kind of magic protection.

His hand shot out and he grabbed me by the throat.

I scrabbled madly at his clawed fingers, but his grip didn't loosen, so I kneed him in the groin as hard as I could.

The teen's eyes widened, and he slid to the ground with a low, sputtering groan.

Oh good. His magic protection was only on his head.

The tremors finally stopped all at once with a surprising suddenness.

I braced a hand on the counter, panting and rubbing my throat with my other hand.

Edgar curled up in the fetal position, but his skin was normal again.

Before he could fully recover, I crouched down. "Token," I hissed into his ear, "or I do it again."

He twitched a couple times, making small hurt animal noises. "U-under the register," he managed at last in a strangled voice.

I helped myself to all three basic tokens. Other than the dent and "H" stamped on each, they could have been any metal coins.

"Want to fight again sometime?" Edgar wheezed. "Most fun I've had on the job ever."

"What is wrong with you? Go join a boxing club. Now, where's the fixed entrance?"

"Broom closet." He jerked a couple fingers toward the back of the café.

"You could have saved me a lot of time and yourself an insurance claim, but okay." I scooped up my phone. "Ella?" I had to call her name three more times before she processed that I was alive and well. "Sorry. Had a bit of a mishap."

"I was scared that whoever killed Carol—"

"No. Just poor customer service."

"Okay?" she said dubiously. "What on earth happened?"

"I literally just wanted a coffee and—"

"Not that. Carol," Ella said with forced patience. "Why were you arrested?"

Oh.

"I just wanted job advice," I said, opening doors in the café hallway. The first one led to a restroom. Ick, no thank you. "Wrong place wrong time. Hang on, how do you even know what happened?"

"Kaitlin's wife is on the force."

Right. Perrault Biotech's receptionist. That grapevine was alive and well. How much longer before the news hit our entire local scientific community? Woody's money laundering had certainly spread like wildfire.

I had to find Baba Yaga before my arrest went public. Once she was eliminated as a threat, Levi would smooth over any rumors.

Meantime, Dr. Nakahara could not hear about any of this.

"Please don't tell anyone." I rattled the knob on the broom closet. "I better not need a key or I'm taking back my tip," I called out.

"First the lab, then Woody disappearing, now Carol." Ella was frantic. "Are we all in danger?"

"But you tipped on a card," Edgar called back weakly. Before I could describe the violence I would inflict on him for this sass, he had the sense to add: "Also, the door sticks."

Of course it did. I swallowed a growl. "All is well."

"How can you say that?" Ella retorted. "Nothing has been well since Woody disappeared. I wouldn't be surprised if he was the one who—"

"Don't even think it, okay? I know Woody left you in a really shitty lurch, but he's not a killer."

"Why do you keep believing in him? He's not your mentor anymore. Far from it. He blew up the lab and destroyed the off-site data. You understand that, right?"

I understood better than anyone what Woody had done —and why. But I took a deep breath, reminding myself that she was just concerned. "Of course I do. Look, my feelings around Woody are…" I rubbed my temples. On top of everything else, I didn't want to have to explain my complicated feelings toward my mentor to his former colleague who was clearly hostile to him. I needed my head in the game to face another man who'd turned out to be different from the person I'd believed him to be. "I can't get into this right now. If you hear anything about a celebration of life for Carol, let me know." I'd go as much to pay my respects as to check out who else showed up. "Otherwise, we'll talk soon, okay?"

"All right. Take care of yourself."

"You too." I brushed my finger over the darkened screen, like I could physically gather up her concern and wrap it around me like a soothing blanket.

My relationship with my own mother had improved in the past couple months, but it didn't have the easy acceptance of my choices that Ella gave me. Mom was in North Africa installing a high-end security system and we'd talked a couple of weeks ago.

She still shied away from any details about the experiments that Robyn and I had endured, but she was coming to terms with the fact that the abduction had happened and, hopefully, would one day accept that it wasn't her fault and I didn't blame her.

She'd gone from showing little interest in my life out of guilt that she'd failed me as a parent to making up for it in an outpouring of excessive support, offering me a job, a place to live, and financial help. The trouble was that it was all predicated on keeping me close and, more importantly, keeping me safe. Like I was still a toddler in need of protection.

It was driving me crazy. Especially since I couldn't share

anything more than superficial details about my life. We'd had a lot of talks about poetry lately though. Mom's love of it throughout my childhood hadn't died, and reminiscing about some of the poems she'd shared with us was our way of dipping our toes into conversations about Robyn and Dad.

Eventually, maybe we could talk about them instead of talking around the hole they'd left. But for now, the poetry was nice. It was a small rope bridge over a massive chasm, but it was still a bridge.

Which reminded me: I still had miles to go before I slept. Well, I wasn't quite sure how mileage worked in Hedon—distance was strange enough over in that slice of reality—but the thought was the same. Time to kick off the Baba Yaga World Tour. I clutched one of the basic tokens and stepped through the door.

First stop: get the band back together.

Chapter 7

I rolled my eyes at the little kids shrieking on the swings behind the sandbox. They weren't even going high.

It was so unfair. We were ten. Totally old enough to go to the store on our own. But noooo. Instead, we were stuck at the stupid playground across the street. If I was old enough to get an allowance, then I should be old enough to spend it. Mom could have let me go buy candy and not sent me here like I was a baby.

I should never go back. Just like Dad had told me Einstein didn't go back to Germany because of the Nazis. That'd show her.

I threw my orange peel. It skipped against the concrete, then bounced out of the hopscotch square. I sighed and dropped my piece into place. "Your turn, birdbrain."

Robyn licked her Fudgsicle. "After I finish my ice cream. You know, the last one from the freezer that Mom said I could have?" She licked it again. "It's sooo gooood."

"If you love it so much, why don't you marry it?" I kicked a pebble at her.

Her ice cream splatted onto the painted lines of the game and she gave me a stricken look.

"I didn't even hit you." I stomped my foot. "You big faker. Owww!"

She'd dug her nails into my arm so hard that drops of blood popped up on my skin.

"Get over it," I said. Drama much? Except when I looked more closely, my sister was as white as a ghost. Her mouth was hanging open and she was gasping for air. My stomach twisted. "Robs?" I shook her shoulder.

"How nice. You remember me," said a woman with an accent. "Which twin are you?"

It was the voice from my nightmares, the very secret ones. The ones I told only Robyn about because she had them too. A trickle of pee dribbled down my leg. I told myself to turn around, because it was worse not seeing the woman, but my legs wouldn't move.

She gave a happy laugh. "I figured it out. You're Robyn."

A tear ran down my sister's cheek.

I grabbed her hand and squeezed tightly. There was the Cave and there was the Voice. Sometimes the Voice had asked me and Robyn to do different things. We'd be cold and dirty and separated, and sometimes when I didn't do things fast enough the Voice would hurt Robyn. We didn't tell anyone about it. Even though it felt so real, it was simply a weird twin thing, right? We finished each other's sentences, so why not have the same dreams?

It just sucked that we only ever shared nightmares.

Now here was the Voice, with that strange sharp accent, right behind me. My throat went tight. The smell of bitter, too familiar chemicals surrounded me, jarring me.

Not this. Not again.

"You can't have her!" I tugged on Robyn, ready to bolt, but she was frozen stiff with fear.

A callused hand gripped my shoulder.

"Don't make a scene," the woman said quietly in a stern voice. She pushed me forward, and since I was still holding

Robyn's hand, we were like a weird train, making our way to our destination bench.

It should have been funny.

"Mom," I squeaked. It was too quiet, but I was too scared to make my voice louder.

"Let's sit down." The woman shoved me onto the wooden seat.

I scrounged up my courage to look at her. No claws or massive teeth. The lady had poufy blond hair, brown eyes, and an ugly pink dress with ruffles. Her right eyebrow had this gross red scar through it that ran down her cheek, the skin a puckered white line that caused her right eye to droop slightly.

Good. I hoped it hur—

～

I TUMBLED NAUSEATINGLY ONTO A COLD, damp floor, bashing my elbow as I landed in an undignified sprawl.

"Who is she, chica?" The Queen of Hearts stood over me, tapping the toe of a red boot with heels that were skinny and pointy enough to fit between my ribs. Her voice was colder than the flagstones that made me shiver through my bulky sweater or the icy wind that buffeted me.

I took in the heavy metal door and bars on the high narrow window, then scooted back on my ass. My chest was tight, as if in preparation to be encased in rock. "No one said I wasn't allowed to come to Hedon."

"Who is the woman from your memory?" Her violet eyes flashed.

Her Majesty's gross violation of my mind was bad enough. However, I accepted the cost of reliving a memory that she became privy to as the price of using the token.

Her alternate reality, her rules.

Or, rather, I would have accepted the cost had it not been *that* memory. The one where Robyn and I had once more come face to face with the woman who'd scared us so badly that even when we were furious at each other, we'd never willingly left the other alone. Not until the night she ditched me at a party for some guy.

I swallowed through a tight throat.

I'd thought I'd give Robyn the cold shoulder for abandoning me, but the joke was on me, because it was pretty hard to freeze someone out when they lay unconscious under a sterile burn sheet. It was even harder when I buried the person who was supposed to grow old alongside me.

Sitting on Robyn's lower bunk promising my firstborn and indentured servitude to any higher being if they would only let me wake up from this nightmare didn't work either.

Shaking off the past, I probed my bruised elbow and winced. If I wasn't in trouble, why had the Queen thrown me in a freaking dungeon? It's not like I could demand a phone call. Though I did have my phone.

"There's no cell service," the Queen said brusquely.

"How did you…?"

"Why do scientists always think they are the first ones to have an idea? Answer my question, Dr. Montefiore."

"I don't know who she is," I said politely, though my teeth chattered. Had she designed this cell as a wind tunnel? Because it was ridiculously cold in here.

"No?" The bronze-skinned fifty-something ruler wore a red leather catsuit that hugged her curves. It rustled when she bent over and hauled me to my feet. "This woman scared you so badly that you urinated and yet you have nothing?" Oh, good. She'd seen that highlight of my preteen life too, had she? "Cariña. Eres lista. Stop pretending."

"I'm not. Believe me," I said bitterly. "I'd be delighted to give you her name and home address so you could add her to your sculpture collection. All I know is that when Robyn

66

and I were three, that woman took us to some cave and experimented on us."

The Queen's expression softened. Not enough to release me from the dungeon, mind you, but concern had appeared like the first rays of light peeking out from under storm clouds. "Is she part of Golden Radial?"

She knew about them? I nodded. "I believe so."

"Where did she take you?"

"No idea."

The Queen raised an eyebrow.

"We weren't given a commemorative map." Whoops. I fiddled with one of my ear piercings to center myself, not making eye contact. "It smelled like wine, but that's all I remember. Maybe Switzerland?"

"Her accent in your memory was Balkan. What evidence is your supposition based on?"

I explained about the muscular dystrophy trials that produced the shifter prototypes.

An undecipherable expression flashed over the Queen's face. She stepped closer and I swallowed. "So many connections," she said softly. "Research from *your* mentor, Gideon's abilities from *your* serum, and *your* preschool teacher in those trials."

"I'd be thrilled to have this not be all about me." I rubbed my throbbing elbow. I would have told her about Lausanne, a name that Woody insisted was important, except I didn't know what it signified, and I wasn't up to more of the Queen's scorn regarding my lack of knowledge.

"What was the purpose of the experiments? The ones conducted on you and your sister." Her piercing gaze bore into mine, reminding me of advisor meetings where I'd failed to meet expectations. Except this was somehow worse, because unlike grad school, I had no idea how I was disappointing the Queen of Hearts, only that I was.

"Why do you care?" I gasped and clutched at the air like

I could grab my nosy question and stuff the words back in my mouth. Ash had warned me never to ask the Queen personal questions.

"Many years ago, she kidnapped someone close to me," she said darkly. "Well, she tried. I've searched far and wide, but I've never found her."

Baba Yaga had escaped this ruler's dragnet? If she was part of Golden Radial, she had a lot of resources at her disposal: money, powerful connections across the globe. I'd still have bet on the Queen every time. A prickle of cold sweat ran down my side. How could I pit myself against her?

I shook off the negativity because I couldn't let anything deter me from finding Baba Yaga. "I suspect she had one of my colleagues murdered last night. Let me out and give me permission to speak with Gideon. I'll convince him to locate this woman with me. You do want her found, right?"

"The experiments," she prodded.

"Levi thinks they were because I had magic and Robyn didn't. Like she wanted to flip a switch in us."

Her Majesty's lips pressed into a flat line and two red spots hit her cheeks.

My pulse spiked, but the rational part of my brain kicked in. My cousin wasn't in trouble; the Queen was upset about something else. I didn't ask what since our sharing relationship only went one way—plus Her Majesty had vanished in the blink of an eye. *Almost like the Queen had a gold token of her own. Duh, Raisa.*

After a good, long, frustrated scream, I pulled out my phone, but there was, indeed, no cell signal, and now I had a headache. I should have drunk my order of Brewtiful before I antagonized Edgar. Ah well, too late now.

The important thing was that I was in Hedon, and based on our conversation, my hypothesis was that something I'd said made her rush off. Not that she intended to keep me prisoner.

That was all well and good, but I wasn't waiting around until she remembered my existence, and thanks to my decision to keep Levi and Ash free from any repercussions of this visit, no one else knew I was here. While that might not have been my smartest decision, I didn't beat myself up over it.

No point wasting energy I needed for my great escape.

Hunger and thirst would only wear me down more the longer I stayed. I rose onto tiptoe, squeezed my hand through the bars of the glassless window, and waved the cell around, but I didn't pick up reception.

Banging on the thick locked door was equally pointless. I stood next to the lone tiki torch bolted to the wall and rubbed my hands in front of the flame to thaw out. The walls and floor were stone, and the door was metal. I couldn't burn my way out, but the fire was still light I could draw upon.

A gust of wind blew through the cell and snuffed out the torch. I shot the universe double middle fingers, hurried back to the window, and hopped up and down until I saw the eerie orange crescent moon to the west of me. Good. It wasn't overcast.

Hedon experienced perpetual night, a fact I'd never been so grateful for. I narrowed my eyes, running through how best to do this. Moonlight was difficult to weave since, as essentially reflected sunlight, it wasn't direct from the source. In addition, its infrared was only a tiny fraction as intense as the sun.

I stroked my chin. I couldn't use its heat to melt the metal bars. Could I wrap it around the bars and pull them free? It seemed unlikely but I gave it a shot. My Weaver magic rose up fast and itchy, covering my hands in a pale orange glow. Standing as high up on tiptoe as possible, I thrust my hands through the bars, my face mashed against the dank, rough wall. My connection to the moonlight fell into place with a satisfying click, and I used my powers to separate the light into strands, like yarn, which I braided together as if they had substance. Which, thanks to my magic, they did. Then I wrapped the braids around the bars.

I braced my feet against the floor, my toes at the wall, fastened the ends of my light braid around my hands, holding tightly to the ends, leaned back, and pulled.

And pulled.

And pulled.

Results were, unfortunately, as expected for a nerd who never hit the gym, much less regularly trained their upper body. The bars remained firmly in place.

I shook out my arms and massaged my shoulders, debating what to try next.

Weavers used their magic in different ways. Some manipulated thread deftly enough to unravel clothing, which they could reform into anything, from a net to a solid spike. Others wove plant material while a rare few could weave water or fire. It all depended on power level and training. A low-level Weaver might stitch a fallen hem with their magic and not much else. Most Weavers were employed as ward builders, magically binding a client's blood into doorways, which was the career pivot Mom wanted me to take. It'd pay well, but I wanted more than a boring job, no matter how juicy the paycheck.

A sudden spark of inspiration hit me. Thank you, Mr. Khan, and our compulsory eighth-grade woodworking class. I found myself humming in excitement. The execution of this move was tantalizingly complex, like a brainteaser made just for me. It would take every ounce of concentration and skill I could muster, but the challenge was intoxicating.

I closed my eyes. I didn't require vision to work my magic, and it was easier to center myself this way. Once more, I rose onto my toes and thrust my hands out the window. This time, instead of braiding the moonlight, I mashed it into a malleable ball like Silly Putty. Carefully, I drew it inside the cell with me and fashioned it into a hacksaw, a thick blade with lots of teeth, capable of cutting metal.

It was depressingly crude at first, more of a stick with lumpy protrusions than a useful tool, but I stayed with it, painstakingly refining the blades. Sweat ran down my neck, and my back screamed in protest from me remaining bent over the light while I worked, but it all finally paid off. One of the teeth drew blood when I poked it lightly.

I grinned and raked a sweaty lock of hair off my forehead. Weaving light into human cells was cool, but I'd done it so many times in the course of my research that the novelty was long gone. I didn't get to solidify light as often, and the ability never failed to awe me.

I'd certainly never pulled off anything this intricate. I dusted my knuckles against my chest at my mad skills.

My rush of adrenaline sent a much-needed surge of energy through me. After the fight with Edgar, calming Ella down, and enduring the Queen's interrogation, it was amazing I was still on my feet. On top of all that, I had to summon the energy to cut through those damn metal bars keeping me prisoner, and I had to do it with the magic hacksaw above my head.

Hoping that I didn't make enough noise to attract attention, I carefully sawed through the metal, keeping my face averted from the sparks that flew off the blade of my makeshift tool. I was breaking out of this prison, and I was doing it with my own two hands. Hot damn!

I grew heady with the thrill of my flight, whistling the theme song to *The Great Escape* while I worked, one of Dad's favorite movies.

The metal squealed and fell away, the bars clanging onto the floor.

I flicked my fingers to make the saw splinter into prisms

of moonlight that hung in mid-air then blew them away into the sky. Heh. Let the Queen wonder how I'd bolted.

After a running jump to hoist myself up onto the sill (which took only three tries), I leaned out through the glass-less window, taking care not to scrape the back of my head and neck on the rough stumps of metal still attached to the top of the frame. I had been in this cell for far too long, and the cool night air on my face was delightful.

The view as I dangled half-out of the dungeon, not so much.

The Queen of Hearts had these expansive gardens where she displayed the people she entombed in stone, their special forever home.

I'd naively assumed that the entirety of her collection was there, but oh, how wrong I was. Dozens, possibly a hundred statues stretched out before me in this backlot, bathed in moonlight, just like the White Witch of Narnia's courtyard.

A shiver ran down my spine. Would I find myself permanently stationed out there because I'd busted out of this cell? Too bad I didn't have the ability to weave light around myself and become invisible. Given how exhausted I was, now wasn't the time to waste precious energy attempting it.

I poked one of the sawed-off metal stumps. Well, the damage was done now, and she hadn't confirmed that I was a prisoner. Exactly.

I looked over the sea of figures. Did Her Majesty switch them out like seasonal displays? Was there a living statue curator? Or were these simply her second-tier enemies, not even worthy of being displayed? *Hey, I know you crossed me badly enough to be stuck as a statue forever, looking out on the world but never a part of it, but to add insult to injury, I think so little of you that you don't even rate being shown off as a warning.*

They were probably dusty too.

I squeezed through the glassless window and wriggled onto the weed-choked dirt. These poor fuckers didn't even get nice spongy grass beneath their feet. Not that they could feel it, but it was the principle of the thing.

I hurried through them as quickly as possible, doing my best not to look at anyone, but it was hard not to catch glimpses of the intricate details etched into stone: creases in their clothing, mouths that were angry slashes, and more than a few spears and swords that they were forever condemned to hold as a perpetual reminder of their failures.

They weren't set out in neat rows like silent sentinels, rather the figures were strewn haphazardly. I came across a bald dude and, unable to resist, ran a hand over the top of his head. I rubbed the dirt that came off between my fingers. Just as I thought. No housekeeping for these losers.

Add in all the shadows they cast, and it would have been creepy enough had they really been statues, but their eyes put goose bumps on my goose bumps. They were alive, aware, and followed me like villains in a *Scooby Doo* cartoon.

Spying a gate in the high stone wall that surrounded this torture museum storage center, I picked up my pace.

A hand shot out from a statue and grabbed my elbow.

OH MY GOD! Bald dude had broken free and was angry I patted his head without consent!

I screamed, kicking and punching with all my might. I encountered flesh, still solid but not stone, which was great for my hands and feet, but not so much for my brain, because I was convinced that someone had gotten free and was coming for me zombie-style.

I went for the instep and then the groin.

My attacker grunted. "Fuck, Raisa, watch the balls."

Recognizing that raspy growl, I stopped, planted hands on my hips, and glared at the man who was still wincing from my hit. "Gideon Stern. Nice of you to bother showing up."

Chapter 8

He looked good, damn him. I'd sort of hoped he'd lost all his hair and wasted away to a husk, eaten by regret for not contacting me. Nope. His skin was sun-kissed like he'd been vacationing in the Bahamas, making his hazel eyes pop, and his dark blond hair boasted tawny streaks, same as his wolf fur. Gideon was not one to sit at a salon, though he had visited a barber recently. His shaggier locks had been trimmed, though he hadn't gone as short as the fade he'd sported when we first met.

He wore a blue linen shirt and slightly darker pants, looking like he'd been styled for a *GQ* shoot. He hadn't lost any of the muscle mass he'd acquired from the shifter magic, but despite his large physique, he clearly wasn't a gym rat. He was a predator.

However, if he thought he could play Mr. Top of the Food Chain and intimidate me into leaving, he had another think coming.

"Raisa, what in the hell are you doing here?"

I stomped past him, heading for the gate. "You don't call, you don't write."

He dogged my heels. "I had good reasons."

"Oh, well then. That clears it all right up, and I have no choice but to understand perfectly."

"Could you—" He blocked my way.

I sidestepped him and kept walking. "I'm not sticking around the gruesome graveyard. If you finally want to have a proper conversation, let's do it somewhere civilized." I opened the gate, then stopped so suddenly that he ran into me.

He was so solid and warm, his scent of rich earth and cool air wrapping around me like a comfy blanket.

I spun around.

Gideon stepped back, rubbing a hand over the blond stubble along his strong jawline, his expression wary. "What?"

"The only way you could possibly have found me is if you knew I was in that cell to begin with."

He opened his mouth. Closed it.

"You asshole." I punched his arm.

Gideon caught my next swing, but at my glower, released me. "I was sent to get you out, but when I got there, the cell was already empty." His mouth quirked up in the half smile that haunted my dreams. "Nice work, by the way."

I clenched my fists so I didn't do something I'd hate myself for, like grin dopily at his compliment because it was so good to see him healthy and here. Except he'd been healthy and *here* this entire time. Plus, missing him was not reciprocated.

All urges to smile gone, I marched through the gate and onto a dirt utility road, my stomach rumbling. "On second thought, our reunion is unnecessary. I've revised my plan and I don't need you for it." I totally did, but this would rile up the contrary jerk while I got some food and waited for him to come to me. "That said, I promised to give you a message so here it is: call Janna. She's worried about you. Goodbye, Gideon."

As last words went, those were pretty good. They even had the desired effect of rendering him speechless, left behind in my literal dust.

"Janna?" he said. "Explain."

I spun around to find him standing right behind me and scowled. "Back off, Weeping Angel."

"Huh?" He shook his head impatiently. "Look, you can't go creeping through my past and expect me to not ask about it. How do you even know Janna? Did you go looking for her?"

"Where, oh where to begin unpacking all the insulting implications of that statement?" I kicked a pebble out of my path. Should I go left or right?

"No. I mean—see—I didn't realize you knew her?" Ordinarily his flustered stuttering would have been a balm to my pissed-off soul, but he looked so worried, and based on the last two months of radio silence, it wasn't on my behalf.

My post-escape high left me in a rush. Gideon was still my first choice to help me find Baba Yaga, but that hunt would be perilous enough without every exchange being wrapped in barbed wire. I didn't have the emotional energy to waste on personal interactions.

I simply wanted my life back and to start my job on January 4 without adding to my body count.

As in, people who had died because of my involvement in this case. Not like sexy body count, although—

Gideon quirked a confused eyebrow my way.

Nope. I was stopping that thought before it even left the station.

Perhaps this really should be goodbye? Surely, Levi had an operative who I could team up with. Someone easygoing and biddable?

"My cousin hired your ex to bail me out of prison," I said. "Talk about a small world, huh?"

"Why were you——"

"I wish you all the best. I really do." I jabbed a finger at the fork directly ahead. "Now, if you could point me in the right direction to that neon ramen place, I'll be out of your hair."

Hedon, while it was colloquially known as the magical black market, encompassed a lot more territory than that one area. My stomach rumbled. I couldn't jump between specific locations with these entry-level tokens, so I'd have to walk. Hopefully the market wasn't too far.

Gideon caught my hand, brushing his thumb across my palm. "Will you answer my questions if I feed you?"

Years of being in school and then living with student debt made the offer of a free meal irresistible. Satan himself could have volunteered to make me pancakes and the only deal-breaker would have been if the maple syrup wasn't real. Maybe not even then, if it was toward the end of the month when my finances were stretched thin.

I shrugged and pulled away. "Well, I certainly won't be forthcoming on an empty stomach. As for the rest, you'll have to take your chances."

He pinched the bridge of his nose, his complexion dangerously red.

"I've said my piece and I'm happy to continue on my merry way. Ball's in your court, Lobo Cop."

A muscle ticked in his jaw. "Why can't anything about you be easy to deal with?"

That stung. I wasn't the proverbial pebble in his shoe of life.

"Like working with you was all cupcakes and rainbow trolls?" I snapped.

He frowned. "You mean cupcakes and rainbows?"

"No, I do not." I wrapped my arms around my stomach,

hoping to mute the noise of its rumbling. "Rainbows are a pain in my light-weaving ass. The phenomenon is basically light that is slowed down and bent, with white light scattering into seven different colors. That change from its normal behavior interferes with my magic abilities. To me, rainbows are nothing more than brightly colored static. Rainbow trolls, on the other hand, are cute."

He was staring at me with an undecipherable expression.

I arched an eyebrow. "Yes?"

He did a poor job of tamping down a grin. "I missed you."

My eyes bugged out of my head, and I swear angry steam clouds exploded around me like I was a cartoon character. "You—that—bullshit!"

He slipped his hand into mine, our fingers intertwining like they were puzzle pieces that fit together. We needed to be in physical contact to use the gold token. "Food, then we'll talk."

I was still gaping at him when we vanished, but my incredulity over his comment turned to surprise over where he'd brought me. He'd used his gold token to take me back to his cabin on the beach. It was still in Hedon, mind you, but not where I expected to end up.

I'd envisioned the black market where we'd be surrounded by people and noise, not alone on the sand with his small home to one side of me and water stretching out to the vast horizon on the other. Bobbing dots of light in primary colors shone along the curve of the shore in the distance.

I blinked. Gideon had brought me *here* to feed me after admitting he'd missed me?

I glanced over. The fire pit by the shore where we'd laid ourselves emotionally bare, exchanging a truth for a truth, was cold. There weren't even cut logs around to light. We weren't going to remain outside; he was inviting me in?

A tingling feeling of anticipation hit me, but it was more as if I'd just bitten into a lemon and hadn't quite decided yet whether I liked the sharp taste.

This man had exiled himself from his friends, family, and police squad, so my entry into his home felt like more than him allowing me into a physical space. However, he'd also ghosted me for two months.

Unless I was reading more into this than it was: food.

"What are you waiting for?" He paused at the top of his back stairs.

"Just getting my bearings." I hurried after him into the cabin.

A tiny kitchen at one end of the narrow rectangle flowed into the rest of the space. There was a small wooden table with one chair, which, given his closed laptop, also served as a desk. Beyond that was a sofa positioned across from an old-fashioned woodstove, which hulked in the corner. Gideon had just enough room to comfortably stretch his legs out in front of the blaze from that hearth.

A flight of stairs led up to a loft where he presumably slept, next to the closed door that must have been the bathroom.

It could have felt lonely, but the exposed pine planks and beams that braced the pitched ceiling gleamed, infusing the jewel of a home with the scent of the forest, and the curtains drawn tight against the endless night and couch cushions were patterned with large, bright poppies. Was that his doing or had the previous occupant been endowed with a sense of whimsy?

Gideon opened the freezer compartment on his small refrigerator and pulled out a round tin. "Coffee?"

"Do you have milk?"

He checked the fridge then nodded.

"Then please," I said frostily.

Gideon pulled out the milk along with a bowl of large brown eggs, a fat loaf of bread, and a package of bacon.

I sat down on the single chair in the place while he went to work, filling the stovetop coffeepot, cracking eggs one-handed, and toasting bread.

The more the room filled with delicious breakfast aromas, the more my stomach growled, and when he tossed bacon into a hot cast-iron pan to sizzle, forget it. There were rocket launches that had been quieter than my belly.

I was too hungry to be embarrassed, plus I was wound up, waiting for his barrage of questions about why I'd been in prison and my meeting with Janna.

They didn't come. He stood at the stove, calmly cooking.

The tension inside me cranked tighter and tighter.

By the time the coffeepot whistled, I'd woven about three different conversations in my head, and at that signal, I started talking with the speed and urgency of Formula 1 race cars.

"If Dr. Nakahara had found a solution to the turbo cancer, none of this would have happened, but she couldn't. So, I proposed a different approach. That in turn required me to find whoever doctored my serum and learn everything I could about that process to use as a starting point to create a short-term immune system booster." I took a breath.

He flipped the bacon.

"I couldn't exactly learn what had been done without finding out which of my colleagues was behind it, and I was very crafty in how I went about it."

Gideon set a caffè latte down on the table in front of me and returned to the stove.

I brushed a stray sugar crystal off the table. "At least, I thought I was being crafty. I'd visited Dr. Carol Shaw, the only scientist who could have done it, and had a conversation with her. In reality, she was already dead and illusioned to look like a dog. The killer was disguised as Carol and talking with me the entire time."

There was a loud snap. Gideon had broken the metal spatula.

I braced myself for some growled admonishment about how much of an idiot I was, but he searched my face. "Did they hurt you in any way?"

I pressed back against the chair. None of this interaction was going as expected, and my solid reality had turned to quicksand. "Not physically, but seeing her body, with the multiple stab wounds?" I shivered. "Not exactly the kind of career trajectory I told her I wanted her advice on."

Gideon turned on the tap and, a moment later, nudged my elbow. "Have some water." He crouched down beside me. "I'm sorry, Raisa. I wish that you hadn't gone through that. Certainly not alone."

I nodded, barely able to force more than the tiniest sip down my thick throat.

He swore under his breath. "Have you spoken to anyone about it?"

"Not like you mean." I traced the rim of the glass with my finger.

"If you need to, you can talk to me."

His concern was too much. I slammed the glass on the table, sloshing water over the rim. "*Why?*"

He sucked his bottom lip into his mouth. "Let's eat first. You need to keep your strength up, because knowing you, you've been going full tilt ever since this happened." He moved back to the stove, taking his warmth with him. "What happened next?"

I wrapped my arms around myself like I could squeeze out the morass of emotions swirling inside me. "The killer timed my presence to the cops showing up to find the body and obviously Golden Radial is behind it all. More specifically, I'd bet my life on it being the woman who experimented on Robyn and me."

Gideon plated all the food, then carried it, along with our cutlery, to the table.

"But I didn't kill Carol, and Janna got me out of those bogus charges." I picked up the mug and took a drink. "This is excellent coffee. Thank you."

Gideon's head was down while he served, and I couldn't see his expression, but his shoulders shook.

I stabbed my scrambled eggs. "What is so funny?"

Gideon's laughter broke free, lighting up his face. "You would make the world's worst criminal. We spent five seconds together in silence before you had to start talking."

I swallowed the slight moan at the taste of those buttery fluffy eggs. There was a hint of some spice that I couldn't identify. "It was longer than five seconds," I said huffily. "And if you manufactured that silence to make me feel like a suspect and spill, I don't appreciate it."

Gideon sat down on the arm of the sofa, facing me, and stretched his legs out. He was still chuckling when he picked up his fork and dug into his own heaping plate on the table in front of him. "That wasn't an interrogation technique. It was me cooking so we could eat faster."

I chomped into my toast, baring my teeth at him, and pulled my feet under my chair.

"Message received," he said, biting into a strip of crispy bacon.

"I didn't say anything." I shoveled down more food. The confusion he inspired was doing my head in, but the food was outstanding.

"You want me to help you find that woman." He carried on methodically eating.

Was that a yes? A no? Did he enjoy making obvious statements? Could this man, for once, just use his freaking words?

A throbbing started in my feet, racing up to the crown of my head like mercury in a cartoon thermometer. I threw a piece of bacon at his chest. It didn't leave a grease mark, and I hadn't stabbed it into his flesh with my fork, so he'd gotten off easy.

He ate the bacon.

"I want nothing from you," I declared.

"Yeah, you do," he said calmly. "That's why you came to Hedon. I have the necessary experience and training, plus, other than you, I'm most personally affected by this woman's actions."

Damn his astuteness. That said, finding Baba Yaga would be difficult and dangerous on its own. I didn't have psychic powers to understand Gideon on top of that, should we partner up.

Also, and this was a huge also, I deserved an apology from him for ignoring me these past couple months after everything we'd experienced together. Didn't surviving death attempts qualify us as texting buddies at the very least?

"I, very briefly, entertained the notion of working together," I said, "but after our delightful time today I've decided otherwise."

"Why?"

My grip tightened on my fork. He was going to make me spell it out? "I appreciate that Janna is your ex, and I was your temporary investigating partner to find Woody, not to mention the woman who ruined your life, but I—" My voice cracked, and I bit the inside of my cheek to toughen myself up.

"Raisa." He wiped his mouth off with a napkin.

"I naively believed we'd formed a connection," I said, my voice oddly steady despite the pang knocking hollowly against my rib cage. "I assumed that perhaps you'd want to let me know how you were doing. Maybe even check in on me." I tossed my head, trying to untangle the mess inside me to find my balance on this tightrope knotted to self-preservation on one end and the urge for clarity on the other.

"For fuck's sake, Donatella."

I refused to soften. "I will allow Raisa. I prefer Dr. Montefiore."

"Then you shouldn't have first introduced yourself as Dr. Donatella Mutant-Ninjaturtle, hyphenated," he snapped. "You think I didn't want to contact you?"

"I don't think; I know, and I have concrete proof of my hypothesis."

"Jesus," he muttered.

"You had the opportunity and plenty of time. Also, technology nowadays makes communication incredibly easy, even from this alternate realm. No knowledge of signal fires or Morse code required."

"I needed distance from you."

I flinched. "Don't sugarcoat it or anything."

"I didn't mean—"

Outside an owl hooted, its cry low and clear.

Gideon tracked it with a yearning that showed how badly he wished to go with the bird and fly far away from this conversation. "I had to come to terms with being a shifter."

"You didn't have to accept your magic if you didn't want to." I ate some bacon, regretting losing a piece as a porcine weapon. "I promised to try and remove it, remember? I also would have respected your decision to keep your magic if you'd made it for your sake, not mine. Your body, your choice. The thing is, you unilaterally determined what was best for both of us, in terms of my serum and our communication." I pushed my plate away. "That hurt, Gideon."

His eyes flickered with regret. "I know, and I'm sorry."

"Then why?"

He shifted his weight from side to side like this admission was a physical burden, but he didn't know how to relieve himself of it without losing his balance.

A full minute went by without him speaking.

I pushed my chair back and started to rise. This was ridiculous. I wasn't going to sit here in silence while Gideon stewed.

"Because Woody was right," he blurted out. "There's no going back for me. This magic, these abilities, they're here to stay. I was trying to make peace with that. Among other things."

I sat back down. "But—"

He pointed at me with a butter knife. "On my own, because you're so damn stubborn when it comes to keeping promises that you would have kept trying to help me at the expense of what really mattered. The serum and your promise to your sister." He softened his gruff tone. "After everything we went through and all you risked to get your data back, I couldn't let you do that." He gave a one-shouldered shrug, his expression tightening self-consciously. "But I'm selfish enough that if you'd been with me, I would have let you, even knowing it was pointless and wrong."

"We don't conclusively—"

He speared me with a weary look. "Don't we?"

"Not conclusively."

He raised his eyebrows. "Truth."

I rolled my eyes. "It wouldn't be easy to get the magic out of you, and it wouldn't happen quickly."

"If," he prompted.

My shoulders slumped. "If it was possible at all."

"There. Was it so hard to admit I was right?"

"Yes." I tapped my chest. "It burns inside."

Gideon crossed over to me in two steps and placed his hand on my shoulder. "I didn't mean to hurt you, but I ended up doing that anyway." His voice was thick with self-disgust.

I sighed and leaned into his touch, feeling the warmth of his hand through my shirt. "Pull your head out of your ass, Stern."

He jerked away. "What?"

"Seriously. Are you done with your pity party?" I pitched my voice into a mocking approximation of his gruffness. "*I must stay away because me noble man even if me big bad wolf.*"

"I'm glad you find my hard-won honesty such a lark."

"Oh, you misunderstand. What I meant to convey was that I find you constantly beating yourself up so yesterday." I had no time for useless emotions on this hunt—in myself or Gideon. I flapped a hand. "Look, if you hated me, I'd understand, but you fed me, so you don't."

He watched me without responding.

"Chime in anytime, buddy."

"I'm too busy beating myself up," he said dryly.

"Yeah, well, quit it. Wolf shifter or not, you're a good man, Gideon Stern. I wouldn't be here if you weren't." I tapped an imaginary watch on my wrist. "I'll give you ten seconds to kvetch and rend your shirt, then I want my competent partner back. Got it?"

"You'll be playing Bad Cop then?"

"Only when I have to. Well? Will you help me find Baba Yaga?"

"Will you quit with the pop culture speak? There's no Google Translate for you."

"Baba Yaga is way older than most pop culture. She's a figure in Russian mythology, the witch in the woods with the house on chicken legs. I can't help it if you're illiterate." I widened my eyes. "You can read, can't you, Jacob Black?"

Gideon massaged a temple with his finger. "You're invoking *Twilight*?"

"*That's* the pop culture reference you know?"

"Janna's niece made us watch it," he mumbled.

That sounded nice. Not the *Twilight* part necessarily, but

a family unit that watched movies together. Did he and Janna have pizza nights and play fight over their film options?

I'd never had anything like that. I'm sure I would in the future, but I felt a very rare-for-me moment of regret that I'd spent my twenties without much of a personal life.

Also, monopolizing Gideon with this investigation would continue to hurt his ex, and she didn't deserve that. "About Janna…" I said.

He sighed heavily. "I am going to say this once so listen up. I know how to get to Toronto, and if I wanted to be there instead of here, doing this with you, I would be. Okay?"

Like I said, he was a good man, so of course he'd say—

"I'm not just saying it," he growled.

"I wasn't even thinking that."

He leveled a flat stare at me. "Look," he said a moment later, "I get that Janna gave you a message for me, but like I once said, she broke up with me months before I ever met you."

"You also said that she wanted to reconcile and the thing that stopped you was being a shifter."

"No. I didn't answer her at the time because my world had turned upside down. I never said that's why we didn't resume the engagement."

"Would you have gotten back together if your life had continued normally?" When he didn't answer, I nodded tightly. "I see. That's—"

"Not a fair question," he finished, shooting me a dark glare. "Because it didn't. Besides, she was right to end things. If we'd made up, it would have been out of loneliness or because on paper we were a good match. We might have even gotten married, but it wouldn't have stuck. We texted about it when I came back from Marrakesh. We agreed we're over."

I dropped my fork. "You *texted*? Oh my God. Of all the clueless—"

"What? That's how we'd been communicating since the breakup. She didn't want to speak to me on the phone or see me after it happened. Only text and even that was infrequent."

Wow, okay. They were both chickenshit when it came to confrontation. Not like I had any room to talk, never having had a serious relationship, but they'd planned to spend their lives together and Janna clearly needed some one-on-one closure.

Gideon did too.

It was good to know I could crush on him guilt-free, but it was also a huge red flag in terms of letting my feelings go any further than that. I understood why Janna wasn't the first person he turned to after he got shifter magic, since they were no longer together, but I also wondered how much he'd let her see any part of him that was less than perfect.

Inspector Gideon Stern loved his rules, a fact I knew very well from our first encounter when he'd shown up with the warrant. He'd gone from being a staunch defender of justice to working for the Queen of Hearts. No wonder he'd ghosted Janna. He probably didn't recognize who he'd become.

But if his first reaction when he lost his way was to cut and run, then should I squelch any attraction now before he did the same to me? Or rather, did the same to me again?

"Are you going to eat or just push food around while you think a billion thoughts?" Gideon said.

There'd be plenty of time to worry about my feelings once we stopped Baba Yaga. For now, though they'd only interfere with my goal. I mean, I still had to work with Gideon, but we'd be friends, like partners in a good buddy cop film should be. That had been fun before and it'd be fun now.

"We can join forces," I said. "This woman must be taken down."

"I know and I'm in." He waved a hand across the air. "Donatella and Lobo Cop, the farewell tour."

Gideon was already putting an expiry date on whatever we were? Nope. I didn't care. Only our goal mattered, and this was a huge first obstacle cleared. I'd gotten his assistance, which was the fastest way to get my life back and my research on track.

He poked me gently in the center of my forehead. "Farewell to Golden Radial, dummy."

I stepped back. "Enough already. You can't read minds."

"I've become fluent in your expressions, and you wear your thoughts on your face." He rolled his eyes but didn't keep the fondness from his voice.

My heart skipped a beat. "I'm not going to be impressed until you also understand all my excellent pop culture references." I imagined catching Gideon up on all the best shows he was woefully out of touch with. I had a feeling he'd like the Twelfth Doctor.

"Yeah," that cultural neophyte said pleasantly, "don't hold your breath."

I snorted. Okay then. One farewell tour, and not the Cher kind, where she kept coming back. Then it was "Good night, Hedon," and our final bow before I showed up to my new job on January 4.

The Baba Yaga World Tour. I was totally making T-shirts.

Chapter 9

I had never actually considered the massive amount of logistics involved in world tours. By the time I'd charted our first stop, back to Toronto, I had a newfound respect for band managers. Anyone who could coordinate getting at least one entire person and their stuff across countries (or realities) had my undying respect.

At least it took only about ten seconds to get the Queen on board with us finding the mysterious Eastern European woman, provided we delivered my tormentor to Her Majesty.

Did I experience any qualms at the deal, knowing I should have sought justice instead of vengeance? Let's just say the Queen promised me that when I brought my nemesis back, I'd be allowed my choice of benches and topiaries by the new installation. Motivation? Twisted, but definitely there.

Gideon transported me to my apartment so I could pack. I'd texted Levi to say I'd be there tonight to stay with him and would explain when I got there, to which I received a thumbs-up emoji.

My partner sat on the edge of my bed while I threw

clothes into my large suitcase, telling me about his interview two months ago with Gus, the magic forger and Golden Radial minion who'd tracked us to Marrakesh. Moran had taken him into custody.

Gus was committed to a "the less I know about these people, the better" survival strategy. The only person at Golden Radial he'd ever met was Jeremy Wade—the Mundane lawyer who Woody dealt with and the person who'd supplied my mentor with wolf DNA for all his research.

Once the Queen learned that Gus was working for Golden Radial, she was determined to uncover all its tentacles in Hedon. She had no problem with black-market transactions going down in her territory, but she expected to be looped in on the players.

She'd heard of the venture capital firm, but just its public face, and this displeased her. Gus had learned the extent of this displeasure since he was still imprisoned in one of the royal dungeons. Dude had tried to kill me twice; I wasn't shedding any tears over his current digs. If he couldn't break out of Hedon's dungeons then that was on him.

Gideon had then pulled favors from old friends and informants whom Moran placed at his disposal in order to investigate Golden Radial when the Queen decreed it his main assignment.

"Did you come across any mention of Lausanne?" I said.

"The city Woody told you about?"

My mouth fell open. "You heard that? How? He whispered it in my ear, and you were near death from the bullet wound."

"Shifter hearing, remember? I looked into it."

"You didn't tell the Queen about it though. You didn't mention the shifter trials either."

He shook his head, his brow furrowed. "I followed the rules with my reports to my superiors at the Toronto Police

Service, and I've gone above and beyond to keep Her Majesty apprised of everything on this investigation."

Fair. She was way scarier than any cop boss.

So, the Queen knew about the shifter trials before I told her. I balled up a pair of socks and slammed them into the suitcase. Relationships in my world were fairly black and white. Sure, I'd dealt with backstabbing and politics in grad school, but every interaction with the Queen was a chess match of Machiavellian proportions. The less I interacted with her, the better.

"Gus is the only direct link between Hedon and Golden Radial." Gideon stretched his legs out and leaned back on one elbow.

"I wish I'd asked Woody how he met Gus. Oh well." I pointed at a pile of sweaters on the bed next to him and he handed them over. "I searched Jeremy's name. He's the guy I told you had followed me." The one who'd worn the same cologne as my father and who'd broken into my apartment.

"I thought as much, based on the description you'd given me. My gut says he's got a lot of power in that organization, and I don't want to go after him directly. Better to squeeze what we can out of lower-level employees and use that information to come for Jeremey Wade."

"We should go to the clinic in Switzerland." I rubbed my hands together. They'd performed atrocities on people, but the scientist in me was curious about the facilities. They were probably state of the art. I wrangled my bulging suitcase closed, trying not to think about whether that made me a bad person.

"It was shut down soon after the fire at Perrault, and before you ask, no, the private clinic wasn't in Lausanne. It was on the outskirts of Sion, which is a small city up in the mountains. The clinic was situated on large grounds surrounded by a high fence and bordered the forest."

Gideon's lips curled into a sneer. "Perfect for their wolf subjects to roam at will with no one the wiser."

"Except the staff." I wheeled the suitcase into the living room.

"Yeah, well, the staff have disappeared." He snapped his fingers. "Into thin air. All digital records were wiped, and when I went to Sion to ask around, no one had any recollection of names or descriptions. Apparently, people at the clinic kept to themselves."

"Still, someone should have seen or heard something. Those trials ran for years."

"You'd think."

"Awesome." I put on my boots. "So where do we start?"

Gideon pointed to my laptop, his eyebrows raised in question. Off my nod, he unplugged it and wound the cord up. "Lausanne."

"We *are* going to Switzerland? The world tour wasn't supposed to go global that quickly, but okay."

"Less European leg, more Asian. We're going to a private members' club in Bangkok. It was a mega-disco in the '80s, but the club went bust in the late '90s. The property sat empty for years getting more and more run-down, until it was bought in 2015, and the owner renamed it Lausanne in homage to the city where the Thai king—not the current one—spent most of his youth." He paused. "Guess who originally staked the club owner?"

"Golden Radial." I raised my eyebrows. "Clubs and biotech. That's a strange diversity for their portfolio."

"They must have expected the real return to be from the members," he said. "Connections are powerful things, especially where information gathering is concerned. The owner paid them back, but it's worth speaking to her to find out what she knows of the group."

"How will we get in?"

"I tracked down a resident of Hedon who's a member

and persuaded her to give me a visitor's pass to check it out and see if I wish to join."

"Persuaded like…?" I made claws and an "arrrr" sound.

"Do you want to come with me or not?"

"I'm going undercover?!" I jumped up and down.

"Keep behaving like that," Gideon said, "and no one will suspect a thing."

"Can I pick my name?"

He crossed his arms. "I would be the stupidest person alive to let you do that, and you know it."

"I want to be a countess. Oh, and have a shady past with three husbands that no one is really sure what happened to."

"Keep dreaming. Let's get you to Levi's. We can reconvene in the morning."

I put on my jacket, grabbed my purse, and surveyed my place. I had everything I required for now. I gave him a regal nod. "The countess is ready to depart."

Gideon shook his head and blinked as though clearing his mind of an unpleasant thought, then he took my suitcase in one hand, twined his other with mine, and we were off.

Between being in Hedon and Toronto, I felt like I'd been experiencing days in dog years, and my disorientation deepened when I hit Vancouver to find the sun still setting. Would today never end?

Gideon waited with me at the fence surrounding Levi's Mediterranean-style villa until I'd been buzzed in. He bid me good night and vanished back to Hedon.

I dragged my suitcase up to the large home painted a mellow gold. The ruffled nightmare of a wedding dress which had been speared into the lawn the last time I'd been here was gone, either tactfully removed by Levi or dragged back to the hell from which it came. I'd have to ask Ash if she'd picked out a dress.

The door flung open when I was still halfway up the walk, and my cousin bounded out in his socks to sweep me up into an enormous hug that lifted me off the ground. I relaxed into his embrace, all my worries erased by pure happiness.

Robyn and I were twins, but when Levi was around, we were the Three Musketeers. He'd always been more of a brother to us than a cousin. An older brother, as he annoyingly liked to point out, though by only a few months.

Our twelve-year estrangement after Robyn's death had been horrible, but between weekly Zoom calls, late-night text exchanges of stupid memes, and a lot of happy wandering down memory lane, we'd carefully and lovingly repaired our relationship.

Levi gallantly took my suitcase and escorted me into his home. At six foot two, he was a couple of inches taller than Gideon, though he wasn't nearly as bulked up. He had more of a soccer player's build, which he used to flaunt his impeccable taste in clothing. He'd rolled up the cuffs of his—no doubt Italian-designed—shirt that he wore with a pair of pinstripe trousers. He'd foregone a tie and suit jacket, and he'd raked his fingers through his hair, shaking out the black locks that were usually swept off his forehead to accentuate his sharp cheekbones and jawline.

"You couldn't dress up for me?" I teased, unlacing my boots.

His blue eyes, twins to my own, warmed in amusement. "Well, it's not like you're company, Red."

Laughter floated out from the kitchen.

"Speaking of company," I said. "Am I interrupting something?"

"We had friends over for the first night of Hanukkah."

I dropped my boot. "Oh."

Levi frowned. "You're not interrupting."

"It's not that." I used to love Hanukkah. It meant eight days of presents, fried foods, and best of all, Robyn, Levi, and me being reunited, since we lived in Toronto and he was in Vancouver. But over the years, I'd stopped celebrating. My mom was never around, probably deliberately, and it became too depressing to light the candles by myself.

Even the few times I'd been invited to a friend's house, the celebration had a hollowness to it, and somewhere along the line, I'd blocked the holiday out entirely.

Like tonight. With everything else going on, I'm not sure I would have remembered it at all, and that was really sad.

Levi crouched down beside me. "You don't have to come meet everyone, if it's too much. I can ease you into them in tiny amounts when you move here."

"So, about that."

His face fell.

"I got a job in Toronto and I start on January 4. I'll be working under the leadership of this really smart scientist who's excited to have me on board." I hung up my coat in the closet by the front door.

Levi looked at me for a long moment then laughed. "That was the most miserable-sounding description of a fabulous new job that I've ever heard. I'm thrilled for you, and if I have to root for you from this side of the country, so be it. We have planes and phones and a gold token. Four thousand, two hundred and seven point four kilometers are not going to come between us."

I pressed my lips together, but a snort escaped me. "You looked up how far apart we are?"

He ducked his head for a second, a faint blush hitting his cheeks, then notched his chin up with the haughtiest expression. "I rule from out here on the west coast and Toronto is Canada's largest city. It seemed prudent to be aware of the distance."

I bowed, extending my arm in a flourish. "Of course, Your Royal Bullshitter."

Levi smacked my shoulder. "Shut up."

I smiled. "Come introduce me. I want to see Ash and finally meet your friends." I paused. "Friends you've said suspiciously little about, leaving me to wonder if they're actors you've hired."

"If only. Then I could send them away."

"Hang on." I fished the flash drive with my data out of my purse. "Can you keep this for me for a bit?"

"Of course."

We detoured into his office briefly where he locked the flash drive up in his hidden safe, then he led me into the living room, with its wide bleached wood planks, modern furniture that was stylish and comfortable (an impossibility on my budget), and picture windows showcasing a wide sweep of private beach. I'd mostly gotten used to Levi's wealth on my last visit, but I still checked my socks for holes in the toes.

The lifestyle-magazine vibe was lessened by wedding sample tat covering every surface: tottering piles of invitations in more neutral colors than I realized existed, candles in glassware of varying shapes and sizes, now-dead flower arrangements, veils, tuxedo accoutrements, and dinner wear. There was even a life-size cardboard cutout photo of Levi and Ash standing on a beach at sunset with hearts floating off into the sky.

It had been stabbed multiple times, so I was guessing they hadn't posed for that delightful item.

I squinted into one corner. Yes, that was a heap of cake topper figurines, and they weren't even all human. "Are you having a dinosaur-themed wedding?"

Levi threw up his hands. "It's like no other House Head has ever gotten married. Every supplier and their dog is sending us shit." He grabbed an abstract metal sculpture that was about two feet high with a large tulle bow on it. "You know what this is?"

"Not even with all my degrees."

"Me neither. But apparently, I can use it at my reception."

"Couldn't you hire someone to deal with this?"

"We did. This is the overflow that didn't fit in the storage locker." He winged the sculpture onto the sofa. "The wedding has taken on a life of its own."

"That…sucks? I'm sorry for your overabundance?" I patted his shoulder. "All joking aside, I'm sure that in the end, it will be beautiful and the most important part, the commitment between you and Ash, will shine."

He sighed. "I hope so, because Ash hates this even more than I do, and I've got almost two more months before she's legally stuck with me." He shook his head. "Enough of that. Come on."

Hopefully what awaited me in the next room wouldn't be scarier than the wedding hell in this one.

Chapter 10

Levi's kitchen was my favorite place in his house. Even though it was a big room, it was cozy and clearly the heart of this home. Round spice tins were stuck to a long magnetic board, near the braids of garlic tacked to the window frame, while red appliances added a touch of whimsy, the entire space anchored by gorgeous blue glass tiles.

In the middle of a table filled with dirty dinner dishes sat a gleaming gold menorah with melted red candle wax on the rightmost holder and on the raised shammash. I smiled at the sight of my nonna's menorah, happy that Levi had taken good care of it.

Four strangers lounged around the island in the middle of the kitchen. Between them were almost-empty platters with grilled vegetables, some slices of roast chicken, a lonely square of kugel, and a handful of potato latkes.

I hovered by the door. "Hi, I'm—"

"Dr. Raisa Montefiore!" A dazzlingly handsome man clapped his hands and jumped off his stool at the counter. Of Asian descent, he had sharp cheekbones, full lips, and black hair that floated free to his shoulders. He wore a crop top reading "Dudes Taste Better," spotlighting his ridiculous six-pack. Or was that an eight-pack? I had the weirdest urge to go over and count.

The other three had also cut their conversation short to stare at me, wineglasses in hand.

I rubbed my thumb over the post of one of my piercings, but sadly it wasn't sharp enough to inflict damage in case I had to fend off these gawkers. "I feel like it's feeding time at the zoo."

"Inside voice on the outside!" Handsome guy beamed at me.

"Arkady," the lone woman of the new group warned, pronouncing it "Ar-KAD-y" and not a place with video games. "Don't overwhelm her." She had a black bob I envied for its perfect straightness, sparkling green eyes, and brown skin that was complemented by a cool turquoise tunic.

I tugged at my hoodie, but it didn't transform into something more glamorous.

"I only have the one mode of operation, darling." Arkady pointed at my shiny piercings. "Besides, we share a magpie's love of treasure. Now, sister from another mister..." He drew a circle at the graphic on my sweater. "Levi says you're some kind of science genius. Explain for the masses."

It was the AC/DC logo with the thunderbolt separating the two pairs of letters, but DC was replaced with GT.

"Adenine, cytosine, guanine, and thymine," said the third stranger. "They're the four types of bases found in a DNA molecule." His posh British accent matched his bow tie, but who actually wore those aside from grooms and the Eleventh Doctor? Granted, he was nerd-hot, giving off a kindly Giles librarian vibe with his short reddish-brown hair, pale white skin, and those glasses, but I believed that act about as much as Clark Kent's fumbling innocence.

The woman beamed at him, while the final man, a huge

guy who seemed to simply be a giant muscle sculpted into human parts, leaned away from the others like he could disassociate himself from them. He had buzzed blond hair and serious brown eyes, and he looked vaguely familiar, although I couldn't place him.

"He's right," I said, nodding at the British man. "It's a DNA joke."

Levi caught my elbow and led me to the counter. "Gin and tonic?"

He'd remembered I didn't drink wine. The smell of that cave when I was little had put me off it forever.

"Make it a double." I stuck close to my cousin's side while he pulled a bottle of gin out of the freezer. "You all know who I am, but I haven't had the pleasure." I could hazard a fairly reasonable guess on a couple of them, but I didn't want to flub names as a first impression.

"Because Levi and Ash hogged you all to themselves," the vivacious woman said.

"What am I being accused of?" Ash exited out of the basement stairwell, holding another couple of wine bottles. "Raisa!" The dark-haired woman dumped the bottles on the table and raced over to hug me. "It's so good to see you."

"You too." The more I'd gotten to know Ash, the more I adored her. She was smart, funny, fiercely loyal, and, best of all, did not hesitate to bust Levi's balls. I pushed aside the small sting that she never got to meet my twin and vice versa. They probably would have been thick as thieves.

The fridge rattled as Levi dispensed ice into my glass. He set it on the kitchen island in front of me.

Arkady planted his hands on his hips. "Can I do the introductions now?"

Ash grabbed a corkscrew and one of the bottles. "Go nuts."

"Very well." He smoothed a hand over his shirt. "I'm Arkady Choi. Do not call me Ark. I'm Levi's favorite operative. This is Priya Khatri, Ash's best friend, and a computer wiz."

"Priya!" I shook her hand. "I'm so happy to finally meet you, and thank you so much for all your help." Without her hacking abilities, I'd never have found Gideon in Marrakesh and finally tracked Woody down.

Arkady sniffed at my interruption, then pointed at the man next to Priya. "Rafael Behar is our British import."

"You're Ash's partner in Jezebel Investigations." I shook Rafael's hand as well. "Nice to meet you."

"You as well, Raisa."

Arkady glared at Levi and Ash. "Why does Dr. Raisa know who Pri and Rafael are, but showed no sign of recognition at my name?"

"We figured you were best experienced with no preamble." Ash topped up his wineglass.

"Uh-huh." He patted Muscle Man's shoulder. "This fine specimen of a man is Miles. My boyfriend and Levi's best friend."

"I'm also head of security for House Pacifica," Miles said. He glared at Arkady, but it was pretty feeble and his boyfriend just grinned.

"Miles Berenbaum," I said, dredging up an old memory of one of our visits here when I was a kid. He'd been Levi's best friend forever. "We met years ago."

"Yeah," Miles said. "I wasn't sure you'd remember."

Ash handed me a plate. "Help yourself."

That kugel was calling my name. I grabbed a clean fork and dug in. "Mmm. This is your mom's recipe," I said. Traditionally, people made sweet kugel with cottage cheese, but my zia Nicola always used mascarpone and it was so much better that way.

"It is," Levi said. "I can't believe you remember."

"It's delicious food, dummy. Of course I do." He'd even layered the noodles, creamy cheese, cinnamon, and raisins perfectly so the eater got a complete experience in every bite.

Arkady tore off a piece of latke and popped it into his mouth. "Now that we've met the newest member of the wedding party—"

I choked on my mouthful of kugel, gripping the counter with one hand because I felt knocked sideways. "Wedding party?"

"Down, Arkady. I haven't had a chance to ask her yet." Levi sipped his wine. "I'd love you to be as involved as you're comfortable with."

"We both would," Ash insisted.

"It would even out Levi's side of the wedding party with Ash's," Priya said, "which would be great." She turned to me, pulling out her phone and scrolling. "How do you feel about a tux?" She held up an image from a Pinterest board.

"It's not something I'd ever considered my emotions about." I mumbled into my gin and tonic. I was thrilled to be invited to the wedding, but standing up with Levi? I took an especially long swig.

As happy as I was to meet these people, tonight was a lot. I spent most of my time by myself in a lab. Sometimes I'd consult with another scientist for a while, working through a particular problem, and yes, we'd eat together in the staff lunchroom, but those were short bursts of social time where we mostly discussed research. Not personal matters.

I no longer got juiced up on larger social gatherings like I had back in high school, and my energy was being drained here at a rapid rate. I couldn't remember the last time I'd cared about making a good impression on a group of people, while everyone here, including the one person who mattered most, expected an answer about a very next-level personal commitment.

"So, Priya," I said, very much avoiding answering any of

the questions currently before me, "are you planning the wedding?"

She looked up with a scowl. "No. I'm only allowed to handle affairs relating to the bridal party."

"You're busy enough that you shouldn't even have to deal with any of this," Ash said, "but you're the only one I trust not to have me look like a Disney princess on my wedding day."

"Nice save," Priya said, her grin back.

Ash winked at her.

"How do you figure Raisa's presence would even out the numbers, love?" Rafael said to his girlfriend. "Ash has you and me, while Miles and Arkady are standing up for Levi. The numbers are even already."

"Mrs. Hudson, duh. Ooh." Priya stopped scrolling. "This tux is nice."

"Y-you're having your pug in the ceremony?" I shot back the rest of my G&T, pretending I hadn't seen the picture that Priya waved.

"First I've heard of it," Levi said.

"Me too," Ash said.

My cousin slid his arm around his fiancée and murmured something in her ear that made her laugh and give him a private, knowing look. Here he was, starting a new life with the woman he loved, while I was stuck in my past with emotional baggage instead of cheering him on.

"Like Mrs. H's involvement had to be discussed," Priya scoffed.

"We already have her outfit," Arkady said.

Oh. My. God. I nodded at Ash. "The wedding dress that I saw stabbed to the ground outside last time is making a lot more sense."

"I can get an extra sword," Ash said with a bit too much enthusiasm. "Feel free to use it to protest any of their suggestions."

"Your optimism that a sword can stop Pri is…" Rafael frowned.

"Think carefully about how badly you want to be searched at customs the next time you fly home to London, sweetheart," Priya said without looking up from her screen.

"Delusional," he said.

"Oh. That works." She eyed me like she was measuring me, shook her head, and kept scrolling.

Levi placed a hand on my shoulder. "Please don't let them drive you away." He glared at his friends. "I really want you here, and as blood trumps all of them, they can all leave now. Everyone except Ash."

Nothing about being in the wedding party let me remain smart, logical, and laser-focused, or helped me reach my goal. My God, all the emotions it would bring up, like how Levi's mom, who I still hadn't spoken to, would be there. I'd planned to enjoy his big day safely from the sidelines, not front and center fielding pitying looks about my dead twin or assuaging Zia Nicola's guilt over abandoning Mom and me after Robyn's and Dad's deaths.

But it was *Levi's* wedding, and I'd do anything for him. Perhaps standing up with him was exactly the public declaration I needed to make. Not for anyone else, but for me. Once I stopped Baba Yaga, wouldn't I also be starting a new chapter of my life? Shouldn't I celebrate that fact?

I sighed. The key word was "stopped." The image of Carol's bloodied body hadn't faded yet, and I didn't want to make promises I might not be able to keep. I squeezed Levi's hand. "Can I give you my answer once my other business here is wrapped up?"

"Of course." He sounded empathetic though understandably sad that I didn't say yes immediately.

"Wow. Potentially mortifying rebuff." Arkady crossed one leg over the other.

"It's not a rebuff," I insisted.

"Uh-huh. What brings you out west, Dr. Raisa?"

"Besides a tuxedo fitting?" Priya eyed me.

"I haven't agreed yet," I said.

"We'll call it a just-in-case tuxedo fitting. It takes time to order things, so I'll need your measurements. When are you free to book an appointment at the shop?"

"I—uh." I shook my head. "I'm not sure how much time I'll have."

Three-months-ago me would never have shared Operation Baba Yaga, but a lot had happened since then. Besides, this was Levi and Ash's inner circle, and I'd already given Levi permission to share the details of my search for Woody with his most trusted people.

Still, the deeply ingrained habit of not talking about myself because I was tired of rehashing the loss of my sister made me pause.

"I trust these people with my life," Levi said. "More importantly, I trust them with Ash's and with yours. They can keep a secret."

"Appearances notwithstanding," Miles said, nodding at Arkady.

His boyfriend gasped, then shrugged. "Fair."

"It's not any of you," I said. "I was on my own for so long that having people in my corner is…" I shook my head, my throat thick.

"There's your problem," Arkady said sagely. "We're not people. We're the finest examples of the human race."

My shocked laugh released any tension left in me. The fact that I both could and should share this with them left me feeling relieved and warmly happy.

Once I told them about Carol's murder and my arrest, I didn't require much more explaining about why I had to find Baba Yaga. These people understood far too well.

"I looked into Inspector Stern," Miles said. "He was a good cop and he'll be a good partner with a personal investment. You made the right call convincing him to come on board."

"Being a wolf shifter doesn't hurt either," Priya said.

"Speaking of looking into," Levi said. "We didn't find any dirt on Jeremy Wade. To all appearances, he's simply legal counsel for Golden Radial. His worst offense is a couple of speeding tickets."

I grimaced. "I'm disappointed but not surprised."

"Have any of you heard of that club Lausanne?" Ash said, circling back to my explanation of where Gideon and I were going next. "It's not a name I've ever come across."

"It's in Bangkok," Rafael said. "It's neutral meeting ground for Nefesh and Mundanes of a certain caliber." He wrinkled his nose in distaste.

"Have you been?" Miles asked.

"None of us have the cred to get within ten feet of the front door." Rafael toyed with the stem of his wineglass. "No offense, Raisa, but are you sure you'll be allowed in?"

"Or pass even if you do?" Arkady said. "I mean, look at you. You hardly exude power."

Priya hit him, but he shrugged. "She's wearing a science pun hoodie. I call it as I see it."

"You're not wrong," I said with a sigh. "Gideon seemed confident of our access, and he'll fit in fine. I'm the weak link."

"Screw that," Ash said. "I'm the master of undercover work. By the time I'm done with you, no one will doubt your authenticity. Let me go to Hedon and talk to Gideon. I'll get the details of your cover story."

She'd vanished using her gold token before I could say a word.

"Makeover!" Priya squealed, clapping her hands. Then she fixed me with a steely glare. "And future formalwear decisions."

I looked to the men for help because things were

spiraling out of my control, but the cowards were fixated on such scintillating items as light fixtures and their feet.

Well, all except Arkady, whose shrewd gleam turned to a knowing grin when I caught his eye. "Hot wolf cop isn't going to know what hit him." He raised his wineglass. "L'chaim, baby."

Chapter 11

Gideon showed up the next afternoon.

I opened the front door since everyone else had decamped to Rafael's place for Christmas celebrations. Maybe I'd be part of them next year? I could fly out over winter break. My smile dimmed. Any winter breaks I enjoyed in the future were dependent on two things: 1) me having a job that did not explode, figuratively or literally, and 2) Baba Yaga safely in topiary prison and not gunning for my blood.

I'm sure I could move here to Vancouver and find a job, but I wanted things the way I wanted them. That meant stop Baba Yaga and start working with Dr. Nakahara back in Toronto on January 4.

Gideon strode into the foyer in a navy pinstriped three-piece suit and pair of tortoiseshell-framed glasses. On other mere mortals, the getup would look conservative, even fussy. On him, it conjured up naughty banker role playing ideas. "Ready when you—"

My getup left him speechless. Good.

I'd been putting him off via text for a few hours because

my undercover transformation had been nowhere as easy as throwing on a fake mustache and glasses. I'd been tweezed, squeezed into shapewear that I was pretty sure contravened the Geneva Convention, and, thanks to Ash's undercover kit, made to wear the equivalent of a small nation's GDP in makeup. The woman could contour, who knew?

Given Gideon's reaction, the torture was worth it.

I smoothed a hand over my black shirt with lace cuffs. Over it I wore a bloodred velvet jacket with a high collar, a row of black velvet buttons, and swirly black embroidery on the front. When I pronounced it the coolest item of clothing I'd ever worn, Priya pointed out—with a meaningful look— that it was basically a colorful tux jacket, but left it at that.

Ash also forced me into a pair of black leather pants that left no room for breathing, much less a sandwich, but made my ass look spectacular. All of it was topped off with spiky black heels that she assured me could, in a pinch, kill a person.

I'm not sure what it said about my life that I simply accepted this both as a need-to-know fact, and that she was in possession of it, with nothing more than a nod.

I turned in a slow circle. "Do I pass muster?"

Gideon let out a slow whistle. "Yes, Contessa, you pass."

"You made me an *Italian* countess?" I flung my arms around his neck. Ash hadn't been allowed to reveal my undercover identity, but she'd assured me I'd like it.

Gideon's eyes widened briefly. Probably because I'd practically climbed the poor guy in my enthusiasm.

I stepped back but his arm came around me like a steel band.

"I made you the widow of a minor Italian count," he said, his hazel eyes boring into mine. "I wasn't sure you had the language skills to pull off being Italian yourself."

"I don't," I admitted. I'd always had a knack for

languages, be it French in high school or the Italian that Dad and Nonna spoke to Robyn and me, but I hadn't had the time to really study one the way I'd need to in order to pass for fluent.

Gideon traced a finger up my neck and gently set the dangly fake emerald earrings that Ash had lent me swinging. "You look naked without all your piercings."

"Do I?" I swallowed to get the huskiness out of my voice.

"Yeah," he said gruffly, "but this fits your persona as Luciana De Angelis better."

It was the oddest conversation, exchanging information necessary for this mission while our bodies were plastered together. His chest rose and fell in a steady rhythm, and heat poured off his skin through all the layers of my clothes into the center of my torso.

"Light of the angels," I murmured. If I stretched my fingers, I'd be able to thread them into his soft waves. "Cool. Who's my husband?"

"Roberto. Old guy. Dropped dead of a heart attack about six months ago, but there were questions because he cut his kids out of the will."

"Questions." I sighed happily.

A tight expression flashed across Gideon's face. He stepped back and cleared his throat. "Since he was older, the two of you kept a low profile, but now you're untangling Roberto's estate, and want some background information on investors for a medical research firm that was in his portfolio."

"Clever. So why do I need you?"

He bopped the end of my nose. "I'm your lawyer, Rupert Harris." He spoke his name in a British accent so sharp, it could cut glass. "I'll do the talking."

Naughty lawyer can speak all he wants. I shook off my

inappropriate thoughts, processing what he'd said. "Wait. I'm a prop?"

"A silent one. Yes."

We'd see about that. I smiled my compliance and grabbed the final piece of my disguise—a small black hat with a netted veil that fell to my bloodred lips. I'd been confused about why I had to hide my face, but it made sense now. Contessa De Angelis, the grieving black widow.

"I did some research on Sion last night," I said, referencing the Swiss city where the muscular dystrophy trials were held. "And guess what one of its main attractions is?"

"Cheese? Something tame and quaint and charming?"

"Not even close. A witches' tower. It was used to imprison and torture the hundreds killed in witch trials from the fifteenth to eighteenth centuries."

"That's good?"

"Not the trials part, but it's insight into our Baba Yaga. Mountains, forests, witches, wolves. What are the chances that the cave Robyn and I were brought to was located in a mountainous area? One with a forest?"

"Geographically that would make sense. Let's see if we find anything to support that." Gideon pointed to my purse. "Leave your cell here. If anything happens and they get into it, they'll not only find your real name but have contact information for everyone close to you."

"What about you?"

He patted his pocket. "Burner phone. There's nothing on it to connect Rupert Harris to Gideon Stern."

After a split-second transfer through Hedon, we landed in Bangkok in front of a small, partially knocked down building that was covered in panels of colorful graffiti. Benches had been set out for admiring the art, and even though it was the middle of the night, a couple of kids skateboarded on the wide concrete stairs to one side. With squat buildings pressing up on either side of this property, there wasn't enough room for a former mega-disco.

A subway car with a few sleepy commuters whizzed by on its elevated track, and a Thai pop song drifted out through an open window somewhere.

Sweat beaded my skin, the weather still warm and humid, even this late, and these clothes made it worse. If we didn't get inside soon, I'd melt like the Wicked Witch into a puddle of makeup. All of Ash's contouring would be for naught.

"This way." Gideon headed around the side, halfway down a narrow road to a dingy stone fence. Other than a profusion of lush plants, which draped softly over the top of the wall, it was too high to see anything behind it. The gate was comprised of two tall wooden doors with a repeating pattern of ornately carved lotus flowers.

Gideon looked confident that we were in the right place. He pressed a button in the panel to the side of the gate and rattled off a string of numbers and letters into the intercom.

One of the doors silently swung open, and he motioned me inside.

No sooner had we stepped under the cool outdoor canopy in a dozen shades of dazzling greens than the gate closed behind us, sealing us off from the concrete and all sounds of the city. I worried at my bottom lip. We should have still heard something from outside the fence walls.

However, when I combined the lack of sound with a night sky that glittered with brilliant stars instead of one cluttered with light pollution, all became clear.

"Architects built this." I wasn't referring to the occupation, but the rare Nefesh ability of people who could stitch together alternate realities. Hedon was the largest example, and kept very need to know, but even I had heard rumors of tiny pockets scattered around the globe, where a person would walk through a door and find themselves in a magic world.

I'd always hoped to find one when I was younger, like the Pevensie kids in *Narnia*.

Gideon rubbed his thumb over the top button of his shirt. "My token doesn't work here. The hum I usually feel against my skin is gone. I can't shift either."

I stretched my fingers into a sliver of moonlight between the leafy shadows, but there was no sense of connection. "Yeah, my magic is dead too."

"I can take you back," he said.

Going into this situation without magic was risky, but who was to say that using it would be a smart move anyway? This was a concrete step forward, and the two of us would be together, with our combined skills, experience, and intelligence.

"I'm staying." I pushed him forward along the path.

Giant flowers in DayGlo colors not found in nature kept company with bamboo reeds as thick and tall as my partner, while the scent of orange blossoms gently perfumed the garden.

We entered another tall door with lotus carvings, the temperature and quality of light cooling yet again. We'd gone inside, but I had no inkling as to the size or shape of the place because the jungle had crept in through cracks in the walls and up from the floor. It crowded the snaking path.

The entire place was one rainy spring away from being reclaimed by Mother Nature. A blue butterfly fluttered past my face, and when I turned to watch it fly away, a large flowering bougainvillea shifted sideways, creating space for a banyan tree, which rose up, slowly unfurling its branches.

"Outstanding," I murmured. The space was masterfully designed, both in terms of its beauty and its ability to catch people off guard.

"Sawade krab, Mr. Harris and Contessa De Angelis.

Welcome to Lausanne." A soft-spoken Thai man in a rough-spun linen shirt and parachute pants—with a dropped crotch, baggy legs, and fitted at the ankles—greeted us, but there was a steeliness behind his smile and assessing gaze that put me on high alert. Not to mention that he'd already identified us, even with me in this veil, and I hadn't seen a camera anywhere. "I am Kasemchai. How may I assist you?"

Gideon replied in his crisp English accent. "I was hoping to meet with Ms. Suwan, if she's available? I did send word."

"That won't be possible," Kasemchai replied in no uncertain terms. "But may I offer you a drink? Or a visit to the spa? We encourage all interested and eligible parties to enjoy our facilities once before applying for membership."

It was good that our cover stories were sound, but what would happen if he decided our visit was over? Our eviction wouldn't be as simple as being tossed out on the street. I shivered at the image of him throwing us through a crack into some endless void, or into a special torture chamber of the Architects' making. My imagination was quickly conjuring pocket dimensions that made the Queen's dungeons seem positively hospitable.

Gideon returned Kasemchai's polite smile, with a hint of challenge. "Perhaps you could tell Ms. Suwan that Ramona Alverez assured me she could be of assistance?"

Ramona must have been the Hedon resident who got us in.

The Thai man blinked and went still, his gaze growing distant for a moment.

Gideon subtly touched his ear. Oh, Kasemchai had an earpiece.

"Ms. Suwan will meet you in the bar," he said. "The other members are being moved to the lounge so your privacy is ensured. Please follow me." The jungle rearranged itself to get out of his way. Trees slid smoothly aside and plants shriveled in on themselves before being sucked back in the ground, all to create a serpentine path.

I tried not to be tense, but it was tough, given one wrong move and the jungle would wrap itself around me and feast.

Gideon's body language and expression were relaxed, so despite being down the use of his gold token, he wasn't worried. However, his gaze bounced all over, so maybe even without his shifter senses, his cop instincts were cataloging something beyond my abilities, drawing on years of experience to clock all the details in every new situation.

My shoulders descended a notch. "How do people find their way around here on their own?"

"An attendant is assigned to each member." Kasemchai stopped in front of yet another door with carved lotuses. "They remain with the guest during the entirety of their visit so that requests may be fulfilled immediately. Our service at Lausanne is unrivaled."

I didn't think I snorted out loud, but Gideon shot me a sharp glance.

Our "attendant" pushed the door open, revealing a thoroughly modern room that was perfect for the discerning corporate raider.

Tasteful recessed lighting showcased teak furniture with clean lines and neutral fabrics, all the better to allow the showpiece of the room to shine: a wall of windows with a jaw-dropping panoramic view of the Bangkok skyline.

Or was it? Frowning, I strolled closer to the window, attempting to determine its authenticity.

A woman chuckled softly. "It truly is Bangkok."

I turned to the silver-haired Thai woman wearing a sheath dress, low pumps, and a strand of pearls. "Ms. Suwan?" I pitched my voice a bit lower than normal.

"Yes." She extended her hand. "But please call me Anchali."

"I'm Luciana. A pleasure." I shook first, then Gideon.

"I appreciate you seeing us," he said.

"I'm always happy to help a friend of Ramona's," Anchali said. "How is she these days? Still playing hooky in Gstaad?"

"I doubt it very much," Gideon said, maintaining his Rupert voice. "She's currently recovering from hip surgery, preferring the warm weather in Bora Bora."

Anchali snapped her fingers. "That's right. I forgot. Kasemchai, get our guests some lemonade."

Lame test, lady. Gideon, on the other hand, was remarkable. For someone who now had this wild, feral side, he still rocked at methodically removing every obstacle from an investigation.

Smart. Logical. Laser-focused. I smiled. It was also super sexy that under this polished, buttoned-up persona lurked a wolf.

Kasemchai withdrew to the curved bar crafted out of a deep azure glass, while Anchali led us to a table by the window. A beach separated the club from the Bangkok skyscrapers in the distance, the tranquil water the size of a small bay.

I'd bet a kidney that the occupants of that tower didn't see us.

Once we sat down, Gideon-as-Rupert got straight to business. "The late count had a portfolio that included a number of successful medical research facilities. Luciana would like to expand them, but that requires funding."

Kasemchai brought three frosted glasses over on a tray. The pale yellow lemonade was so fragrant that my mouth watered in anticipation of the tartness. A fat colorful bloom floated in each glass, while a thick row of pink sugar crystals circled the rims. He deposited one in front of each of us and then returned to the bar.

Anchali picked up her glass. "I'm sure you have many eager investors."

"These facilities have some delicate requirements." Gideon gestured out the window. "As, I'm sure, this gem of a club did. We have a short list of one, but before we extend an offer to Golden Radial, we'd appreciate your impression as someone who's been in bed with them. So to speak."

"I didn't have much contact with them during our brief relationship," she said. "Most of our interaction was done through lawyers." She put her glass down without taking a sip. What was wrong with these people that they hadn't immediately started sucking down the beverage like I had? "I'm sorry that I can't help you." She brightened. "Did Kasemchai ask if you'd like to visit our spa? It's top-notch."

I started my job in ten days, so while yes, I'd like that spa visit at a later date, I wasn't leaving here without getting one step closer to Baba Yaga.

Golden Radial's investment in this club had bothered me ever since I heard about it. Sure, information was valuable, but my gut screamed that Baba Yaga didn't require some private club for her intel gathering.

There had to be another reason why they invested.

I mashed my straw against the crushed ice in my glass. In science, we used inductive and deductive reasoning. Inductive reasoning started at one fact and led to another: Anchali was useful to them, and so Golden Radial had financed the club. Deductive reasoning went the other direction: Golden Radial had financed the club. Why had Anchali chosen them, approached them out of everyone else?

A hunch tugged at my gut. "Did you visit Sion to check out the clinic for yourself?"

Lobo Cop (British Edition) glared at me for going off-script from my prop designation, but that was on him for believing I would really keep silent.

Anchali tensed just the tiniest bit before she schooled her features into a bland mask. "Sion? Where's that?"

Even though his shifter magic was nulled here, I'd swear the tight smile Gideon shot me involved longer canines than normal.

"We're intelligent women. Let's dispense with the artifice." I infused my voice with the haughtiness befitting minor aristocracy. "There's no reason why you would have gone to a venture capital firm with no known interest in a club of any sort, or conversely, why they would have invested in yours, were there not a personal connection. And Lausanne?" I took a sip of lemonade. It was nicely theatrical but also it kept me from being too obvious in my gloating that my educated guess had hit its mark. "The connection to Thailand's former king is a nice story, but those of us in the know understand the real significance of Switzerland. Who were you connected to in the muscular dystrophy trials?"

Anchali flinched.

Kasemchai crossed the length of the room in a magic blur. Nice that his magic worked, since neither my partner's nor mine did.

That didn't stop Gideon from slowly and deliberately pushing back his chair to stare Kasemchai down. Impressive, given he was still seated.

The other man didn't attack, and while the air had grown charged, until it sparked and blazed I'd keep talking.

"How long did they live once they got in?" I spoke softly, my concern genuine.

"Seven years." Anchali stabbed her straw into her drink. "By the end though..." She shook her head, her voice cracking.

"Someone I once cared about was in the trials as well, and I recently saw its...end results on another man." I clasped her hand. "Golden Radial is on record as the owners of the clinic, but the person involved in those experiments isn't on any public-facing documents. It's a woman, isn't it? From Eastern Europe? What's her name?"

"I don't know." She pulled away and wouldn't make eye contact.

"We can protect you," Gideon said. "Get you somewhere safe if you help us."

Anchali met our eyes, her pain clear. "Where would that be?"

"Hedon," Gideon said. "Say when and I'll have someone here to transport you."

"You're not who you claim." She sipped her lemonade. "The less I know, the better." A familiar refrain. She exchanged a long look with Kasemchai.

He studied Gideon and me, then nodded.

"I don't know her real name," Anchali said. "She was only ever referred to as Lausanna, the original Roman name of Lausanne, but..." She sighed. "Her real name is an anagram of Lausanna."

I leaned forward eagerly. "Do you have a list of the possible solutions?"

Anchali looked aghast. "My curiosity is not worth my life. I wouldn't attempt to solve it for all the money in the world, and I advise you not to either. Let this go."

Gideon snorted, but at my glare, turned it into a cough. "We'll take that under advisement," he said.

I almost cracked my knuckles, I was so ready to dive in. I loved a good anagram and had immediately figured out that the spin-off series *Torchwood* was an anagram of *Doctor Who*, not to mention guessing Lord Voldemort's origin. I couldn't wait to solve this.

"Do you know where she is?" I said.

"No." Anchali shivered. "I only met her once and that was enough."

"Do you want to go to Hedon now?" Gideon said.

Anchali shook her head. "I must get some things in order first, but I'll contact you."

I stood up. "Are you sure?"

"Yes," Kasemchai replied calmly. "No harm will come to her before she goes."

Gideon texted Anchali the number of his burner phone. The club owner would eventually learn our real identities, but the Queen of Hearts would secure her silence.

Kasemchai escorted us out. There were so many twists and turns that I was hopelessly lost. However, I still expected to exit through the front door. Instead, Gideon and I stepped out onto the sandy beach. Before we could ask any questions, the door shut behind us.

And disappeared.

The sky clouded over, the many shades of gray broken by patches of darkness that stretched toward us like skinny fingers. A rumble of thunder shook the ground, followed immediately by a lightning bolt that cracked the night like a whip.

Gideon jogged over to the end of the building, then strode back, his shoulders set. "Well, this isn't good."

"You think?" I beat on the now-blank wall, but no door appeared. "She played us."

He pulled his tie off in one smooth movement.

"What are you doing?"

"There's no way around to the front. We have to swim across and hope for an exit on the city side."

I threw up my hands. "They wouldn't have let us out of the club if we could escape. Our magic is still nulled, and there's obviously some giant kraken or great white shark or something that is going to…" My brain stuttered on Gideon's bare sculpted torso, laid out in glorious high-def. "To kill us."

"Maybe, but we'll die for sure if we stay here." He snapped open the button of his pants with such graceful efficiency that I nearly had a heart attack.

"Fine," I said and spun around in a fit of frustrated pique. I tore off my hat and shrugged out of my beautiful jacket hoping Ash didn't get mad that I had to leave it behind. Talk about the most unsatisfying reason for Gideon and me to be stripping.

Resisting all urges to sneak a peek over my shoulder, I unzipped the leather pants. Not only was I grunting and doing weird contortions to get the stupid things off, but the leather made fart-like squeaking noises. I kicked the clothing away, snapped the high waistband of my shapewear, and grimaced. I wasn't taking them off, but it was, hands down, the unsexiest undergarment for Gideon to see me in.

I grabbed one of my killer heels.

Gideon was in his boxer shorts, which hung low on his hips. Huh. That was pretty thin fabric, and once it got wet, everything would be out there in stark relief.

I snapped my eyes up so I didn't check out any bulge he may or may not have had. I mean, that he hopefully and probably had, since he wasn't a Ken doll, but now was not the time. "You should shift."

"No magic, remember? But even if I could, I wouldn't." He held up a hand to cut off my protest. "Not out of stubbornness. Wolves can swim, but I haven't tried it yet in that form, and I'd rather not have to unless push comes to shove. Especially if I need to help you, because it's going to take at least a good forty minutes to get to the other side."

Robyn and I took lessons for years and spent summers hanging out at the pool or beach. I was a good swimmer. My determination to not play damsel in distress was also excellent motivation.

"I'll hold my own." Murder shoe in hand, I waded into the cool water. Luckily the waves weren't too bad, given the storm blasting above us, and the water was really clear. I got thigh deep and a wave hit me in the groin. I sucked in a breath. "Cooch shock."

Gideon, splashing into the water behind me, laughed.

I focused on easing into the bay, doing my best to block

out the thunder and lightning. When I'd made it in up to my chest, I took a deep breath and dove under the waves.

I came up with a high-pitched squeal.

"How's your cooch?" Gideon swam over.

I grimaced. "Acclimated, thanks."

"Stay close," he said, and at my nod, dove under.

Chapter 12

Tiny yellow and blue fish darted playfully, oblivious to the booming thunder and the lightning reflecting off the increasingly choppy waves. I didn't get seasick, but it slowed my front crawl.

I sliced through the water behind Gideon, admiring the view.

His back muscles rippled with every powerful stroke. He was a beautiful swimmer, his movements certain and economical, utterly at ease in the water. He adjusted his pace to remain one length ahead of me, though every so often he checked in with an okay sign.

I always flashed it back, even though no one could be all right in this situation. However, I decided that being alive was the only bar I had to meet, and on those grounds, yes, I was fine. The biggest problem was that between my anticipation of being fried by lightning or my soft underbelly torn into by one of the fish that got bigger and darker in color the farther out we swam, I was a knot of tension. I tried to relax because stress was tiring me out faster, but I was so damn exposed.

On top of everything, our magic was still nulled. I'd

never gone this long without my abilities. No one had ever done a study on the correlation between magic, circulation, and energy levels in Nefesh, but those would have been useful results right now, because I swear prolonged lack of magic was dulling my motor functions.

About halfway across, I looked up. The storm had passed, and dawn brightened the sky with ribbons of soft pinks and golds. We'd lived to see another day. I let out a deep sigh, savoring this win.

Something brushed against my leg and I screamed, striking wildly around in the water with the pointy shoe I had in a death grip. For fuck's sake, universe!

Gideon was instantly at my side. "What's wrong?"

I scanned the depths, shaking from the adrenaline coursing through me and coughing from the pint of salt water I'd swallowed when I screamed.

About ten feet down, a long eel circled us.

My heart pounded. "Eels don't normally come in blood-red, do they?"

"You're more bothered by that than its dragon scales?" Gideon said.

"Thought I'd stick with the lesser of two evils." I squinted into the depths where the eel swam back and forth in an almost leisurely way. Sure, it had all the time in the world to kill us.

"Just focus on the skyline, okay?" Gideon pointed across the bay. "We'll be there—"

The eel shot up toward us, its face splitting open into five petals with a round center made of teeth. Like the Demogorgon in *Stranger Things*. I would have cracked a joke to Gideon about that, except everything was happening too fast and that jerk wouldn't even get it.

I fell into an oasis of calm. Or a PTSD-induced numbness, but whatever. All my trauma from unethical experiments, mutated wolf shifters, and aquatic abominations coalesced into a hard knot. I was done with all attacks on my person.

A war cry tore free from deep inside me. I dove under the water, ignoring the sting of salt water in my eyes, and slammed the shoe into the eel's mouth.

The eel's petals stuttered in a five-eyed blink, and its mouth muscles spasmed, but it couldn't work the heel free.

I pointed from my eyes to the general vicinity where its eyes should have been.

The eel turned tail and fled.

I burst back above the surface, shaking one fist. "Mess with me and I will fuck you up! You hear that, you genetically modified freak shows? I have history to make, and nothing is going to stop me!"

Gideon gaped at me. Very slowly, he reached out and moved my tangled locks out of my face. He shot me one more piercing look like he was checking it was safe to turn his back on me, then resumed swimming.

My rush of energy propelled me another quarter of the way across. Unmauled, even. Whatever was down there had gotten my message because I didn't see any more sea life. Unfortunately, once my energy left, it whooshed right out of me. A fine edge of fatigue bladed through me, but I forced myself to press on, buoyed by dreams of revenge on Baba Yaga.

I'd formulated six or seven solid scenarios of what I'd do to her when we finally met when Gideon flailed backward so fast that he knocked into me.

"What is it?" Bobbing in the water, I pulled my legs into my chest.

"Holy shit." Gideon stuck his face under the surface.

I did as well.

A manta ray slid silently out of the darkness, and my heart skipped a beat or seven. These creatures were peaceful filter feeders who ate mostly plankton, but they were large.

Ours was a good eight feet across, with the two cephalic horns on the top of its head lending it a devilish air.

I froze, floating facedown as stiff as a surfboard.

The manta ray glided up underneath me, its giant mouth open, but there were no strange teeth, just its regular gaping maw. It performed a barrel roll, flashing its white belly and gills and flipping within an inch of my still body, and a sense of awe washed over me.

Its massive size and graceful movements were a sight to behold, and everything around us looked like a watercolor painting. The refraction of the sunlight coming down through the water cast the sea floor in soft contrast to the dark blue depths, while bioluminescent creatures shimmered white with a slight orange tinge similar to the light of fireflies.

I lifted my head out of the water and giggled like an excited child. Being this close to this playful giant was so freaking cool.

Gideon let out a giddy laugh.

The mantra ray shot forward toward our beach destination.

I wasn't one for signs, preferring facts, but the fact was it hadn't eaten us. It was a normal manta ray and it was playing guide. The universe had heard my insistence to back the fuck off, just this once, and obeyed. This war wasn't over yet, not by a long shot, but all I had to do was get out of here and live to fight again.

I took off after the manta ray.

Finally, my feet touched ground. A brutal pins-and-needles sensation momentarily swamped me, but I didn't care, my magic had come back. The water still came up to my nose, but I was on terra firma. Well, terra silty, but it was magnificent. I curled my toes under, not even caring that I was the one huffing and puffing from the long swim.

The manta ray glided around Gideon and me in the

water. My partner stood with his hands on his hips and his head thrown to the sky, his eyes closed and a small smile tugging at his lips.

I trudged forward to the shore on rubbery legs.

Sunlight rippled up off the sand a few feet from shore, revealing a door, and I swung around to Gideon to tell him we were back in business.

The manta ray soared out of the water, its pectoral fins extended like angel wings.

I beamed at it, confused when Gideon stiffened.

Two needle-sharp fangs descended from the manta ray's enormous mouth and the creature landed on Gideon's head.

"Not another one! I told you we would run into seaborne terrors!" I was weaving light into a staff before I'd processed my actions, but before I could knock the animal away, Gideon was shifting.

Intellectually, I knew that his tearing flesh and multiple snapping bones weren't actually louder and more brutal than usual. It was merely that sound amplified when traveling over water, but that didn't prevent my magic light from falling apart in the wake of the gruesome sound, or the wolf's growls from hooking into me at a visceral and physically painful level as he battled the manta ray.

They were such a blur splashing in the water that even though I waded closer, I couldn't get a clear shot at the ray.

The wolf tore off one of the manta ray's cephalic horns. It thwapped me on the cheek, followed by sticky red viscera. I couldn't tell which animal the gore came from, and I couldn't find an opening to inject my magic and help my partner.

The water turned to blood; roiling crimson clouds frothed overhead.

Our exit pulsed in and out of visibility.

I scrambled back onto the heaving shore, screaming for

Gideon to get out, and threw myself against the door—still closed and now blinking in and out at dizzying speeds.

There was a whooshing sound behind me, and the air was sucked away like it was being vacuumed. I swallowed and glanced back.

The water rushed backward to curl into a massive wave.

Gideon streaked across the sand toward me, bloody droplets flying off his tawny fur.

I threw myself against the door one more time. My shoulder smacked the wood painfully, but it gave way.

As did the sand under my feet. I tightened my grip on the handle, but the pull was too strong. I slid backward to the sound of a deafening roar.

A shadow fell over me.

The wave crested.

Frantic, I stumbled forward, my legs sticking in the sand with every precious step.

Gideon knocked into the backs of my knees, and I grabbed on to his fur so he could use his gold token and get us out of here.

The tidal wave crashed down, propelling us through the door, but breaking us apart.

For one horrifying moment, there was nothing but darkness. Up was down, the water seeming to reach inside me and replace not only air, but blood. I couldn't see Gideon, but my foot hit the edge of the door. I kicked backward, praying I shut it.

The water disappeared, and I fell facedown onto the concrete. I banged my wrists protecting my face, but nothing was broken.

I lay there in a dank puddle, my head turned to the side, unable to do anything beyond cough.

The wolf brushed his cold nose against my side with a soft "arroo?"

I pushed myself up. We were in an abandoned storefront. A faded blue logo in Thai script was painted across one wall. Bare wires hung down from the ceiling, and the only light was the hazy blur of sunshine coming through tears in the papered-up windows. "I'm okay. You?"

Gideon's hazel eyes were as much man as wolf while he looked me over. He yipped sharply and tilted his head.

"What?"

He yipped again.

I wanted to snap at him that he should shift and use his words, but maybe the effort was too much for him. Besides, after he batted his head against the backs of my knees, pushing me toward the door, I understood his question.

Being alone at Levi's place while he was out celebrating Christmas with his friends—his found family—would suck. I rubbed a hand over my heart. I could patch myself up with a first aid kit and ask to join them, but while I liked his friends, they weren't my people yet. Hopefully one day they would be, but for now I needed easy and familiar.

I eyed the wolf. One of the two would have to suffice. "Can I go back to your place and dry out?"

Gideon immediately wormed his furry head under my palm.

"Right." I gently gripped his fur and we vanished.

Chapter 13

As soon as we hit Gideon's living room, the wolf nosed me toward the shower, but I argued that it was his house, and he should go first. I'd feel bad otherwise.

Ignoring his furry bristling, I took a towel from a small laundry basket in the corner of the bathroom containing clean, folded clothes, wrapped it around myself, and headed for the main room. "The longer you keep me waiting, the colder I'll get."

He growled, went into the bathroom, and kicked the door shut.

I wiped myself down with the towel, looking forward to a shower, dry clothes, and getting out of this godawful shapewear. Then, I checked myself from head to toe for injuries. Other than my skinned palms and wrists, and a twinge in my right shoulder, I was okay. Physically.

Mentally and psychologically? Well, let's just say that by the time Gideon returned in jeans and a T-shirt, his hair damp, I'd come up with another five artfully plotted revenge scenarios.

"Hey." His eyes searched my face; he smelled faintly of

orange and sandalwood. "On a scale of one to Godzilla, how are you?"

"Other than wanting to clean up so I can hunt Baba Yaga down like the rat she is?" I shrugged. "We survived. I suspect that's going to be the bar for a while."

"You think Anchali was telling the truth about the anagram?"

"Yeah. She didn't have any advance notice that we'd ask her about that, and it's not exactly a go-to lie."

Gideon patted my shoulder. "I showered first like you stubbornly insisted. Now go. I put some clothes you can wear on top of the laundry basket, along with a fresh towel and the first aid kit."

"Thanks." I headed for the bathroom, but my legs buckled.

Gideon caught me before I hit the ground, one arm around my waist and the other behind my neck. His gaze licked over my décolletage, sending delicious flames of warmth across my skin.

I gave a full-body blush.

"You should get out of those wet clothes," he said, his voice rough.

"Uh-huh."

His hold on me tightened, bringing our faces closer together.

I saw the light dusting of blond stubble on his jaw, and dark flecks in his hazel eyes.

I also saw the need in them.

"I really want to kiss you," he murmured. His lids lowered halfway.

I wanted it too.

I wanted his mouth to claim mine so badly that I had to briefly close my eyes against the image. I wanted to lose myself in him and feel more alive than I had in years.

"Not like this." I gently disentangled myself. "Not when I'll always wonder if it was because we almost died."

"It wouldn't—"

I met his eyes. "Or if that's why I kissed you back."

He bit his bottom lip like he was holding back arguments, then nodded. "Go shower."

I didn't let myself look back.

Once I'd freed myself from my clothing prison, I set the water temperature a touch cooler than was appropriate to boil a lobster then stepped under the spray, one hand braced on the tiled wall and my head bowed. I swear the ground still slipped away like the sand had, and no matter how many times I rinsed my mouth, I tasted salt water.

At least my ciccia was free of the confining garments. I patted my belly with a wistful pang. Ciccia was the Italian word for "fat," but it was also this weird term of endearment used on both genders in the same way as sweetie. Dad had called Robyn and me ciccia all the time.

The hot water pounded over me, releasing knots upon knots. It was heavenly. I stood there until the water swirling down the drain was mostly clear, then I lathered and soaped up. The orange and sandalwood soap was nice, but Gideon's lingering natural scent was better.

My stomach untwisted and my shoulders relaxed. I was one hundred percent a feminist. This wasn't about feeling safe because of a man. It was Gideon-specific, a *person* who'd had my back over and over again. It wasn't about romance or intimacy, it came down to a scent-based reminder that this individual and I had fought together and survived.

He almost kissed me.

Out of nervous habit, I went to fiddle with my piercings, but I didn't have the jewelry that I typically used to center myself. I'd left them all with Ash, along with my chai pendant since they didn't fit my undercover persona.

I raked my fingers through the knots in my hair. I didn't

regret saying no to Gideon. Well, my body regretted it like crazy because I could have had a much better reason for this shower than washing off evil manta ray goo, but I stood by the decision. I still wasn't happy about why he'd ghosted me after Morocco. He could have explained that he needed time to figure things out. Even via text.

Instead, he'd run away from me because that's what he did.

Except, that wasn't totally fair. When it came to his feelings he ran, but when it came to this investigation or having my back, he stepped up with no hesitation.

He hadn't run from the kiss. That was on me. I shook my head, flinging water droplets. That wasn't running. It was being smart, logical, and laser-focused.

Plus, the entire pretext of my visit was to deliver a message from his ex. They both needed closure that would come only from a face-to-face conversation.

I wouldn't deny that Gideon and I were attracted to each other, but we had to keep our wits about us. Having sex, scorching as I imagine it would be, would only complicate things.

I smacked the wet shower tiles on the wall. And didn't that just suck massively? Well, I could stay here and pout or get back to finding Baba Yaga and putting all this behind us so we could figure out our feelings for each other in normal daily life.

Whatever that looked like.

After I dried off, squeezing as much water out of my short hair as possible, I applied magically boosted arnica cream to my scrapes and banged-up shoulder, then pulled on the basketball shorts and jersey that Gideon had left me. I grimaced. Both were branded with the Toronto Raptors logo of a basketball with claw marks shredding it.

I left the bathroom. "I want to register my official complaint against wearing sports-themed clothing."

He looked up from the table where he was hunched over his laptop, grinned, and held up a fist. "We the North."

"You're the worst."

There was a knock on the door.

Gideon crossed the cabin to open it. "Insults won't get you fed."

What was the Hedon equivalent of SkipTheDishes?

He threw open the door.

I swallowed and shrank back because Moran stood on the other side.

One hand rested on the pommel of his sword, the other held a brown bag emitting the mouth-watering aroma of grilled meat. The flat look he speared me with said he hadn't decided which way this encounter would go.

Gideon looked confused. "I didn't expect a royal delivery."

"I thought I'd drop by for an update," Moran replied in his nasal voice. He didn't take his eyes off me.

Despite my stomach plummeting into the soles of my feet and the strongest urge to hide under the table, I forced myself to remain calm. "Great."

It took Gideon three tries to tug the food away from the other man. Frowning, he gave Moran a quick summation of what we'd learned. "If that's all?" my partner said.

Moran didn't move.

Enough with the intimidation, dude. I wasn't doing anything wrong. "The Queen sent Gideon to free me from the dungeon. She knows I'm with him, so your decree no longer applies."

"Decree? What are you talking about?" Gideon looked between us.

"I'm ensuring that there are no distractions to the mission at hand," Moran said. "Her Majesty is most insistent that this be wrapped up as soon as possible."

"That's what we're doing," I ground out.

"Good." He stepped back, taking his hand off his sword. "Enjoy your *cheeseburgers*." I'd heard less disdain for a meat and dairy combo from Hasidic Jews.

Gideon closed the door. "Want to tell me what that was all about?"

"Moran found me in Marrakesh after you left. I'll fill you in another time." I sent all the good karma to whomever had made the huge juicy-looking burgers and fries that Gideon plated and handed over, hefted the hamburger to my mouth—and paused midway. "This is beef, right?"

"Go with yes."

I grimaced, shrugged, and took a big bite. My mouth flooded with the perfectly seasoned meaty flavor. Beef, lamb, the last unicorn, whatever this baby was made of, I was polishing off every last bite.

Between the food and the heat pouring out of the iron stove that Gideon had lit, I started feeling more like myself. "What have you got on the Lausanna anagram?" I said, my cheeks bulging with food.

"Her most likely first name is Anna," Gideon replied.

I mentally deducted the letters. "That leaves 'L,' 'A,' 'U,' 'S.'" I munched on a couple of fries. "She's Eastern European. Can you search surnames in that region with those letters?" I really regretted not having my phone or laptop to do my own search.

"I'll try. You want something to drink?"

"I'm still full from the swimming pool's worth of salt water I consumed, thanks." I considered standing over Gideon to help him search faster since two brains were better than one, but there was no way he'd allow it.

"Quit fidgeting," he growled a few minutes later. "This isn't a straightforward search. I'm going as fast as I can."

"Who said anything?"

"You didn't need to." He nodded at the napkin I'd

shredded and stacked on my plate and pushed the laptop closer. "You want to take over? Have at it."

I'd snatched it away before he even finished his offer. He'd found a letter combination generator, which yielded twenty-four results. The first four he'd plugged into a search with "Eastern European surname" didn't get us anywhere.

I methodically went through each letter combination, cross-checking it with known Balkan surnames. I got excited when I hit on "Salu," but it was Estonian, and as I learned, the language spoken in the Northern European country was Finnic based, not Slavic. I researched what a Finnic accent sounded like, but it didn't fit my memory of her voice.

Gideon placed a mug of tea on the table within arm's reach. "Here. You sound scratchy."

"Is that your subtle way of telling me to shut up?" I'd relayed every new detail to Gideon as I learned them. I'm not sure if he found them as interesting as I did, but he hadn't encouraged me to keep them to myself either.

"No. I'm stating a fact. You like those."

"Yeah," I said, already searching a new combination. "They're a kind of foreplay with me."

Gideon choked on his own sip of tea.

I looked up with a horrified expression. "Not that I mean that you…that we…" I sipped my tea to cover my discomfort. It was delicious, with a lot of lemon and honey.

He narrowed his eyes, regarding me with a slash of dark hazel framed by thick sooty lashes, and for a second, I was positive he was going to kiss me.

I wasn't sure I had the stamina to say no twice in the same day.

"Did you know that André Breton, the founder of surrealism, made up an anagram for Salvador Dalí?" he said.

I blinked at him, disappointed yet grateful he'd changed the subject. "He did? What was it?"

"Avida dollars, which in Spanish roughly translates to 'eager for dollars.'"

"Ooh, burn." Also a cool fact, but in light of my foreplay comment, I filed the interaction away to be dealt with at the same later date as the kiss and my feelings. I moved the laptop onto my knees to hide my face. "Aslau is a possibility. It's a Romanian surname, but then her first name would be Ann, which doesn't fit."

"Don't be discouraged," he said. "If anyone can crack it, you can."

I smiled. "Thanks."

On my sixteenth try, I hit possible gold. "Get this. Sula is a predominantly Eastern European surname. It's in a few different countries there, but one etymology puts it in the Czech Republic and Slovakia. Given the age of the woman, she would have been born when those two countries were still Czechoslovakia."

"Don't they both have forests and mountains?" Gideon wiped down the counter. He'd cleared all our dishes, but I'd been too caught up in the search to notice.

"Yeah!" I bounced in my seat. "The Bohemian Forest and the Carpathian Mountains, both of which are steeped in mythology."

"For a scientist, I'm surprised you're extrapolating your nickname for this woman and a love of fairy tales into proof of her origin."

"This is my hypothesis, not the proof." I kept typing. "Holy shit. Sula is also a city in Slovakia. Okay, okay." I held up one hand. "I have another thought to plug into this hypothesis."

"I would never have guessed."

"You're not funny."

"Agree to disagree."

Whatever. "The anomaly of investing in Anchali's club aside, Golden Radial's focus is genetic research involving science and magic. Wherever they created those things in the bay, they had an isolated place to dump them after. Like the lab where they created the hybrids."

"The clinic in Switzerland *was* isolated." Gideon stroked his stubbled chin. "Who knows what happened to those hybrids once the trials shut down."

Thrown out and left to survive? I doubted they'd been so lucky.

I unclenched my fists and wove that fact into my latest revenge fantasy. "Then there's whatever cave Robyn and I were taken to. The one that smelled like wine." I maximized another screen. "Look at this. Slovakia has a long history of wine-making."

"Oenology," Gideon said. At my confusion, he clarified. "It's the science of wine and wine-making."

Science facts? *Foreplay.*

I squirmed in my seat. "Yes, well. There's one other item of note. The Carpathian Mountains, which have forests and caves, also have myths involving wolves. Dracula is tied to it as well because the mountain range runs through Transylvania."

"Is that supposed to be a plus?" Gideon added more hot water to his mug. "Vampires aren't supposed to exist, but then again, neither am I." He set his cup down hard enough to make the liquid slosh over the top. "I've had my fill of these people's creations."

"Forget vampires. Baba Yaga is tied to the Carpathians as well. Whether or not that's actually relevant, I like that it all fits." I shoved the laptop at Gideon. "Use your police databases and find something to connect an Anna Sula from that region with Golden Radial. She's probably in her seventies now."

Apparently, Gideon had access to more than police databases, he also got on some dark web forum, his access courtesy of Moran.

Meantime, I called Levi and asked him to check House databases around the world for any Anna Sula of that age. There was no proof she was Nefesh—or that I was right about her name—but there was no proof to the contrary either.

My hypothesis was vindicated when in a matter of minutes, Levi found a Nefesh with Healer magic bearing that name and in the correct age range who was registered in the archives of the Czechoslovakian database.

She didn't have Illusion magic to have made me believe Carol was a dog, but she could have been there and murdered her.

Using the record that Levi provided, Gideon found a Dr. Anna Sula who'd had her license suspended for unethical practices about thirty years ago. Healers didn't have to attend medical school in addition to their training in order to practice, but those who did generally went on to become leaders in their field.

This doctor had lived in Bratislava. The Slovakian city was nestled in the foothills of the Little Carpathian Mountains (part of the larger range), an area known for caves and wine-making.

Thanks to all those details, we unearthed an old address for the doctor.

"We've got our starting place." I shut the laptop, rubbing my sore neck. "Bratislava with an eye to any setup she had or has in a cave in the Carpathian Mountains."

"Red and the wolf going into the woods." Gideon propped his hip against the counter. "One of us might not come back."

Any self-respecting fairy tale connoisseur knew that a forest was a dangerous liminal space. Unsuspecting characters were forced all the way into its darkness and beset with terrifying challenges with their lives on the line. Once inside, I couldn't rely on modern technology; the only way out was by my wits. But the very wildness and unpredictability of the forest made crossing it wondrous and magical, the greatest of adventures.

Forests were also places of incredible temptation, like with Hansel and Gretel.

I mean, if the trade-off was a candy house lunch? What a way to go. "One of us might get eaten," I agreed cheerfully.

A slow, wicked, and very wolfish grin spread across Gideon's face. "I meant that since it's December, the mountains are covered in snow, and even with the help of my token, crossing them could be dangerous. And while I agree there might be wild animals, I don't think that's what you were implying."

I'd meant witches. What did he think...? I rewound my words. Yup. I heard it now. I buried my face in my hands. Damn phrasing.

As Gideon laughed himself hoarse, I plotted out our destination on a map and googled the closest inns and restaurants. Next stop on the Baba Yaga World Tour, here we come.

Chapter 14

I was braced for the dark scary woods of my childhood imaginings, so when Gideon used his gold token to take us to Bratislava and we landed under a soft purple-gray evening sky, outside huge walls lit up with gold floodlights and a turreted white castle straight out of a fairy tale overlooking the snowcapped city? Well, it took me a moment to adjust.

Impatient to get to the inn that we'd booked, Gideon was already tramping through the medieval gate in the fortress walls and into the winding streets of the Old City.

I adjusted the straps of my daypack over my lightweight down jacket, amazed at the technology that kept me toasty but not sweaty. Gideon had outfitted me from head to toe in the best outdoor gear since nothing I'd brought to Levi's place—or owned—was appropriate for a trip into the mountains of Slovakia. Even though we'd be using Gideon's gold token to get anywhere specific, he deemed it best to be prepared for any eventuality.

I'd been fascinated yesterday watching him put together the list of gear, succinctly explaining to me the pros and cons of every item, from high-protein snacks to biodegradable toilet paper and a lightweight packable shovel. He clearly had experience hiking in extreme weather conditions.

All the unexpected variables in this kind of hobby seemed odd for such a stickler for rules and order, but maybe it was the perfect thing? Maybe for Gideon, his love of outdoor adventure was like an investigation: something to tackle and triumph over, step by step, thanks to his knowledge, experience, and determination.

I had to resist the urge to fan myself more than once while observing him.

I'd stayed over last night. It might have been weird sleeping on his sofa, especially after that near kiss, but we were both so wrung out that we crashed hard.

It didn't matter that yesterday was Christmas and stores were closed, once Gideon told the Queen what we required, she pulled some strings, and voilà. By this morning everything had been delivered to his cabin.

I'd protested the expensive purchase on the grounds that I didn't want him gifting this stuff to me and I couldn't pay him back, but he said it was on the Queen's dime.

I accepted it as her apology for throwing me in her dungeon.

All she expected in return was the woman from my memory. Hopefully Baba Yaga was Dr. Anna Sula, otherwise, we'd be starting from scratch, and Her Majesty's orders to "Find her and rapida, chica" were hardly subtle.

Neither was the fact that she'd issued them from that awful statue graveyard. Point taken, thanks.

We had our gear and our marching orders. We were ready.

Just before we left, Gideon snuck into Levi's place while my cousin was asleep and retrieved my phone for me without getting busted.

However, when I called Levi, he almost shit a brick when I told him the plan was for Gideon and me to hie off across the world and venture into a mountain range, in the middle of winter if necessary, to track this doctor down.

It was so sad that the cell service in Hedon grew unexpectedly spotty and I lost the call.

All of which led to me now following Gideon through the silent streets of Bratislava past holiday lights twinkling in the slumbering city like our own special fairy beacons.

The inn we were booked into was clean and basic. We said good night outside our rooms, agreeing to meet up for breakfast and go to the address we had for Dr. Sula bright and early the next morning. Neither of us expected her to be there, but if it was her family home, or the current owners knew her, we'd be in luck.

I shucked off my clothes and fell onto the bed. I'd had two narrow escapes in as many days; it was tough not to keep from obsessing over how long my luck would last. Anchali had certainly ratted Gideon and me out to Golden Radial.

They may not have been able to track us when we decamped to Hedon, but we had the anagram info and those people were formidable. If we'd surmised correctly about my tormentor's real name, then they—or rather, Dr. Sula, as the one truly in charge—would have people here waiting to greet us.

I had a lot of time with these sobering thoughts since I'd stayed awake for ages thanks to the time change wreaking havoc on my sleep cycle.

Gideon appeared just as rough the next morning. We fueled up with a hearty breakfast and a lot of coffee and headed off through the old town.

The narrow stone house at our destination was tucked away in a small courtyard. Its windows were boarded up with iron grates over top, and although it shared the same smart façade as the squat buildings it was wedged between, the place gave off a disconsolate vibe.

Before approaching the building, we patrolled the neighborhood, on the lookout for anyone who might be with Golden Radial, but the few people we encountered were shopkeepers opening for the day, and a harried mom trying to get her slouchy kid to hurry up.

We returned to the courtyard, and Gideon rattled the home's handle.

A short, wrinkled woman about Dr. Sula's age, in a shapeless black dress and thick wool stockings, hurried out of the small grocery store next door to yell at us in Slovakian.

Gideon pointed at the house. "We're looking for a person who lived here? Anna Sula? She was a doctor?"

The old woman crossed herself and ran back inside. Wow, she was spry. Okay, her reaction wasn't auspicious in terms of what we were about to learn about Sula's personality, but in terms of this mission? An excited curl spun out inside me.

Gideon stepped into the store—and was promptly thwacked on the shin with a broom.

The old woman banished him like he was an evil spirit, hitting him again and again, not caring what part she smacked, while continuing to yell.

He hopped farther and farther back, his hands jumping around to protect his body parts. It would have been hilarious if it wasn't so disconcerting. Between the shifter experiments and the shit pulled on Robyn and me, I figured Dr. Sula's evil had been contained to work she'd done with Golden Radial. However, I doubted this broom wielder knew about that, so what had garnered this reaction?

Another woman raced outside in bejeweled Crocs, waving her arms. "Mama!"

When her mother didn't stop the smackdown, she wrestled the broom away, pointed at the store, and said in no uncertain terms to go inside. In Slovakian, but some things were universally understood.

Her mother obeyed but not before bestowing a glare of such animosity on Gideon that I was pretty sure she'd cursed him with the evil eye.

The daughter sighed.

I slid my backpack off and set it on the ground. "Do you speak English?"

"Yes." She had a softer version of the accent from my memories of Dr. Sula.

I swallowed. "I'm sorry we upset your mother," I said. "We're simply trying to get some information. This is Inspector Gideon Stern from Interpol. I'm Dr. Raisa Montefiore and I'm consulting on his case."

Gideon received a doubtful glance, which was understandable, given his trekking clothes and backpack.

"Anna Sula is a person of interest in our investigation, and we understand she lived here." I spoke with my hard-ass voice, one pitched slightly lower. I'd used it many a time on certain professors and fellow grad students when my plethora of facts was not enough to convince them that the blonde female actually knew what she was talking about. "Can you tell us anything about her?"

"She left suddenly one night." The woman headed for her store.

That was it? I opened my mouth, but Gideon shook his head.

"Were your family good friends with her for a long time?" he said.

The woman stiffened, her back still to us.

Way to go, Lobo Cop. He'd insulted her by suggesting a connection to the bad person.

She slowly spun around. "Yes. She was my mother's best friend."

I only gaped a little.

Gideon angled his body toward her, mirroring her crossed arms and her stance with one foot slightly ahead of the other. "Losing her must have been hard. Like a death."

The shopkeeper's expression remained wary, but she nodded.

"Was this before or after she lost her license?" he said.

"After." She said it in a sigh, her entire body slumping. "I think she would have stayed, maybe found a different job, but on top of her girls dying, it was too painful to remain."

"She had kids?" The shock literally made me step back. How could a mother do what she had to Robyn and me?

Gideon placed his hand on the small of my back. "Steady," he murmured.

The woman nodded. "Maria and Nina. We used to play together."

"What happened to them?" Gideon said.

"They were born with a disease." The woman frowned, then mimed using crutches.

"Muscular dystrophy?" I sputtered.

"Yes. They died very young, and Anna was…" She shook her head. "Very sad."

"She was broken," I murmured. "What was she like before?"

The woman brightened. "Funny. She loved riddles. Sister Viktória still tells them to the kids at the orphanage where Anna volunteered."

Saint Sula. Gideon elbowed me and I dropped my sneer.

"Do you have any photos of her?" he said. "Even an old one would prove useful."

"Wait." She walked back into the store, returning a moment later scrolling on her phone. "I kept it for Maria and Nina. It's not very good but it's all I have." She handed me her cell.

She'd photographed one of those old Polaroids, which showed three girls, maybe aged seven or eight, outside on a sunny day. The one kneeling on the grass with healthy limbs was obviously this woman. She had one arm on each of the wheelchairs on either side of her, holding the turned in hands of the girls sitting in them.

I blinked, violently shaking my head. *They were twins*?! My brain stuttered over the revelation because this made the situation a million times more horrible.

Gideon stroked a hand slowly up my back in comfort. I pulled my shit together and refocused on the photo.

The two girls' wasting limbs hadn't stopped them from being kids; the photo had caught them laughing, maybe at the game they'd been playing with the dolls in their laps.

My eyes pooled with tears, which flash froze when I saw the woman to the side of the photo, coming toward them with a tray of drinks, a fond expression on her face. She wore an ugly ruffled dress similar to the last time I'd seen her, but she was also in bare feet, her blond hair was longer and softer, and she didn't have the red scar through her eyebrow that disfigured her cheek and caused her eye to droop.

"It's her," I murmured.

We'd done it. We'd confirmed that Baba Yaga was Dr. Anna Sula. *She had twins and they'd died.*

I swallowed down the taste of bile.

Gideon asked if he could get a copy of the photo, and the woman reluctantly AirDropped it to him.

"If your mother was good friends with Dr. Sula," I said, "why did she react that way when Inspector Stern inquired about her?"

The woman's expression shuttered.

Gideon held up a hand. "I understand you don't want to speak badly of someone you were close to, but we have to find her. She's hurt people."

"She's a good person who got lost," she said decisively.

149

I clenched my fists. That wasn't enough. "I had a twin sister too."

The woman threw me a startled glance, then shook her head vigorously. "Anna only wanted to make sure no other children died. She didn't mean to hurt any others."

"Others? There were others?" My voice rose to a screech. I'd only meant to form a connection by mentioning I'd been a twin, but this information was reprehensible. I stepped forward with a snarl. She was going to answer every single question I had if I had to tear it out of her.

The woman stumbled backward, then turned and fled inside.

Gideon caught my arm. "Raisa," he said softly and nodded at my hand.

It glowed pale orange.

"I don't care." I pulled free. "We're not leaving without answers."

"You can't force them from her. Come on." He walked out of the courtyard, but when I didn't follow, he crossed his arms. "That woman has never gotten over losing her friends when she was a kid, and Anna Sula will always be their nice mom. Her emotional and intellectual understanding of the situation is rooted in her childhood and that's understandable, but it also means we've gotten all we can from her." He shuddered and glanced at the store. "I hope her mother doesn't take the broom home with her at night."

My anger and sulking evaporated and I followed him down the street. "How did you know that her family was friends with Sula? I would have guessed the opposite."

"Loss often produces the most violent emotions in people."

We set ourselves up at a pub with outdoor tables that had a clear view of the courtyard, and Gideon got us food while we mulled over our next approach.

"I'm not hungry." I pushed my pirohy around on the plate.

"Suit yourself." He reached for the plate to slide my food next to the massive steak he'd ordered for himself, but I smacked his hand away.

"I'll eat, but only because we need a reason to loiter here until we come up with a plan B."

His lips twitched. "Yes. All your cop show watching has come in handy."

"Nothing about this is funny." I bit into my, admittedly excellent, potato dumplings.

"I know," he said somberly.

"I don't care that she has a tragic origin story." I stabbed another dumpling. "Every two-bit villain has one."

"Or that she enjoyed riddles like Baba Yaga."

I blinked at him in shock. "How are you now in possession of Baba Yaga facts?"

"I looked her up last night so I'd know what you were talking about. Baba Yaga was a witch, but she helped people too."

I leveled a flat stare at him, incredulous that Gideon, of all people, was throwing out this defense. "The ends justify the means? Where was that forgiving attitude when I saved your life with my serum?" I shook my head. "Also, I don't buy the whole 'helping people' BS. The shifter abilities those people in the muscular dystrophy trials got weren't side effects. They were deliberately developed. That woman is a monster."

"Deliberately developed because it would save them?" Gideon said, not unkindly. "The way they saved me from developing cancer from your serum?"

"Is that a backhanded thank-you?" I dropped my fork so I didn't stab him with it. I'd endured his anger and a metric ton of guilt over injecting him, but when it came to Anna

151

Sula, he saw her side of things? "Don't you dare compare me to her. I had no idea the wolf DNA was in there."

"Woody did," Gideon said. "And you never called him a monster."

"He didn't put the stem cells in the serum."

"What if he had? What excuse would you have given then? Your serum is a good thing," he said. "But what if the only way for it to work without subjecting the recipient to terminal cancer is with abilities created at the expense of the men and women who were in those trials?"

"I have other avenues to pursue," I said hotly. "An amplified immune system that—"

"What if the shifter side effect is the only way?" he said evenly. "Will you throw out all your work? Your promise to Robyn?"

"I couldn't proceed under those conditions. It's unethical."

He looked away, strangely silent.

"What?" I said.

"You could have found a way without my consent to get blood or tissue samples from me and try to re-create your serum, but you didn't."

I twisted my hands together in my lap and made the sound of a buzzer. "Sorry, contestant. The correct answer is 'what did Raisa think about doing more than once?'"

"Thinking something bad isn't the same as doing it." He flashed me a too-bright smile. "I mean, you're still standing, right?"

"Ha. Ha. Still."

"Still nothing. You have a strong sense of ethics, and even if you thought about it, you didn't take advantage of me for your own gain." He drew his brows together. "But the serum is connected to another reason why I didn't contact you."

"I don't understand." I stared at him, my heart pounding

inside my chest, wondering what else he was hiding from me.

"You didn't want to kiss me because you weren't sure if it was attraction or the rush of having survived." He shrugged a little too casually. "Well, I'm never sure if you want to work with me because I'm the only one with the serum inside me. The only connection to your dead sister."

"If you'd asked me," I said, "I'd have told you emphatically that wasn't the case."

"I'm sure you would have said that." He smiled sadly. "Everything you've done for over a decade has been in service to that promise. You've spent your adult life memorializing one aspect of your sister—her death."

I slammed my hand on the table, rattling the dishes. "That's not true."

"Being a shifter threw me for a hell of a loop," he said, "but I had a full life before and I will again. Sometimes, though, you look at me, and I'm not sure you're seeing me or a means to an end. From the little you've shared, you've lived like a ghost of yourself. Did you go on weekend getaways with friends? Have hobbies? Relationships? Or were you always so zealously dedicated to your work?"

I sucked in a breath. Who was he to judge me for how I lived my life? And how dare he imply that all I cared about was the promise? I cared about Robyn, but she wasn't here to give that stupid laugh...

I froze. I couldn't hear her laugh in my head anymore. I heard her gasping wheezes in the hospital but not her laugh, and when I tried to remember how she sounded when she sang, all I heard was a voice laced with pain. The fading one of her last days.

My stomach was a tight knot, and my jaw was clenched so hard that I feared I'd crack a tooth. "I'm going back to the inn." I pushed away from the table, threw my napkin down, and left.

Chapter 15

It was a minor miracle that I made it back to the inn, given my eyes were blurry with tears. I'd been so focused on giving meaning to Robyn's death that I'd forgotten about the part that mattered most: her life.

Once inside my room, I rested against the headboard, my knees drawn into my chest.

I hadn't once cracked open the book with her drawings that I'd stashed in my closet, and I actively avoided hearing her favorite songs, even leaving stores when they came on. Why wasn't I revisiting our memories, like the time Dad was teaching Robyn to drive stick?

I'd been in the back seat since my turn was after hers. Instead of shifting gears, she accidentally pulled up the hand brake. Everything went into slo-mo, the car drifting in a wide circle like we were in a music video. Robyn let out this long "Shiiiiiiit" while Dad screamed in this high-pitched voice "My baby!" with his hand on the dashboard. When the car finally stopped, all of us unharmed, Robyn and I couldn't stop laughing. We teased him mercilessly for caring more about his car than his daughters.

I swiped at my eyes; I still couldn't hear her laugh.

Could Mom? All these years she avoided any mention of her husband and daughter. I'd rebelled against her way of dealing with grief, feeling self-righteous for keeping our loved ones alive. But was I doing that when all I'd focused on was their deaths?

Should I have taken the lab's destruction as my cue to make a clean break? I thought long and hard about that before deciding no. I genuinely enjoyed my area of research and was looking forward to this shift into working on a short-term immunity boost to make the serum a reality. Regardless of my serum's origins, I wanted it out there to save people from the same pain and distress that my sister had faced.

I blinked and pressed my lips together in a flat line, Gideon's words ringing in my head. I was determined to help people live, so why wasn't I doing the same for myself? My personal life had been pathetic since Robyn's death. I'd walled myself off, avoiding prom and turning down invitations from roommates when I was an undergrad. I'd gotten a little better in grad school, but my socializing had mostly been contained to lab hours. Admittedly, I spent most of my time there, but still. I rarely asked anyone to hang out.

Even Anna Sula had kids and friends and enjoyed volunteering before she turned to the dark side. Not that I could blame her for the recluse I'd become. Being abducted and experimented on as toddlers had messed my sister and me up, but it hadn't stopped me from being an extrovert. I'd genuinely loved people and being at the center of the action.

I reflected on my teen years. Hadn't it been an almost frenetic need though? Keep being shiny and live at warp speed so I didn't have to stop and be alone with myself? I was still subconsciously dealing with the trauma of the experiment, even though I'd buried the memory by that point. Maybe I'd have been slightly less of an attention hog, slightly less reckless and far calmer, had I processed it all.

It wouldn't have changed my essential nature, but would I have stopped trying to outrun myself?

Robyn was the opposite of reckless; she maintained total control of her environment and only took on challenges she would excel at, not anything that would knock her down. She left it to me to push back against every boundary, fighting against anything that might snare me.

I'd assumed that my twin went to the party as me that night because it gave her the courage—and the in—to hook up with Aaron Rothstein. We'd never spoken about what Anna Sula had done to us, and I couldn't remember my sister's personality before the kidnapping because we'd been too young. I didn't think her more introverted nature was an act, but I couldn't say for certain.

I hugged a pillow to my chest. Was *that* why she pretended to be me? To see if my skin fit her better than the one she stitched as her protective armor all those years?

If we'd stayed home, would she have grown into a skin that stretched and fit her perfectly?

There was a soft knock at my door.

"Raisa," Gideon said. "Can I come in?"

For someone who'd mastered running away, he couldn't leave me alone now? I sighed.

"One sec," I said in a wavery voice. I quickly splashed cold water on my face and blew my nose before opening the door.

His gaze zeroed in on my red eyes. "I'm sorry."

I opened my mouth to brush it off, but all that came out was a defeated "I can't remember her laugh."

"Oh, swee—" He caught himself with a headshake, stepped inside the room, and gathered me into a hug. "That's really rough."

His muscular arms anchored me.

I pressed my cheek to his solid chest, holding him tightly. "I'm going to remember it again."

"I know you will." He kissed the top of my head.

I stilled, then he did too.

Gideon cleared his throat and tried to step away, but I held him fast.

"I'm sorry if I made you feel like anything other than a smart, experienced man that was my first choice of partner in crime," I said vehemently, tilting my face up to his.

"Thank you," he said softly. He brushed the back of his hand along my jaw.

I had to force myself not to rise up onto tiptoe and bring my lips in line with his.

"I'm not going to kiss you," he said.

I snorted a laugh and stepped away. "Good, because that's the last thing I want."

He arched an eyebrow, a cocky look on his face.

I threw a pillow at him, which he caught one-handed as he lowered himself carefully onto the chair in the corner.

Drained, I dropped onto the bed, my elbows braced on my thighs. "I was thinking how maybe when Robyn pretended to be me at the party, it was her first step to becoming a different version of herself." I laughed wryly. "Taking me as a role model wasn't the smartest or healthiest way of doing it, but she was seventeen."

"It was a compliment."

I pursed my lips. "Perhaps, but in the end, it was a death sentence. If I'd been more responsible, more like her risk-averse self to begin with, the way I am now—"

Gideon gave a surprised laugh. "We literally faced down fanged manta rays the other day."

"It's not like I saw them and jumped in the water to pet them. It was unexpected."

"You stabbed an eel with a heel." His shoulders shook.

"That sounds nothing like 'thank you.'"

"Raisa, you haven't reshaped yourself anywhere close to what you think you have."

I opened my mouth, prepared to argue, but was disarmed by his fond look.

"Did you ever consider that Robyn needed to be you that night," he said, "not because you were reckless, but because you're fearless?"

"With a reckless edge."

He shrugged. "Nobody's perfect. Especially not teenagers. You grabbed life by the balls and kept going despite what happened when you were little. You're still doing it. I mean, how many other scientists went on a crazy hunt for Woody after Perrault burned down?" He held up his fingers in the shape of a zero. "They found other jobs. You know, like risk-averse people?"

I shot him the finger and he laughed. But I grudgingly admitted—to myself, he didn't get an ego boost—that I'd never given up trying to live life on my terms. The terms themselves had changed to accommodate my promise, but if I was really risk averse, I could have tried harder to find a job at another lab after the fire. Or even gone to work for my mother.

Gideon wagged a finger at me. "You're thinking about how right I am. I can tell."

"You're annoying."

"And you, Dr. Raisa Montefiore, are brave in the face of seemingly insurmountable odds."

Blushing, I covered my face, overwhelmed by my feelings for Gideon. He saw me like no one else did, not even Levi, but the timing sucked. I couldn't be distracted by the fact I was crushing hard. Once we'd delivered Anna Sula to the Queen though? Gideon and I were going to have a long talk.

One that hopefully ends with us being naked and sweaty. Oh God, could he smell my arousal? My blush deepened.

"I saw the aftermath of a lot of car accidents during my time on the force," Gideon said, mercifully steering us back to mood-killing ground. "It's entirely possible that Robyn had no idea that guy was drunk. Not everyone presents like a stumbling, slurring mess, and it doesn't take much alcohol to badly impair someone's driving abilities. Give your sister the benefit of the doubt that even if the hookup was a bad choice, she didn't knowingly get in a car with a drunk driver."

Because Roth didn't seem drunk or because Robyn was too wasted to tell? No, I couldn't believe that her desire to be with Roth trumped her natural caution.

Levi had assured me that Robyn's death was an accident, Gideon not only reinforced that, but he also showed me that she might not have known Roth was too drunk to drive.

Her death was nothing more than a horrible, tragic accident. I couldn't blame it on stupidity or some nefarious plot.

Was it fucked up that I wanted to? That having nothing to rail against made this worse? My life was devoted to cause and effect, to concrete explanations. Dad died because he lost his daughter. I could cling to that knowledge; it wasn't comforting, but it made sense and had allowed me to mourn him in a healthy way that gave me closure.

Without anything or anyone to blame for Robyn, her death was pointless and senseless. How was I supposed to just accept that?

A perverse part of me acknowledged that I didn't have to. I could absolve Robyn, even absolve Anna Sula and Golden Radial of this single event, but there was one person left to blame.

Me.

"If Robyn hadn't pretended to be me," I said, "she couldn't have cozied up to Roth that night. He had no use for good girls and wouldn't have hooked up with her."

Gideon rolled his eyes. "You sorely overestimate the morals of teen boys. She was your identical twin, right?" Off my nod, he jabbed a finger at me. "I promise you, even if she'd approached him as herself, he'd have been interested."

That was gross, but it got me thinking. My sister was legendary in our family for her patience and determination and could well have gone through with her plan.

Even if I'd said no to the switch, the tragedy might not have been avoided.

When Robyn died, it was like I hit a brick wall, and as I staggered back, stunned, I became more like her: quieter, more focused, and responsible. Had taking on my twin's characteristics been a way to honor her—or penance for being the one who lived?

For all that I berated Gideon for his avoidance tendencies, how was I any better if my total commitment to my serum was a guilt-fueled refusal to accept that my sister was gone?

Maybe it was time to stop living with survivor's guilt.

I probed that idea as cautiously as I would a sore tooth, braced for further sharp pain. Say I accepted that this was a tragic accident with nothing and no one to blame, and that I didn't have to feel guilty, what did that leave me with?

A single emotion rushed in, pushing at me like prickly needles under my skin. For the first time ever, I let myself feel the one thing I never had: anger at my twin for putting me in that position that night and carrying the guilt of it ever since. I let out a string of Italian curses, flung the closest pillow against the wall, and buried my head in my hands.

I didn't know—yet—how to live without the guilt, but I was positive that I couldn't carry it any longer. I dragged in a deep breath. It had been stifling, like I'd been underwater all this time and, having finally bobbed to the surface, realized I should breathe.

I'd not only lost my twin that night; I'd lost myself. And I hadn't properly grieved either of us.

Finally, I lifted my head. "I need therapy." Gideon

opened his mouth, and I held up a hand. "No comments from the peanut gallery."

I was leaking feelings. It didn't feel right to jettison them, even if I could, but now was the worst possible time to deal with them. Facing Anna would be emotionally challenging enough. I took slow, deep breaths until I had some semblance of control again.

Smart, logical, and laser-focused may once more have been in the driver's seat, but they had some new emotions riding shotgun.

I shook myself like a dog flinging water from its fur. "Thank you for helping me see a whole other side of this. If you want to talk about anything, I'm here for you."

I appreciated his support during my emotional meltdown, but that made our relationship feel really unbalanced. I trusted him with my life, but I still didn't know him that well because he didn't open himself up. He was still playing lone wolf and that didn't bode well for any future together past this world tour.

I gave him an encouraging smile.

"I'm good," he said. "Can we go back to Anna Sula?"

I swallowed my disappointment and frustration that he'd refused this opportunity to deepen our connection, choosing instead to pull away again. "Sure. Before all this we were talking about consent. The patients in the muscular dystrophy trials didn't know they were signing up to become shifters."

"You can't be certain of that," Gideon said. "They were desperate, and we have no way of knowing what they agreed to."

"Even if that was the case for the muscular dystrophy trials, Robyn and I sure as hell didn't sign up for anything. Nor were we playing any role in curing muscular dystrophy. That genetic marker doesn't run in either side of our family. So how does our experience fit into all this?"

"I don't know."

I made a sound of frustration. "It's like we're working on two different puzzles when my gut says it's all part of the same picture. Especially since Robyn and I weren't a one-off event either. There were others." My voice cracked. "Sula pulled the same shit we were subjected to on other people. Maybe other kids who...." I furrowed my brows.

Gideon tapped my hand. "What are you thinking?"

I was still furious, but I was also connecting the dots. "Look at the timeline. Her daughters die, then she loses her license, and leaves. Given the old woman's animosity back at the shop, I'm willing to bet that Sula's experiments started with twins and not with muscular dystrophy."

"Why?"

"Because genetic editing was only developed at the end of the twentieth century, and it was basic. Too basic to have started messing around with wolf stem cells. That wouldn't have been possible until maybe 2010?"

Gideon stretched out his legs and folded his hands on his stomach. "You agreed with Levi's assessment that you and Robyn were placed in a high-stress situation to switch off your magic gene and switch on Robyn's. Can you connect that to the trials?"

I jolted up from my slouch. "Muscular dystrophy is a genetic condition. My God, what if her twins were the first ones she experimented on, using a combination of magic and science as a way of genetic editing the disease? Seeing if she could turn the mutation on and off, so to speak?"

"You just said you and your sister didn't have that genetic anomaly," Gideon said.

"No, but there's a reputable school of thought that believes magic is a disease because it didn't evolve, it invaded us. That it's a mutation as well. But she found us, one twin with magic and one without." I spread my hands wide.

"Still, there couldn't have been many like you and Robyn either."

"Probably not," I admitted. "Though I bet her medical board found out, either about her own girls, or some other twins, and that's why she lost her license. That happened before we were born, but she kept up the experiments."

"That's how Golden Radial found her," Gideon said. "They've been around for quite some time, and Sula must have had help to disappear since there's no death certificate for her."

"This all fits." I ticked the points off on my fingers. "She does her own research on her girls, but when that doesn't work, she conducts further research on twins. Eventually, she teams up with venture capitalists to add in a different approach using wolf stem cells because the technology has advanced enough to be feasible." I slowly shook my head. How she'd made the leap to that solution was beyond me.

"With a side benefit to the project that would make them all a lot of money," Gideon sneered. "Shifter soldiers."

"Even knowing about her own twins, I can't forgive her."

"You don't have to."

My phone chimed with a text from Ella containing the details of Carol's memorial. The police had signed off on Carol's brother taking the body for burial, and the ceremony was the day after tomorrow, on December 29. Ella was asking if we could go together because she'd been jumpy ever since hearing the news about the murder.

I sighed. Telling her I was out of town would lead to questions I couldn't answer, and even if I could, I wouldn't. Ella was freaked out enough about Carol, and she and I were much closer than she'd been with our colleague.

Guess I had my deadline for finding Anna Sula. It was only two days from now, but I'd always worked well under pressure.

By the time I texted my friend back that I'd pick her up, Gideon was searching something on his phone.

"Check it out." He showed me an old newspaper obituary for Maria and Nina Sula, with the name of the church where their funeral was held.

"Is the church supposed to mean something to me?"

"No, but guess where it's located?"

I smiled coldly. "The Carpathian Mountains?"

"Yeah, but not the Little Carpathians, a tiny village in the High Tatras."

"She must have a personal connection to the place if she buried her daughters there."

"I agree. My gut says that's where we'll find the cave where you and Robyn were taken."

The thought of being there again overwhelmed me. I smelled the dampness of the cave, the musty stale air, the thick iron stench of fear. I tugged the blanket around me like a superhero's cape, banishing the memory. This time, I'd be there on my terms.

I texted the name and location of the village to Levi along with a quick recap of what we'd found in Bratislava.

My phone immediately rang.

I hovered over the decline call button, but Levi would keep on me until I answered. "Hey—"

"Pull another disappearing act on me, Red, and I'll—"

"Lock me up? Too late," I said cheerfully. "The Queen of Hearts beat you to that and I bet your cells at House Pacifica are way nicer than hers."

Levi gave a strangled growl.

"Uh-oh," said another man from my cousin's end of the phone. "Levi is turning an unflattering shade of apoplectic. It's Arkady, by the way. You're on speaker. We were having a very dull meeting, yes, in the middle of the night, because someone couldn't wait until morning for a debrief on my latest mission." He paused for air. "I took the phone from him while he was sputtering so we could all chat. Thanks for livening things up."

"You're welcome."

"I like things peaceful," my cousin groused.

"Liar," Arkady sang.

"Let me send a team to this village," Levi said. "If there are any labs there—"

"You didn't sit back and let Ash handle the whole Chariot thing, did you?" I tsked him.

"She took the lead," he protested.

"Levi totally micromanaged that entire ordeal," Arkady said. "He's lucky Ash didn't kill him. And that she has low standards and is willing to marry him."

"Shut up, Arkady," my cousin snapped.

I could feel the other man's smirk.

"Look, I'm not alone," I said. "I've got Gideon. Ask Ash. She'd agree he's the best person for me to work with. I'm safe with him."

Gideon smiled. It wasn't dazzling or broad or cocky. To anyone else, it wouldn't even read as a smile, just an amused tug of his lips. But I was fluent in this man's expressions. I saw the crinkles at the corners of his mouth and the warmth in his hazel eyes, all of it containing his deep joy and satisfaction that we were in this together.

Nothing about this journey we were on followed some rule book, yet he wasn't running. Not physically and not emotionally. Was he realizing that he didn't need to anymore? Not for my benefit, but for his own?

The rush of hope I felt at that thought, made me trip over my next words. "He's on an official assignment for the Queen. We've kept both of you apprised of the situation, and we also have Gideon's gold token to get us out of any danger. We're the A Team, you're the backup. Let us do our thing, all right?"

Arkady laughed. "Levi so does not want to admit that

you're ri—" He yelped. "No hitting. Ooh, was that one of Miles's stress balls? I'm keeping that."

"Technically, I didn't touch you," Levi said.

"See if that holds up with HR," Arkady replied.

"You better come back safely and even out my side of the bridal party," Levi said. "Priya is scaring me."

"I'll come back safely." Once I did, I'd say yes and go for all the tux fittings in the world, but I didn't want to jinx the wedding by agreeing too soon. I didn't trust the universe. Look what happened after one measly joke about kraken.

Gideon made a "wrap it up" motion with his finger.

I nodded. "I'm going now. I love you and I'll call you if I need help."

"Fine," Levi said. "I love you too, Red."

"So do I," Arkady called out.

"Jesus, Arkady," Levi muttered and cut the line.

I exhaled. "That went better than expected."

Gideon stood up. "Ready to confront your past?"

That subterranean darkness, the dank smell, Robyn's cries, they rose up tightening the noose I'd lived with since the memory of the cave had slithered up from the depths of my unconscious. I wouldn't find closure until I stood in that cave again and stopped letting it have power over me.

I turned my face to the window, letting the bright light of day saturate my skin, and nodded. "Ready."

Chapter 16

I inhaled a deep lungful of the crispest, cleanest air that I'd ever breathed and looked down over the snow-covered valley, past the frozen emerald green lake, and along the ridge of jagged mountain peaks presiding in picture perfect fashion over it all. *If I'd had to get here under my own steam, I'd have died about twenty minutes into the trip.*

Gideon studied the vista with a satisfied expression. "Getting to the top of a mountain is an amazing feeling. No matter how prepared I am, something could go wrong. A storm could move in, I could twist my ankle."

"Wow, you're really selling me on how awesome the great outdoors is."

"Let me finish."

I mimed zipping my lips.

"When I reach the top, exhausted, that sense of accomplishment is a rush like nothing else. I made it. I dealt with any problems, I adjusted for unexpected variables, I tested my physical limits. Now I can sit back and enjoy the view. I think there'd be one hell of a view to enjoy out here. One day, I'd like to hike this for real."

I'd like to enjoy that view with you. I blinked. What the

hell was I thinking? Mother Nature was a dangerous lady. I waved a hand at the miles of forest sweeping in a crescent at our backs. "Knock yourself out. You could shift and hunt to your heart's content. Test a whole new set of physical limits."

He eyed the woods, his head tilted, and I raised my eyebrows, amazed he would even consider the idea.

I scanned the sky, which was growing more overcast by the moment. It was eerily quiet up here. Forget traffic noise, there wasn't even birdsong. "Let me know if you see enormous chicken feet tracks." I shivered and picked up my pace.

"Sula isn't actually Baba Yaga." Gideon brushed a low-hanging branch out of our way. "A hut isn't going to run out of the forest and chase us."

"You're right. I'm being silly."

"Not if she has any more wolf hybrids at her disposal."

I smacked his arm. "Is that supposed to reassure me?"

"Yeah, 'cause I'm the biggest baddest wolf of them all." Gideon smirked.

I rolled my eyes, but he wasn't wrong.

We trudged along the single lane leading into the village, leaving tracks in the snow. Honestly, calling it a village was being generous, given it was about two city blocks long, with a cluster of small houses and a gloomy church on a small rise.

Glassless windows faced us like the crooked smiles of gap-toothed children, while more than one roof had caved in. A house on the end listed so precariously, it was in danger of being swept down the mountain with the next snowfall.

I clenched my fists. "I wasn't arrested and pitted against mutant manta rays and forced to endure even a single moment of compassion for this woman only for her to have vanished without a trace. Carol is dead, Woody's career is over, and I'm..." I shook my head. "She has to be somewhere."

Gideon stalked through the snow, carefully examining each abandoned house, clocking a tattered lace curtain blowing in one pane-free window. "I find her absence conspicuous. We managed to tie her to a single address which she hasn't been back to in decades. Okay, I can buy that, but now we connect Sula to another place and the entire village is a ghost town? What happened here?"

A lone wolf's cry pierced the silence.

I stiffened.

Gideon planted himself, legs hips width apart, occupying as much room as possible, his eyes tracking something in the woods. "It's a regular wolf and it's gone." He huffed a soft laugh. "Regular wolf. Never thought I'd say those words."

"Hopefully, it's a sign that we're in the right place." I pointed at the small cemetery to the side of the church. "This entire story started there. I want to see Maria's and Nina's graves."

If their deaths were the event that marked the fork in Anna Sula's life from kind doctor to cold-hearted scientist with about as much regard for her subjects as a driver for a bug on their windshield, then I wanted—no, I needed—to see it for myself and understand that transformation.

Perhaps I also had to assure myself that though I'd experienced a terrible loss of my own, I hadn't chosen to give meaning and worth to that loss by creating something good and important at the expense of my humanity.

I glanced at Gideon, then briefly closed my eyes. I hadn't.

"There's more to seeing their graves than Sula's personal story, isn't there?" he said. When I shrugged, he continued down the street to the church. "You wouldn't believe how many nights I sat by the orange fencing surrounding the ruins of your lab after I shifted, hoping to find perspective."

Another wolf's howl shivered out from the woods.

I speed-walked to stick to Gideon's side. If that wild animal charged us, my plan was to shove my partner in its path while I found shelter. It wasn't like I was flinging it a fresh baby to eat. Gideon in wolf form was larger than a regular one; he'd alpha that bugger in no time.

"Did you?" I said. "Find perspective?"

"No. Just a shitty location for an origin story. An industrial park on the outskirts of Toronto?" Sneering, he waved his hand like he was brushing the idea way. "Get outta here with that."

"Way to discount that it happened while you were saving an injured woman in a lab and that said lab was an inferno at the time, Mr. Glass Half Empty." If Gideon hadn't carried Ella out of the blaze, I might have had to add my friend to the list of all the other people I'd lost.

"Huh. When you put it that way, it kind of rocked." He winked, kicking snow away from the small gate into the cemetery so I didn't have to climb the waist-high fence.

His teasing dampened my fear.

"What happened to her family is awful, but it's intangible. I mean…" I slowed down to read the names on the first grave. "Sula was a constant nightmare for most of my childhood, and I want to find something to humanize her in a tangible way before we find her. Reduce her from the monster under my bed to just another shitty adult."

Long shadows from the wild coniferous trees cast a blanket of shade over the simple headstones, some of which had cracked and eroded thanks to time and the elements.

"Hence the cemetery," Gideon said.

I nodded. "Yes."

It didn't take me long to find the graves of the two girls. I pulled off a glove to brush snow from the stone, almost savoring the bite of cold that penetrated my skin. Seeing their names was proof that Anna Sula existed and that our hypothesis made sense.

I walked back and forth until I caught the faintest cell signal and translated the Slovakian epitaph. "Trust in God."

Gideon clucked his tongue. "They were eleven years old."

Frowning, I resettled my daypack, double-checking the dates they'd died. "Even for the rarer strain of Duchenne muscular dystrophy, which claims patients at an earlier age, eleven is oddly young. Also, what are the chances of them dying that close together? They passed away two weeks apart? This isn't like pneumonia or scarlet fever where that's at least plausible. Not even twins should waste away that quickly and in tandem."

"Did Sula's experiments kill them?" Gideon's words were barely a murmur, but they punched into me like icy spikes.

"I don't want to believe that," I said, "but nothing else makes as much sense. Even if it was accidental—and I'll give her the benefit of that doubt—it's sickening." I tugged on my jacket zipper, though it was already done up all the way, suddenly chilled despite the hundreds of dollars of tech gear designed to keep me warm. "Why did she let Robyn and me leave?"

"She did enough to you," he said, his voice tight with anger.

"Sure, but my promise to Robyn might as well have been a throwaway comment in comparison to Sula's fanaticism to cure muscular dystrophy. You saw that poor hybrid shifter who attacked us when we found Woody. She had no compunction turning a person into a monster, so why did she let us go? She should have kept us until she'd drained every drop of usefulness from us. Until we were dead."

When Robyn and I were about ten, we saw part of a documentary on Josef Mengele, nicknamed the "Angel of Death" for conducting abominable medical experiments on twins in Auschwitz. Most of the subjects died; sometimes that was his desired outcome, other times, it was a tragic result of his horrific work.

Everything about him scared the living daylights out of us.

After Robyn's death, I became morbidly fascinated with him again. What I learned was even scarier because he couldn't be written off as some psycho. The truth was infinitely more complicated and upsetting for it. Mengele was a highly trained doctor, respected in his biomedical field, and one of many such people carrying out experiments under the Nazi regime. I told myself that it was an extreme ideology and that the conditions giving rise to it couldn't possibly happen again, but given the divisive state of our world, I didn't fully believe it.

Dr. Sula might not have operated from a dangerous and false political ideology, but wasn't her grief still extreme and her experiments just as inhuman?

When people participated in legitimate research trials, they received aftercare. We didn't simply take what we wanted, then toss them into the cold. Yet that's exactly what Sula had done to us. We'd been forced to live with that darkness. Too young to explain it to our parents and ask for help, we'd turned it inward and clung to each other for safety.

A wave of despair washed over me. "Maybe it would have been better if Sula hadn't taken us back home."

"Enough." Gideon strong-armed me away from the graves and out of the cemetery.

"Where are we going?" I put my glove back on, my daypack bobbing against my spine in time with my footsteps.

"Somewhere I can talk sense into you without freezing my balls off. Levi's place or Hedon?"

"My entire life has been a dead end since Robyn died." I yanked my arm away. "All my research with the serum was a hamster wheel I was running on because if I stopped, I'd have nothing left of her." My voice hitched.

For the first time in forever, I couldn't see a way forward. I'd been certain that coming to Slovakia would finally get us much-needed answers. It would be my reward for connecting the dots, but here I stood in a graveyard belonging to a dead village under a darkening sky that felt like a portent.

"How are we ever going to find Anna Sula?" I said. "The Queen couldn't. Ash and Levi couldn't even crack the façade of Golden Radial."

"Don't give up. There's a good chance her lab is in these mountains. You said it yourself."

"Look how big this mountain range is. How long do I keep looking? I thought… I hoped we'd find something tangible, but all we have is more death. I can't even start my new job because she had Carol killed and I'm scared about who she'll go after next." I slumped my shoulders, exhaustion etched into my bones. "I'm tired, Gideon. I don't know how to keep fighting a ghost." I marched off.

"Don't run away." His voice grew thin through the fog rolling in.

I opened my mouth to snap that that was rich coming from him, then closed it with a small shake of my head. He'd stayed with me at every turn and had even comforted me when it would have been way easier to avoid my messy emotions.

"I'm not running away. I just need five minutes to myself." I dragged myself up the stairs of the church, turned sideways to get through the warped and bloated wooden front doors, and fumbled in my pack for my flashlight to cut through the dim gloom. I clicked it on, shone the bright beam inside, and flinched.

Soot warred with mold for dominion of the walls, the burned remnants of pews were knocked over, and every window had been smashed, the ground a sea of glass. I could practically taste the rage that had fueled this destruction.

I'd tasted it myself once, though I hadn't had a church to burn down. It was a hospital room too empty, a long beep from the monitors, a sterile sheet covering a still shape on the bed. Syringes and IVs knocked to the floor. A nurse telling me I had to calm down, that it was over, that I had to understand.

After that, I'd turned the fury inward, powering late nights of study, eating when I didn't want to, all because I needed my body for this singular goal. Sometimes I wasn't sure I resided in my body at all because the last glimpse I'd had of Robyn before the chevra kedisha took her away to prepare her for the Jewish funeral was of a face identical to the one I saw in the mirror every day.

I kicked aside a shard. Someone, two guesses who, had taken an axe to the holy water font. She hadn't managed to do much damage to the marble basin, but given the tiny nicks, she'd certainly tried.

Avoiding the mummified corpse of a mouse, I moved slowly through the wreckage, headed for the sun-bleached outline of a large cross in the middle of the front wall. I hoped the church had salvaged it after the fire. This might not be my holy space (that was my lab if anything), but I respected other people's places of worship and always tried to treat them with the respect I expected in mine. *Do unto others* wasn't a bad motto to live by.

"What the everlasting fuck?" The beam of Gideon's flashlight joined mine. It did not make the place look better. "Someone took lapsed Catholic to a new extreme."

"Someone stopped trusting in her god."

Chapter 17

I'd bet my meager savings that until Anna Sula lowered her children into the ground, there had been countless thoughts and prayers in addition to her magic and science. She'd volunteered at a religious orphanage after all, so Catholicism was a large part of her life.

Once her daughters were gone, however, she'd cut out all religion and cauterized the wound with magic and science. I recalled the burn on her face and shivered. That didn't make it better, because the combination I'd also devoted my life to required checks, balances, and a lot of critical thinking and healthy skepticism.

I crouched down, pushed aside a couple pieces of the altar that had been chopped into kindling, and picked up a half-melted silver chalice. I sniffed it. It didn't smell like anything, but the memory of the wine from the cave rose up to overpower me and I swayed.

"Hey." Gideon was immediately at my side. He grasped my elbow to steady me.

"You know," I said slowly, "this mountain range is riddled with caves."

"Okay."

"Caves were used before refrigeration for food storage. Useful for a remote village, don't you think?"

Gideon looked around. "You think the cave you were brought to as a child is under here? That she did this to the church as a red herring to throw people off her track?"

I set the chalice on the side of a pew. "No, I think this was genuinely born of her rage and grief, but while we're discussing red herrings? You spoke to people in Sion and no one believed anything was amiss at the clinic. What if it wasn't? No trace of the staff? No suppliers that saw anything? A lab doesn't exist in a vacuum."

He ran the flashlight in a circle around the main room. "You think she carried out the shifter experiments here?"

The fog grew denser, the wind howling and blowing snow inside the church and dropping the temperature. I pulled a scarf out of my pack and wrapped it around my face, my next words coming out muffled. Better that than my poor nose freezing off.

"A remote village where she'd driven the inhabitants off and where the labs were subterraneous, making them almost impossible to find? Yeah. I do." I shone my beam at the front door. The outside was a blanket of fog, while snow piled up in tiny drifts against the half-open door. I swung the light along the floor. "I'd bet that the entrance is in here somewhere. A giant fuck you to the god and the religion that failed her."

Gideon knelt down at the seam of the floor and wall, tapping the ground carefully with his boot, his light trained on the spot. "I can't smell anything other than mold," he said, "but I might be able to sense a cold spot that regular people wouldn't notice."

"Great. You focus on that." Deciding to hug the left wall, I scanned from floor to ceiling with my flashlight, then pushed on a decorative sconce that had escaped Sula's wrath. "I'll look for the entrance my way."

We worked in silence for a bit, moving methodically through the church.

"When we get the world tour T-shirts," I said, "should we list this as Carpathian Mountains or High Tatras? I vote for the latter since it's more specific and sounds naughty."

"We're not getting T-shirts."

When I didn't immediately agree with him, he sighed heavily.

We kept searching, my swearing at our lack of results growing more frequent.

"I haven't been entirely honest about why I didn't contact you after Marrakesh," Gideon said.

Thinking that I looked at you and saw only my dead sister wasn't enough? I rattled a loose brick in the wall. "You want to get into that *now*?"

"You opened up to me, and I wanted…" He shrugged. "We can talk about the Raptors' current season, if you want."

I shuddered. "No basketball." Besides, I'd rather chop off my left arm than shut him down right now. That said, I adjusted my expectations accordingly. "By all means, dive right in."

"My dad was a consummate gambler," he said with a forced lightness. "Charming and chatty, he never met a person he didn't like." Gideon pried a chunk of burned pew railing away from the floor and stomped on the ground, testing it. "Sorry. I meant, he never met a person he didn't like to fleece. It was always feast or famine at our place, you know? When times were good and Dad filled the house with laughter, he was my hero."

"Times weren't always good though, were they?" I asked softly.

"Are they ever?" He kicked away a piece of pipe. "Anyway, everyone always commented on how much like him I was, always ready with a joke, easily making friends." He stared off into the distance. "Sometimes that was the greatest compliment I could get."

Everything I knew—or thought I knew—about Gideon rearranged itself in my brain with a click. "You became Mr. Stoic, upholder of the law, in direct opposition to everything your father represented."

"That would be Inspector Stoic, but kind of. Mostly, I did it because it was the only thing I could think of to lower my mom's stress after Dad lost everything and fucked off."

"You protected her." I paused. "And everyone else."

"The day I graduated from Police College?" A wistful smile unfurled on his face. "She was so happy. I hadn't seen her that lit up in years."

"But being a cop is risky."

"That's why I steered myself into white collar crimes, instead of undercover work in Vice. I really did love being an officer and helping people, but I went into an area that was easier for my mom to deal with."

"Vice, huh?" I moved aside a large pile of debris in case there was a trapdoor underneath.

"My second choice. My dream was to be a stunt car driver."

I chuckled. "Seriously?"

"Oh yeah. Whenever Dad disappeared on one of his business trips, Mom would watch a lot of TV to fill the time until he got back. She had shit taste most of the time, but both of us were fans of that old series *The Dukes of Hazzard*."

"For very different reasons, I'm guessing."

Gideon winced. "Please don't make me think about my mother lusting after those actors. Anyway, there was a lot of great stunt driving in the show. Tame by today's standards, but still pretty cool to young me."

"You've seen every *Fast & Furious* flick, haven't you?"

"Once or four times," he agreed. "But we're getting off track. I'm trying to tell you that I wasn't always this staid person, nor did I ever expect to be, but I did what I believed was right."

"Just like me with Robyn."

"Yeah. I played it safe for my mom's sake, then picked a partner who reinforced that. Janna was—is—an amazing woman, but when we got together, I even gave up any hobbies that were the slightest bit dangerous." He glanced at me. "Then I met you. A woman who understood acting outside the norm if it let her keep fighting to stay afloat and achieve her goals. You kept flinging us into danger and chaos at every turn."

"Given who you'd become, you hated it." I said it with my back to him. He was only a few feet away, but this entire conversation was digging a canyon between us.

"Nope. I loved it."

I spun around and he smiled at my shocked look. "You felt guilty for it?" I said, wrinkling my brow.

He shook his head. "Not that either. I didn't contact you because you made me remember who I was. I wanted to be that man again, and it scared the shit out of me. I'd worked so hard to become this other version of myself."

"You'd convinced yourself that your skin fit."

"Exactly. I wasn't ready to admit otherwise, so I cut myself off from you, because it was easier than continually reminding myself that I was living a lie. It was hard, since a part of me, deep down, enjoyed my shifter side a bit too much, but I couldn't double down on lying to myself if we stayed in contact. I'm truly sorry that I hurt you though."

Hearing this admission from him wiped away any lingering pain and resentment I'd nurtured. "You're forgiven, but why team up with me again?"

"I couldn't lie to myself anymore."

About who he was? His emotions? All of the above? The wind snaked through the broken window, and I shivered. "If we don't find anything soon, let's get out of here and come back tomorrow."

"Do you remember anyone other than Sula when you and Robyn were taken?" Gideon said from the back of the room.

"I don't even remember *her*, just her voice. My memory of her face was from when she found us again later. Why?"

"You were in Toronto, and she's not a Transporter, so how did she move you two to wherever and back? I can only think of one easy way." He tapped the base of his throat.

"A gold token? But how? I didn't get the impression there are a lot of those coins or that Her Majesty tends to misplace them."

"Another reason the Queen wants her apprehended?" Gideon slipped through an empty doorframe at the back of the church. "I found something in the sacristy."

"The what now?" I joined him in the small bare room, whose once richly stained panels had been twisted away from the wall and warped over the years.

There was still glass in these windows, though between the fog and snow blowing furiously against the panes there was such an oppressive vibe here that I longed for the fresh air back in the chapel, freezing though it was.

"Sacristy," Gideon said. "Where the priests get ready for mass. They keep vestments and sacred vessels and stuff here, but it's not consecrated and not considered a sacred space."

I blinked at him. "That's a lot of Catholic info for a Jew."

"Janna made me go to mass with her a few times for family stuff."

"Ah."

"Check this out." He jerked a finger at what I had taken for a storage closet door. One of those generic beige metal ones found in many an institution. "All the other doors are wood except this one." He examined the lock. "It has a dead bolt that's free of rust."

"Did you try the knob?"

He slapped his forehead. "No. Why didn't I think of that?"

"All right, Mr. Sarcasmo. Well, then pick the lock."

"This may shock you," he said, "but as a former cop, I never developed B&E skills."

"Then huff and puff and break down the door."

"This isn't a fairy tale, and that door is metal." He shook his head. "Not happening."

I was one door away from reclaiming my life; I was sure of it. I cast my flashlight over the dead bolt. "Bring your light here."

With the lock now brightly illuminated, I flexed my fingers. Yeah. I could work with this. I drew a fiber of light away from the wider beam and fed it into the keyhole like I was threading a needle.

Fine. It wasn't that simple, nor did it take one try. I'd never done this before, and my focused magic kept falling apart inside the dead bolt. It would have helped to pull a schema of the lock off the web, but any cell signal had been spotty enough before the storm. Now it was gone.

Gideon suggested we jump to Hedon momentarily and get tools, but I had this weird superstitious dread that if we left, we'd never find our way back. Besides, it's not like the token was going anywhere. If worse came to worst, we could be out of here in a second.

I squatted down, visualizing pins and tumblers while drawing on any scrap of knowledge I had about dead bolts. Believe me, they *were* scraps. I kept having to stand up from the crouch keeping me eye level with the lock because my legs were on fire and my vision was starting to swim. I was sweating, all outerwear long ago discarded in a heap on the floor, but at long last, my magic weaving caught hold of something inside the bolt.

Barely daring to breathe, I fed more and more light into it.

The metal lock gave a sudden bulge outward, and that small victory energized me enough to pick up the pace.

Gideon's breath tickled the back of my neck, his head next to mine and a fascinated expression on his face.

Slowly, the lock rippled and twisted, pulling free from the metal door, until with the most beautiful thud I ever heard, it fell backward onto the ground.

The door swung open.

"Wow. Well done." Gideon shone his flashlight inside.

"Wait." I dug my pair of extra socks out of my daypack and tossed them in, braced for a flurry of arrows.

Nothing happened, except my socks landing in a puddle and getting gross and damp. With a grimace, I retrieved them.

"You good now, Indy?" Gideon said.

"You can't be too careful." I quickly put my discarded jacket, scarf, and gloves back on along with my pack. "Allons-y."

Gideon, already in the tunnel, tapped his boot against the ground. "It's concrete. This is man-made."

"Yeah, it is." I high-fived him. Sula's lab was within reach. I just knew it.

The tunnel was a straight stretch of uneven rock, which sloped gently down. There were enough bare bulbs strung overhead to see by, and while it wasn't bright, we had clear line of sight to the bottom.

We clicked off our flashlights to conserve the batteries while we trekked along the passageway. We were headed for an underground mad scientist's lab via tunnels under a forest famed in fairy tales for its capricious characters and creepy environment.

My heart pounded in my chest, and even though there was only a faint tinge of must in the air, all I smelled was wine. While I stood by my idea of venturing into the tunnels, I couldn't keep all the best doom questions from swirling in my head: would I find myself in the cave of my nightmares moments from now? Were we walking into a trap? Would we make it out alive?

I steeled my shoulders, refusing to let my nerves get the better of me, and slid into my most analytic, deconstructionist mindset. The one I used when yet another serum revision had failed, and even though I longed to smash my computer, I forced myself into a cold, logical state to navigate my troubles one small piece at a time.

"Quit swiveling your head like the kid in *The Exorcist*," Gideon said. "I'll hear or smell anyone long before you do and sound the alarm. Okay?"

"Okay." This had to be a supply tunnel. Would the labs be at the bottom?

We curved around a bend.

My eyes widened and my mouth fell open at the enormous cavern we stood in. The ceiling soared higher and more majestically overhead than any cathedral or university building.

Gideon whistled. "The power of water and time is beautiful to behold."

White stalagmites, some no bigger than my hand, others towering over us, dotted the space. They resembled half-melted candles with rivulets of beeswax cascading down their formations like waterfalls, glowing softly thanks to work lights mounted to the crude wooden walkway snaking through this chamber.

Gideon stomped on one of the boards, giving a satisfied grunt at their trustworthiness. "Stick to the planks." His voice bounced off the walls. "The ground is slippery and drops away in places."

Water dripped on my head. I glanced up while making my way carefully forward over the groaning planks. Fat plops ran off stalactites, adding to the wet humid air that hugged us like a damp blanket. The sound of running water was soft but ever present.

"The stalagmite to our left gets its white color from the limestone and is probably six stories high," Gideon said conversationally from behind me.

"Crazy. I thought it was only ten feet tall."

"The sheer size of this cave makes it impossible to accurately determine the scope of things by eye."

The air grew colder as we descended deeper, and there was the faint hum of machinery. The back of my neck prickled, but I focused on Gideon's calm recitation of facts.

"Why do you know this?" I said.

"I was into caving for a while."

"I'm into patio-ing, but I couldn't tell you the architectural details of my favorite brunch place." That said, my scientific curiosity had kicked in, because when would I ever get the chance to see something like this again? *Hopefully never*, a voice in my head chided.

Again, yes, but this wasn't the cave from my memories. That cave was likely up ahead, and the more armed with information that I was, the more chance I stood of getting us out of here. In the same way that Gideon couldn't bust down the metal door, his brute strength would only protect us so far. This was a battle of wits, and while he was really smart with years of police training and experience on his side, as a fellow scientist, I understood Anna Sula's way of thinking.

Loath as I was to admit it.

I had to believe that even if I was given unlimited funds and left unchecked that I'd be nothing like her, and yet… I shook my head. The only relevant detail in my existential musings was that in experimenting on Robyn and me, Anna had created the petard she'd get hoisted on.

"Tell me about some of your adventures," I said.

"Once you're through the mouth of a cave, it's so alien, you're so cut off. There's almost no one with you, no safety net, no cell service, and a lot of rock pressing down on you. It gets even crazier when you go underwater in near-pitch darkness praying you don't lose your grip on the safety line, or when you chimney up a long drop."

I rubbed my chest. "I'm getting an anxiety attack just listening."

"Seeing the world from a fingerhold while dangling over a chasm or having to focus on one breath at a time in a seemingly impassible tunnel, instead of from my ass on a seat during roll call, gave me a different perspective on the world. On life. Those were some of the times I felt most alive," he said softly.

"You let your stunt car driver side out. My risk-averse self would never do it," I joked.

"Stunt driving and caving, yeah, they're high-octane adrenaline activities, but both require tons of training and preparation and a slow amassing of experience. I followed specific procedures and techniques that I learned, and then, because I understood the rules and methods so well, I improvised as needed. The times I spent out in nature were when I felt whole."

I glanced up, certain there were twittering birds and hearts floating above me because having him open up to me like this was heady.

Thankfully, Gideon didn't notice, busy pointing out thin slices of deposits ribboning along the wall that looked like fish fillets, some with red or black striations in them from mineral deposits.

We ducked low through a gap between two rocks, and I jumped at the bat that exploded out of the darkness to wing across our path. The work lights continued sporadically along the planks, illuminating a small lake on our right.

"The blue color comes from sulfur," my partner said.

"Does that also produce the dildo-shaped stalagmites?"

Gideon sighed heavily.

"Like you don't see it." I pointed at the small mineral deposits scattered in the shallow water. "That is an objective description, not my dirty mind."

"I hate that I can't unsee it now."

"Good enough."

The cavern narrowed and my chest tightened, all amusement gone under the very real awareness how much rock was above us. I really hoped this wasn't earthquake country.

Gideon caught my hand. "Was this where…?"

"No." I didn't let go.

He was quiet for a moment then he cleared his throat. "The tumble of rocks on your left is an example of a landslide that happened likely a few thousand years ago. Excellent for continued cave growth."

Gideon knowing all these cave facts was doing squirmy things to my insides, but I locked them down to enjoy at a more appropriate time.

We passed alabaster spears, some layered mineral deposits that resembled jellyfish emerging from the walls, and another huge stalagmite that was gnome shaped, cap and all. It remined me of the Queen's statues, and a shudder ran through me.

Gideon squeezed my hand tighter.

We rounded a bend and hit a natural archway. Small, thin, razor-sharp rock spears pointed down from the top of the arch. I pressed back against Gideon, my entire body screaming at me not to step into that mouth.

"There's a door just through the arch," Gideon said, turning on his flashlight and peering ahead. He ran a thumb under his necklace. "The magic in the gold token is still alive. I feel it humming against my skin, but this could be our last chance to safely leave. Your call."

My mouth was dry and my tongue was caked in sand. It

was the taste of time running out, the taste of the past catching up in a rush.

We had to move forward to get answers, the same as with any scientific hypothesis. There would be missteps and dead ends and times I beat my head trying to figure out which questions to ask and which steps to take next, but that's where I excelled.

I pried myself away from the big picture and down to what was necessary in this one single step.

"There's zero chance that our presence has gone undetected," I said. "And I don't want to spend the rest of my life looking over my shoulder. I've met Anna Sula twice in my life. We need to meet again."

"Good things might come in threes," Gideon said, "but this doesn't exactly qualify."

"Obviously, but three is important in science, not just fairy tales. Three primary colors, three stages of existence, three times of day, there are countless examples. It's not inevitable, but it feels necessary."

"In that case, ladies first." He swung his flashlight from my face back to the door, and I startled as it passed over a shadow projected on the cave wall. It was the side profile of a witch with a hat and a warty nose. Baba Yaga marking the entrance to her lair.

I yelped, but it was just the shadow from the misshapen stalagmite next to me. Just like those were mineral deposits, not teeth in a mouth.

Get it together, Dr. Montefiore, I told myself sternly.

"You good?" Gideon said.

"Yeah. Fuck once upon a time," I said, and stepped through the arch.

Chapter 18

Out of nowhere, pale orange magic twisted out of me, and I doubled over, crying out in pain. I felt like an old radio where someone had cranked my volume to high.

It splashed against the three work lights strung up in this chamber, and they blew with a sharp snap. I wasn't in pitch black, however, because the tiny cavern was almost blindingly bright from the magic pouring out of me. I couldn't breathe, my skin was on fire, and my internal organs may have been melting.

Gideon's flashlight hit the ground. He leapt to my side, one fist closed on his gold token and his other hand outstretched to grab me.

The token exploded into smithereens under the force of whatever had compelled my power.

A tiny shard scratched my cheek, drawing blood, but I barely registered it, because Gideon's wolf form had erupted into existence in one deafening crack. His backpack broke off and careened down a crevasse.

The sound of his tearing flesh was so loud and visceral that I couldn't help glancing to see if his human skin lay in a discarded puddle on the ground. In a blink, his eyes went from wide and horrified to feral and deadly.

Without any light source my magic turned on itself. My powers were weaving and reweaving into clunky knots that felt like acid anchors weighing me down and eating me alive from inside.

I screamed and crashed to my knees.

Gideon snarled at me, his wide, mad eyes burning hazel orbs.

I couldn't do more than whimper "Stop."

But Gideon didn't hear—maybe what was Gideon in him had gone. He tensed his leg muscles and I threw up my arms, uselessly, to ward him off.

A shadow fell over me and I closed my eyes.

There was a massive thud beside me.

I cracked an eye open.

He lay on his side less than half an inch from my foot, a tranquilizer dart sticking out of him.

"I told you the draw was set too high." A scientist in a starched lab coat, her hair slicked back into a tight bun, stood in the doorway, speaking over her shoulder at someone.

Gideon, still in wolf form, shuddered a final huff and fell terrifyingly still.

The woman prodded him with her foot. "He better not be dead, Bruno. This one's the real deal."

My magic deepened from its pale color, bright and hot. I tried to grab hold of my wildly fluctuating powers and turn them on this stranger, but she simply gave an annoyed sigh, and pulled a smaller weapon that resembled a throwing star off her belt.

She tossed it, almost gently the way you would a frisbee to a small child.

The star spun toward me, slashing through my magic

and absorbing it. Its sudden absence was as shocking as being plunged into a glacial lake, and I collapsed onto all fours, shivering so violently that my teeth rattled. I could barely prop myself up on my arms.

I stretched my fingertips out to bury them in Gideon's fur, but I had to press hard to feel the faint rise and fall of his torso. The edges of my vision were starting to blur, I was breathing as hard as if I'd run up a dozen flights of stairs, and my magic hadn't returned yet.

"Take me to Sula," I whispered.

The scientist laughed. "You're hardly in a position to be making demands." She jerked her head at the doorway, and five other people emerged.

If I'd had the energy I would have laughed because these pale individuals with their pens clipped to their lab coat pockets, a few of whom wore thick glasses, could have been straight out of a Hollywood casting call for "geek scientists."

Four men picked up Gideon and, with much effort, carried him away while the other woman assisted the scientist who'd nulled my magic. They grabbed me under my elbows, hauled me to my feet, and dragged me out of the cave and through the door.

There it was. The lab.

I'd done it.

Too bad I was taken to a smaller area glassed off to the side, and unceremoniously locked in a cave cell next to Gideon's.

"I hope your stay will be enlightening, Dr. Montefiore," the scientist with the bun said, and left me there to rot.

I fell into a fevered state, plagued by dreams of my sister, Gideon, witches in chicken feet houses, and at one point, my mother feeding me broth. When I finally came to my senses, weak and shivering, I had no idea whether I'd been out for a day or a week. I smelled pretty ripe, but I'd been sweaty while feverish, and even a day or two in that condition would leave me stinky so that didn't help me determine how long I'd been here.

I sat up on the narrow cot, shivering against the damp air and clutching a thin blanket. Nulling cuffs jingled on my wrists.

Light from the bare bulb overhead glinted off a few tiny shards of glass on the concrete floor. I shook the cuffs. My magic must have come back while I was unconscious.

My daypack and outerwear were gone. I'd been left with my winter hiking boots, jeans, T-shirt, and fleece hoodie, though the latter had been taken off me and thrown on the cot. I didn't dwell on who'd done it or who'd attended to my needs while I was delirious. Nor did I let the realization that I had no phone and no gold token overwhelm me.

I placed my hand on the wall separating my cell from Gideon's and whispered his name, but there was no answer.

Refusing to think about why that was the case, I shuffled to the bars of my cell, standing in the shadows, my body aching, and studying the lab through the glass wall separating us before any of the scientists grew wise to the fact that I was conscious.

The lab was underground in a cavern, but other than that, it didn't look much different from the setup at Perrault Biotech. Its ceiling and other three walls were smooth and gleaming white, same as the tiles on the floor. Everything was made brighter by the fluorescent lights mounted in rows above the long tables containing the genetic editing equipment, with the necessary supplies stacked on shelving within easy reach of each machine.

One scientist peered through a microscope, another labeled samples, and a third sat at a desk, entering findings from a file into a computer.

If this had been where Robyn was tied up while I was

forced to run through a maze of magic tests to get to her before the timer ran out, there was no sign of it.

I scraped my raw emotions into a metaphoric box and studied my surroundings through a dispassionate lens. The door I'd been brought through into this cell area led back to the caves. The glass separating me from the lab was actually a sliding door, and there was another exit at the back of the lab, though I had no idea where it led to.

Like any good scientist, I was willing to admit when I required more information before I could come to a conclusion. I pulled the cuffs as high on my forearm as possible and squeezed my hand between the bars, stretching forward painfully to tap my fingernails against the glass. Even that short burst of effort left me exhausted, but the scientist who'd helped Bunhead put me in here noticed me.

She said something to a bearded colleague who opened the sliding door and stepped up to my cell.

"How are you doing, Dr. Montefiore?" he said, his face troubled.

"How do you think?" I said, rattling the cuffs. "Dr....?"

"Eggers," he said. "I'm sorry we had to leave you in the cell rather than give you a room, but some individuals react poorly to the pull of the black star, and the cave chambers are the safest place to let them calm down." His American Southern accent really brought out the condescension in his voice.

I blinked stupidly at him. He sounded like a hotel concierge, but he was speaking about space and behaving like I was following along. He also seemed worried and not like a total psychopath carrying out unethical experiments on his boss's orders. Perhaps he was as much a prisoner as I was?

Despite being dirty, exhausted, and foggy, I put on my best professional manners and requested clarification. "Huh?"

"Sorry." Dr. Eggers ruefully shook his head. "I forgot you aren't familiar with all our terminology. We don't generally get visiting scientists, only our test dummies." He chuckled at his little joke.

I continued to stare blankly at him. "By test dummies, you mean the patients in the muscular dystrophy trials? That happened here, right, and not in Switzerland like the official documents state?"

"Correct on both counts. It's much easier to control the experiments here." He paused. "And deal with any unruly subjects appropriately."

These people had victim blaming down to an art.

Still cuffed, I clasped my hands tightly together so I didn't throttle him. Those were patients suffering from a debilitating disease who had worked their butts off to even participate in these inhumane trials, not naughty children. I doubted they got off with a scolding. Then I imagined mass graves down here and shuddered.

"What's a black star?" I said.

"The tool that Dr. Svensson used on you."

"Because it had so much pull that my magic couldn't escape it?"

"Not just yours but all magic. See, we created a special alarmed area outside the lab door to test the full potency of any magic that a stranger might have. Best to be forewarned. We can turn off the compulsion, but that doesn't stop the engaged magic." He shrugged. "The black star is more effective than nulling cuffs because we don't need to actually touch anyone."

"God forbid," I muttered sarcastically, but he nodded. "Where's my partner? Gideon Stern."

"The shifter." Eggers sighed dreamily. "Discovering he had that magic was... Well, I declare...I'd never been so delighted." His eyes gleamed, and he touched his mouth as if checking for drool. Better than if he'd touched his crotch because I'd bet the dude had a hard-on. "Stern is occupied."

"Doing what?"

Dr. Eggers gave an elusive smile and wagged a finger at me. "The world's first healthy shifter. As your collaborators, we should have been informed of our success."

His words made sense only in the strictest dictionary definitions of them.

Collaborators? Informed? Success? Was he fucking kidding me? My fingers clenched around the handcuffs, the metal biting into my skin as a surge of anger coursed through me. Was I expected to take out a personal ad in the newspaper after Gideon first shifted? *Chemical geneticist seeks mystery colleague for celebratory drinks. Furry cosplay optional.*

A vein in my temple throbbed. I'd seen what they did to the people they worked with. I stilled, my rage ebbing away. Damn. Carol's memorial. "What's the date today?"

"December 29, why?"

I hung my head. I'd missed forty-eight hours, but that wasn't the worst of it. Even though Toronto was only six hours behind and the memorial might not have started yet, I wasn't going to make it.

Ella was going to freak out.

How was Levi coping if he believed I was missing? Wait. He knew where I was. Why hadn't he come to rescue me? Was he unable to or…

I dug my fingers into my palms, blanketing myself in sharp pain instead of sharper emotions. "I want to see Anna Sula."

"Dr. Sula wants to see you as well. We'll get you cleaned up first." Eggers wrinkled his nose and unlocked the cell door. "She likes things orderly."

I liked not being experimented on, my research not being fucked with, and not being accused of murder, even as a warning shot. But we couldn't always get what we wanted, could we?

"Understandable," I said, following him through the sliding door into the lab proper.

The two other scientists present nodded at me, like they weren't responsible for fucking with my magic and locking me up. Did Sula have a special psychopath test she administered as part of the hiring process, because my first impression of Eggers was so wrong.

I curled my fingers into a ball, hitting a new low from shame. Despite the gravity of my situation, I wanted to touch everything like a little kid and see if their stuff was better than mine. I glanced at their multi-mode plate reader that was at least one model up from the one we'd had at Perrault. Yup. It was better.

"I have to admit," Dr. Eggers said, "when Dr. Sula suggested your serum as the best pairing for the wolf stem cells, I was skeptical. I mean, Weaver magic has its uses, but I've always regarded it as rather rudimentary."

My pasted-on smile hardened.

He opened the far door, herding me up a set of stairs. "But she was right, as usual. And may I say, congratulations on your excellent work with the rapid regeneration."

"Thanks," I said flatly.

The area beyond the lab was a dormitory. Dr. Eggers explained that this floor was the living quarters of the scientists. The test dummies—I hardened my jaw at that term—were housed two levels down, though they'd suspended those trials, and no one was currently in residence.

"Are any still alive?" I said.

"No. None had the fortitude to survive the shifter magic we gave them."

Of course it was their fault.

"Your serum? It's a game changer." He pressed his thumb to a scanner pad, and the door slid open. "This is you. Once you're ready, press the bell inside and you'll meet with Dr. Sula."

He unlocked the cuffs before he left. "We'll put these back on after your shower, but meantime, don't blow out any more bulbs." He smirked. "Supply requisitions are such a pain, am I right?"

Yeah, paperwork was the problem. Rubbing my wrists, I gave a tight nod and went inside.

The room was sparse but fine. My pack sat on the bed, so I had a change of underclothes, jeans, and T-shirt, though they'd kept my phone. I alternated between shampooing my hair as quickly as possible and soaping up with the speed of a snail. I couldn't decide if I wished to meet Anna Sula right away or put it off for as long as possible.

Once I was dressed again with my fleece hoodie zipped up tight, anticipation won out. I stood up straight and pressed the bell.

I didn't personally know the silver-haired lean man in the doorway, dangling the nulling cuffs off one finger, but his sandalwood and citrus scent was as familiar as my father's scratchy cheek when he kissed me or his off-key whistling.

Because it was Dad's favorite cologne. And this sono-fabitch had left it lingering when he broke into my Toronto apartment.

Even in jeans and a sweater instead of the conservative suit he'd worn when he'd followed me before I left for Morocco to find Woody, I recognized him from his photo on the Golden Radial website.

Hello, Jeremy Wade. Legal counsel to Golden Radial, and, if I was correct, Anna Sula's second-in-command.

"I was promised the boss, not her henchman," I sneered.

"I'm here to set some rules before the meeting."

"Keep my hands in the ride and do not attempt to get off before the safety bar has been released. Got it."

"Not quite," he said with a look like he'd just stepped in

196

dogshit. He made a big production of hooking the nulling cuffs to his belt loop instead of back around my wrists. "Attempt to harm Dr. Sula in any way and we'll kill the wolf. Attempt to escape and we'll kill the wolf. Are you getting the picture?" When I opened my mouth, he held up a hand. "Don't bother protesting that the wolf doesn't matter. Dr. Sula is aware of your loyalty to those you care about."

I ground my teeth. "Oh, she is, is she?" I bet she wasn't aware of how far I'd go to avenge harm to those same people. Robyn, Woody, Gideon—Sula was owed payback, and I was going to dish it out with the fervidity and persistence of student loan interest.

Also, a great deal of joy. So. Much. Joy.

"What's your deal, Jeremy?" I tilted my head and tapped a finger against my mouth. "You're general counsel for a venture capital firm with headquarters based in Chicago, yet you broke into my place in Toronto and now here you are in the mountains of Slovakia to give me some Evil 101 warning. Is your actual title 'Sula's bitch'?"

The smile he flashed contained too much shark to be amused. He must have had orders not to hurt me because his eyes darkened with barely banked rage. "Such a busy little bee buzzing around asking all those questions. Though not too busy that you couldn't land that new job of yours."

It was as much a warning shot as setting me up for Carol's murder had been.

"I'm certainly looking forward to this new chapter in my life," I said. *The one commencing with me dancing in the ashes of everything you people hoped to achieve.* "I also want to see Gideon."

"That'll be Dr. Sula's call," he said. "On that note, let's not keep her waiting. Follow me."

Jeremy escorted me down a nondescript corridor to another cave with a concrete floor. It had a food service area and a number of tables and benches on wheels that could easily be moved aside. The bucket and mop leaning against one wall explained the smell of bleach.

There was nothing to suggest wine had ever been made here, and other than its unusual location, it could have been any corporate cafeteria, but my throat closed up and my heart tried to escape my rib cage.

This was *the* Cave.

I was back in the place that had launched my lifelong fear of losing Robyn. A wave of nausea and dizziness crashed over me, and my vision tunneled to a pinprick. I was back in the dark, and there was no one here but me and the Voice.

A pale orange glow erupted from me, my magic shooting to the surface of my skin with a violence that made me shake.

Jeremy merely raised an eyebrow.

I bit the inside of my cheek hard enough to draw blood, calmed my ragged breathing, and wrestled my panic into submission. My magic wasn't what they had to fear; my intellect was. I would outwit and outplay them; make them rue the day they ever messed with me.

The orange glow disappeared. I fake-smiled at Jeremy.

He kept me company—or guarded me—until his watch chimed, at which point he headed for the door.

I gripped the table, leaving sweat marks. My knuckles were white and my skin was flushed and hot, but my chin was set determinedly.

Jeremy opened the cafeteria door to the click of heels growing closer.

Dr. Sula paused in the corridor to speak to her minion.

I craned my neck but couldn't see past Jeremy for the first glimpse of my enemy in our final showdown.

He stepped aside, but not before gesturing from his eyes to a security camera mounted in one corner. Yeah, they'd be watching me, and any deviation on my part would mean Gideon's death. Got it.

I unclenched my jaw and stood up. This was it. The moment I'd dreaded and wanted in equal measure. I was finally going to look Anna in the face and reduce her from a nightmare to a distant memory before I delivered her to the Queen.

I had no qualms about what would become of the ex-doctor. Not after she'd chosen this particular place to meet.

The woman entered, but it wasn't Anna Sula.

It was Ella.

A choked sound punched out of me because Anna Sula and Golden Radial had fucked with me yet again.

They'd murdered Carol and were doing who knew what to Gideon, but now they'd kidnapped my friend too?

Through my haze of shock, I processed two small yet relevant details. Jeremy had left us alone, and Ella was smiling at me like she was amused.

She strode toward me as calm and collected as I'd seen her in many a lab crisis, her dark hair tumbling to her shoulders. She was in black trousers and a black shirt—not her customary wardrobe, but not a lab coat either.

I stumbled back, swallowing down the taste of bile.

The pieces felt like a Rubik's Cube, which I'd never been able to solve. Someone out there could have put them together correctly, but I kept twisting things around and they never slotted into their proper pattern.

"Carol's memorial was lovely," Ella said. "It's a shame you missed it."

It wasn't my friend's voice. Not the Canadian one that had asked me to solve cryptic crossword puzzles with her, called out the new total every time she pasted on one of the vegetable stickers to track Woody taking his doctor-mandated walks to stay healthy, or told me stories about her travels over our many lunches together.

It was the Eastern European–accented English that had so terrified me that I'd repressed all memory of it for years.

199

My legs gave way, and I crashed onto the bench. My world had been crushed in some cruel fist of fate then discarded on the floor, leaving me with a reality that was nothing more than unappealing trash.

Ella—Anna—winked at me. "Surprise!"

Chapter 19

I shook my head, struggling to draw breath into my lungs. "No," I said in a small voice. "Not you."

The scope and horror of this betrayal made Woody blowing up the lab seem like a nonissue. Had Daleks managed to take over all of the galaxy and turn every sentient being into one of them, Doctor Who would have shrugged it off with an "eh" in comparison to this.

Anna—her Ella persona and our friendship was dead to me—rolled her eyes. "Oh, don't look so affronted." She motioned in a circle around her face. "I had some work done, got rid of the scars from my burn." She shook her head. "You've got your thinking look on. You're trying to decide what to ask me first. It's just like when at Perrault you would—"

"Don't," I said in a hard voice. "This is nothing like that." I gaped at her, struggling to reconcile her terrible actions with her serenity. "How could you murder Carol?"

"That was Jeremy. He went a bit too far in warning Carol about going to the police." Anna shook her head, frowning. "I had very stern words with him and the Illusionist he took with him."

Were they given a time-out? I resisted the urge to bang my head against the table and see if that helped this conversation make sense.

"It was a shame to lose a good scientist," she continued. "I do like to surround myself with the best. Did you have a chance to meet some of my staff?"

This woman had severed all connection with reality. How had she masked that all those years that we worked together?

Or, I thought with a dawning horror, was it not madness, a condition easy to understand and sympathize with in the wake of her tragedy, but something else? Something pernicious?

Smart. Logical. Focused. Anna was me, taken to the extreme of having surgically excised all emotion when it came to achieving her goal.

I'd seen the world through a scientific lens since Robyn died because it was easier to face my life armed with cold, hard facts and not emotions, but everything I'd experienced since the night of the lab fire had torn open the scab I'd plastered over my heart.

I still struggled with emotions, but their return had made me a better person. They made me a better scientist.

Good thing, because right now, I was drowning in feelings: sorrow for Carol, dread at having embraced a path that could have led me to the same end as Anna, and rage. So much rage.

"How could you do that to Robyn and me? We were babies. And now to bring me *here*, to the place that—" My voice cracked.

"Technically, you came to me." Anna looked around the cafeteria and nodded. "Good for you for remembering our first visit. I wasn't sure you would." She sniffed. "It took years to get the stench of wine out of the stones after I took it over from the church and renovated."

I wasn't getting an answer to the question that mattered most. Not that it would have changed anything if I had.

"You destroyed the church and moved in." I moderated my high-pitched tone and massaged my temples because her bullshit was making my head explode. "Why were you even at our lab, pretending to be a Mundane office manager, when you had these mad scientist experiments to attend to?"

"There's nothing mad about them." Her voice dripped ice, and there was a dangerous glint in her eyes.

"Sorry," I mumbled.

She smiled and patted my hand. "I'd trained my team to handle things, and I had to keep an eye on Woody. He'd gotten skittish, and I wanted to be close at hand in case he stopped providing the research I required for the trials we conducted here." She slowly clenched her fist. "Had I known what he was going to do..."

I thanked every deity in existence that I'd never told her that I found him and gotten my data back.

"And of course, you were coming to work at Perrault," she continued. "I was thrilled when your department head passed the job posting on to you. Woody's notes indicated you gave an excellent interview."

My rock bottom dropped another few feet; I was totally unsurprised. "You've been watching me my whole life, haven't you?"

"It's a testament to how special you are. You and Robyn weren't supposed to be anything other than my test subjects, the same as the rest, but you two were so spirited despite your fear. You fought so hard for each other." She reached across the table and took my hand. "You reminded me of my girls."

Completely squicked out, I tried to pull away, but she had the grip of an anaconda wrapped around its prey.

"We were so special that you pretended to be my friend for three years?"

"Our friendship was never fake." She stroked my cheek. "How could you think that? I even fed you broth in your cell and worried like mad about your fever."

My skin crawled. That was—I couldn't even—*Mannaggia!* She'd made sure I worked near her, nursed me after her people imprisoned me—how far did her twisted interest in me extend?

Ask the question.

No. I'd stick to the subject of her work.

I yanked my hand away. "You were testing the concept of genetic editing but with magic, right? If you could get that to work, you could magically use that process on the genes responsible for your daughters' disease."

Ask the question.

"Luckily, CRISPR technology became a lot better," Anna said. "Though, it wasn't until you developed your rapid regeneration serum that it all finally came together."

ASK. THE. QUESTION.

My brain screamed the demand at me. My mouth was dry, and goose bumps dotted my skin. Once I asked it, I could never unhear the answer, and knowing wouldn't bring Robyn back.

Yeah, well, curiosity was hardwired into us. Look at Pandora and the box, Bluebeard's wife and the door, and a long line of scientists before me.

I plucked at the hem of my sleeve. "Did you kill Robyn? Or have her killed to send me down a path that would benefit you?"

Anna's eyes widened, clear and guileless. "No." Her protest was immediate. "You were already interested in the sciences, and I planned to bring you on board at some point, but Robyn was supposed to live a long and healthy life."

I believed her, but the knot in my chest didn't loosen.

"Besides," Anna continued in a matter-of-fact voice,

"why sacrifice the one person I could use to keep you in line? After you came to my side of your own free will, of course."

What a joke. The only free will I'd ever had thanks to this creepy fuck was the promise I'd made to Robyn, and Sula had violated that too.

"Once Carol doctored the sample, how were you going to get the vial out without me noticing?" I said.

"It would have been waylaid when it was couriered to Dr. Nakahara's office, but I got a better opportunity when the police showed up with the warrant. As soon as they got into your office to pack up your computer, I'd take the sample, and everyone would believe it went missing in the chaos. Then the explosive charge went off, and I was trapped under that damn filing cabinet. I missed my chance."

It galled me that I'd ever worried about my fake friend's safety.

"No matter," she said. "It worked out even better than I could have hoped. We can't wait to start reproducing your serum."

I froze, shaking my head because there was no way I'd heard her correctly. "You can't reproduce it."

"Why not?"

The security camera swiveled as if it, too, awaited my answer.

My serum, my rules. No monsters allowed to have it. "Because all the data was destroyed."

Anna gave me a pitying smile, and I fought not to punch her in the mouth. "The moment you gave me that ridiculous story about changing the direction of your research and inquiring about muscle mass, I knew you still had your data. Clever girl. You'd backed it up on your own, despite company policy, didn't you?"

I wrinkled my brow. "That's why you handed me Alexei's name? For me to get to Carol so you could have your killer, Jeremy, interrogate me about the data? Would he have gone too far if he didn't like my answers or were the murder charges enough?"

"Don't be silly." She wagged a finger at me. "He wouldn't have touched you, but you deserved some kind of punishment for letting me believe the data was gone. We make the most advances in the sciences when we're collaborative, Raisa. Hoarding knowledge never does any good and only fosters competition and inefficient doubling of work."

"And help you create shifter super soldiers? No, thanks." Would it even stop at wolf armies? Would I be recruited to mutant up other animals like the eels and manta rays? Who else had Sula sold these side hustle by-products to as magic security systems?

She tapped a manicured nail on the table. "Labs aren't cheap, Raisa, and it's not like we can run these trials through the official books. Not completely," she amended.

"Hence the dummy clinic in Switzerland."

"Shifters are only a minor part of the whole picture. I'm excited about the practical applications of wolf DNA woven into the fabric of cells along with your rapid regeneration serum. It will require tweaking to cure different diseases, but what a gold mine this opens up." She rubbed her hands together. "You'll have every resource at your disposal. You can devote your time to solving the issue of the cancerous tumors that your serum produces with the assistance of world-class colleagues."

"You can't cure these diseases when the trade-off is wolf shifters!"

She flapped her hand like that was a minor detail.

"It's illegal," I said. "Even if this all works, the patients won't be able to go home and live a normal life. Not when the government or some arms dealer or whoever will be after them for their own purposes."

"Laws can be changed. What was illegal and unethical one day becomes the future of humanity the next. Once we

206

eradicate these major diseases, we'll be hailed as saviors," she said. "During our time together, I got to know your hopes and dreams, and now I can give them to you. It's your promise to Robyn kept tenfold. All you have to do is join me in the family business." *And be your Helper Brain in perpetuity?* She gazed at me, misty-eyed, her hand extended.

I barely suppressed my shudder, but with Anna's disturbing pronouncement came a certain amount of relief.

She'd made a critical mistake. I had a family: Levi, the memories of my twin and my dad that I kept deep in my heart, Mom too. I didn't want a replacement, and I didn't want her lab with unlimited funding. Not when turning people into shifters where their lives would no longer be their own was the price. It wasn't just about laws. People's friends and family members would shun them, and work-places would be scared to employ anyone at the mercy of the moon's pull.

I'd found Gideon's ability to shift a beautiful, awesome thing, and I still did, but in spending time with him, I also appreciated the realities of his situation.

Maybe if Anna had proposed doing the wolf stem cell research by the book, like we did at Perrault, I'd have proceeded differently, but that was impossible with the way the laws stood. As it should be.

Any government that would sanction curing diseases by turning individuals into a different species was to be feared. It wouldn't matter if researchers followed all the same proce-dures that I had when investigating the possibilities of magic and science, we'd still end up in the same place. The disease would be stopped, but these people would have to live with being shifters in a world not ready or open to them. Even if they consented, there was no way they'd understand what they were in for.

What about people with a physical disability? Would

they be forced into a "cure" so we could have some fucked-up ableist reality?

I'd seen enough suffering.

I'd *caused* enough suffering.

I wouldn't be a party to causing any more.

"I'm not giving you my data, and I will never join you. Now," I said, in my most imperious voice, "release me and Gideon, because if you don't, both the Queen of Hearts and the Head of House Pacifica will rain hell down on you and hunt you to the end of the earth."

Anna sighed. "Children are such a disappointment." She looked directly into the security camera. "Kill her."

Chapter 20

Jeremy Wade's anger was no longer banked when he led me over a narrow rope bridge spanning a drop so deep and dark that I couldn't see the bottom.

I gripped the railing in case he was planning to push me over the side, but he escorted me farther into the cave system.

A soft sigh escaped me. I was about to die, but it would be in the most marvelous of places, because holy shit.

They'd re-created an entire forest deep underground.

It was filled with phosphorescent trees of different shapes and sizes. I basked in its reverence. Some had greenish-brown leaves, others bright green needles. Shadows and light glowed over green bark like a wash of stardust.

Researchers had been modifying plants for years to achieve luminosity, but the light had always been faint. I brushed my hand across eerie green lichen growing on the trunk. Everything here was as brilliant as the photos of the aurora borealis that I'd seen.

Too bad the specter of death dimmed the majesty of it all.

I didn't know what species most of the trees were, but I'd

guess they mirrored the ones found naturally out in the Carpathian Mountains, because the trees themselves were real. Only their glow was magic.

Their light danced over the rocks high above, and if I squinted, I could believe it was the Milky Way.

Jeremy prodded me forward over slightly spongy ground, past rocks scattered in clusters throughout the dirt.

The nulling cuffs once again manacled around my wrists clinked softly.

The trees creaked, swaying in a gentle breeze, their branches moving left and right like a conductor leading a song of the forest for our journey.

A rustling leaf on a low branch caressed my cheek.

The forest smelled like pine and flowers, a perfume of spring, buried under a real forest slumbering for the winter.

Red and the wolf going into the woods. One of us might not come back, Gideon whispered in my head. I blinked my blurry eyes. Jeremy hadn't answered my question about Gideon when he'd shown up in the cafeteria to follow Sula's orders, but I expected our reunion was eminent.

Jeremy shoved me. "Keep moving."

After all the quips about Red and the wolf and Baba Yaga, it was fitting that our world tour had led to this moment—to these woods. My heart pounded in my chest so loudly, I was amazed it didn't echo across the forest canopy.

I mean, it sucked that I'd been brought here to die, but if there was ever a time to hold tight to the stories of all the other doomed characters who'd survived a dangerous arboreal journey, it was now.

I slid a sideways glance at Jeremy's torn shirt and the cut on his bruised face, which he'd received attempting to put the cuffs on me. He'd killed the overhead lights in the cafeteria first so I didn't have anything to draw upon magically, but I had teeth and fists and feet.

I'd used all of them.

We continued deeper into the forest, the illuminated trees pressing in denser and closer. These woods must have been created to give the patients a controlled environment in which they could run in their twisted hybrid human/wolf shape or participate in specific tests of their motor abilities or cognitive function without some townsperson freaking out and sounding the alarm. This underground forest also removed the obstacle of winter weather.

The amount of time and money it must have taken to hollow out this massive space, plant all these trees, and line the rock floor with enough soil for the roots to take hold and stay strong was unimaginable. Golden Radial must have had quite the labor force, both Mundane and Nefesh, to make this a reality.

What must have happened to those people didn't bear thinking about.

Jeremy stopped and unlocked my nulling cuffs.

I rubbed my wrists, confused. He had to know I could use the phosphorescence against him. He was Mundane, and I didn't see a weapon.

"These trees are resistant to other magic. That includes their light." He smiled coldly and my pulse spiked. "Run. It's more fun that way."

"Fuck you and your games. You want to kill me, try it. Right here, right—"

A short muzzle with pointed canines snapped out of his face, fur blooming on his neck, face, and hands that had become gnarled claws.

Jeremy wasn't just Anna's bitch.

He was one of her test subjects.

Growling, he lunged.

I bolted, stumbling over fallen moss-covered logs and stumpy roots.

The branches of the trees twisted and turned, creating a mazelike path that disoriented me. A chill ran down my spine as I heard Jeremy's not-so-distant howl and strange cackling noises that seemed to come from every direction.

I ran blindly, uncaring of low-hanging branches that smacked me in the face, and I tensed in anticipation of his teeth sinking between my shoulder blades.

My sides burned but I pressed on. I ran longer and farther than I ever had, until heaving, I staggered into a clearing, partially doubled over. I pressed my hands to my sides.

Jeremy loped in after me, not even winded, saliva dripping from his mouth. He wasn't a full wolf, only one of those fucked-up hybrids, so he didn't run on all fours, but the play of phosphorescence and shadow across that mangled monstrosity left me weak-kneed.

He flexed his mutated claws at me—too enthusiastically —and I shuddered. Was that how he'd slashed Carol's throat?

Jeremy could put those murder mittens away, because I refused to die at the hands of a B-movie villain. Here I had a perfectly terrifying evil nemesis and yet her sloppy wolf man was going to kill me? Not today, universe.

He ambled closer, the smell of his cologne that was the same as my father's growing stronger.

Perhaps some of my hatred leaked out through my icy terror because he laughed delightedly. That joyful human sound coming from that heinous face was chilling. If I'd ever sought assurance that I'd made the right choice turning my back on Anna's offer, this was it.

Jeremy was the worst of both species.

A deep howl rent the air so thoroughly that the leaves around me quivered under its force.

Gideon! My heart soared—

Until I saw him.

White foam frothed on lips bared in a snarl around lethal canines, but the scariest thing about him were his eyes.

I'd seen his human amusement and intelligence peeking out when he was in wolf form, I'd also seen a primal deadliness from his beast self, but never this.

They were flat, lightless—even the hazel color had become one shade of dark, dark black.

His fur was still tawny, but clumps of it were missing, and the patches of bare skin were raw from weeping gashes and puckered burns.

Torturing Gideon at all was despicable, but to burn him, given everything he'd been through? My vision clouded with a red haze.

A fat metal collar was locked around his neck. The fur around it was gone, replaced by pus-filled blisters like he'd gnawed himself to get free. The device was keeping him from healing, because otherwise his innate shifter magic would have taken care of his wounds.

"What did they do to you?" I whispered.

The wolf ignored me, prowling toward Jeremy, who'd had the good sense to freeze. Running wasn't so fun when you were prey, was it?

Gideon growled again, his tail high and his ears jutted out horizontally.

I silently encouraged him to bat Jeremy's head off with one swipe of his enormous paw.

Jeremy slowly sank to his knees.

I looked around for a weapon, David Attenborough's voice narrating in my head. *Regard the mutant. Sometimes evolution will grace a creature with a new trait which will allow it to move through the world better than its peers. Most times, however, mutations like this are formed, making the mutant fare significantly worse. It is a cursed existence.*

A decent-sized rock that I could palm one-handed lay a few feet to my right. Keeping one eye on the pair, I inched sideways.

Jeremy mewled and bowed his head, exposing his throat.

When faced with a true alpha, the beta shows what we may construe as the intelligence to acknowledge his superior rank. In reality, this is merely a self-serving move to buy himself time before he betrays the alpha.

Gideon opened his mouth, and very deliberately bit down along one side of Jeremy's neck.

That's right, alpha. Get him. In my head, my Attenborough narrator cleared his throat.

Jeremy's flinch shuddered through him, but he remained in the same position, his claws at his sides. It wasn't a deep bite, just one with enough of an edge that it established who was in charge.

The males now band together to form a new pack to hunt their common enemy, Attenborough-voice continued.

I narrowed my eyes.

Screw that. Attenborough gave his pronouncement and vanished from my head.

I grabbed the rock, jumped forward, and bashed Jeremy across the face. His nose cartilage shattered, blood spewed, and his jaw snapped sideways in a sickening crunch.

He screamed and fell to the ground, curling into the fetal position, his agonized cries unceasing.

Gideon snarled at his out-of-commission beta.

Only the most distant part of my brain was horrified at the damage I'd inflicted. Jeremy had been ready—no, eager —to kill me. It was self-defense—and payback for twisting the scent of Dad's cologne from a comforting and precious memory to one that would haunt me forever.

The wolf raked his paws against the bite he'd given Jeremy a moment ago. Almost like a caress.

Then with a single swipe, he tore out the hybrid's throat.

Jeremy and I made the same gurgled sound of shock and horror.

I spun away from the blood pooling on the ground,

practically hyperventilating. Porco miseria, Gideon had killed Jeremy. Or rather, the wolf had.

Either way, it had looked pretty damn intentional. He'd killed the weak link.

The wolf licked his claws clean.

I shuddered. I'd be next if I didn't get the upper hand.

I held the rock aloft in one hand, my other coated in a magic glow. My magic slid off the light from the trees like it was oil when I tried to grab hold of it, but the wolf didn't know I was defenseless.

"Gideon, it's me," I said firmly. "Raisa. Donatella. We're friends, remember? Let me take the collar off."

The wolf growled, frothing at the mouth. The sound shivered off the trees and up to the ceiling, ricocheting back to me like a boomerang to slap against my skin and make my ears ring.

All righty, he wasn't letting me get that thing off, but if I ran, he'd chase me.

I'd be dead in about three seconds flat.

"Sit." I pointed at the ground. "I command you."

He bounded through the air and crashed into me, pinning me on the ground with one huge paw.

A piece of mangled human skin was caught in Gideon's teeth.

The entire situation was so ludicrously dire, so cartoonishly awful, that something inside me snapped.

"You want to fight with me, asshole?" In the greatest miracle of all time, forget Moses and the parting of the Red Sea, the collar had a latch. It was a useless miracle, however, because the latch wouldn't open without a key. Still, I bashed on the lock with the rock, denting it. "Let me get this thing off and we'll go all twelve rounds."

He snarled, his teeth ripping my sleeve.

I smacked his nose so hard with my hand that he yelped and fell off me.

Honestly, I'm not sure which of us was more surprised, but I was all for keeping any tactical advantage. I wagged the rock at him. "Bad wolf."

He shook his head like he couldn't believe what he was hearing.

Thus emboldened, I continued. "That's also a TV reference you probably won't get, but if we survive this hellhole, I am absolutely making sure you will in the future."

He snarled, teeth bared.

Keeping my eyes on him, I pushed to my feet. I clenched my bladder, ignoring the screams in my head to run. "'The woods are lovely, dark, and deep,'" I blurted, quoting one of my mom's favorite poems, back when she still talked about sadness and death like they were things she could deal with and not disasters crashing through her life. "You are too, Gideon. Fight this. Please."

For a second, I swear his eyes cleared.

He let out a soft "aroo," and my heart surged in my chest.

Suddenly, sparks flew off his collar, and his body was racked with a spasm so violent that his front legs bucked.

The wolf's head snapped up, his eyes fogged with madness.

I swung the rock at his torso as hard as I could, adrenaline dancing through my blood. Before he regained his balance, I kicked behind the knee of one hind leg with my heavy winter hiking boots. Hearing Gideon's bones crack made me feel sick, and his pained yowl shredded my heart, but if I didn't live and get to safety to call Levi for reinforcements, there was no chance of returning and saving my partner.

"Forgive me," I whispered and ran.

The good news was that I reached the end of the forest before either my energy died—or I did.

It was like in *The Truman Show* when Truman hit the

end of the sound stage, but instead of a projection screen, there were the cave walls marking the end of the underground forest.

More importantly, there was a door leading to freedom.

I hoped.

Behind me, Gideon thrashed in the man-made woods, growing too close for comfort.

There was no time to worry about whether I was going from the frying pan into the fire. I threw myself through the door—

Chapter 21

I stumbled out of the cave systems into the wintery woods of the Carpathian Mountains, bitch-slapped by a wind so cold it stunned me into a momentary paralysis.

Gideon knocked into me, sending us both into a snow-drift. He rolled away, but the second he got to his feet, his lame leg buckled, and he collapsed, whimpering.

Jeremy's bloody corpse danced before my eyes next to Carol's. Keep this up and the body count would outnumber the tour stops.

I laughed hysterically, the laughs turning painful when another thought hit me.

Gideon was wrong about one of us not coming out of the woods.

Neither of us were.

I had no jacket, gloves, hat, phone, or gold token, and I was in the snowy woods in winter in the Carpathian Mountains with a gravely injured werewolf.

I shakily pushed to my feet and brushed the snow off as best I could, my laughter fading away to a hollow silence. *Get it together.* I slapped my cheek hard enough to think critically. We weren't going to die. I hadn't delivered Anna to the Queen yet, and if I didn't, Sula would come for me and my data.

Not to mention, I wasn't going to renege on a promise to Her Majesty. Or to Robyn, to actually live in a way that honored her properly while keeping other people from sharing her fate.

The snow would provide us with water, but we had to find shelter, warmth, food, and, most importantly, a way out. And by we, I meant me.

The moon wasn't full. I'm not sure whether that mattered, given Gideon was stuck in shifter form, but it couldn't hurt.

Tentatively, I circled him.

His eyes were open, but there was a glazed sheen over them, and his breathing was shallow. I had to get that collar off him right now so he could heal.

I crouched down beside him, tensed and ready to flee, but he was too far gone to register me. Luckily, in my frenzied fleeing, I hadn't dropped my rock weapon. I slammed it against the collar until my arms were tired, flinching at the sound of every strike and positive the wolf would bite off my hand for annoying him.

It finally broke open.

I slid the collar off his neck, about to throw the metal device as far from Gideon as possible, but on second thought, I tucked it into my back pocket as best I could. Might as well keep it as further proof of Anna's wrongdoings.

Should I leave Gideon here and scout for shelter, or find a neighboring village and call Levi? Sadly, my chances of leaving this mountain on my own were comparable to a woman having sex with a selfish lover: neither of us were getting off.

Leave Gideon behind and I'd never find him again, but how was I supposed to get an injured wolf with no memory of me to docilely accompany me?

I had mere seconds to figure it out, because when Jeremy didn't report back to Anna that I was dead, she'd come looking for me—and find his body. We had to get away. I squinted at the sky, weighing whether enough daylight remained for me to use my magic.

I had to try. The first thing I did was weave a very long leash around the wolf's neck, careful to stay out of biting range.

Next, I pulled all the light from the infrared end of the spectrum, weaving it into his body at a cellular level to heal him.

My magic couldn't reset any broken bones in his injured leg; he'd require his own shifter healing magic for that. With the collar off, that magic would theoretically come back on its own, but I didn't know how long it might take, and we didn't have time to wait.

Lame or not, he had to walk.

I used all the infrared light I could sense from both the ambient external pool and what Gideon emitted. Even as worn out as I was, that part wouldn't have been challenging on its own, but it was made infinitely tougher given I had to maintain the magic leash as well, and the sky was growing darker.

Sweat plastered my already-wet clothing to my body in minutes. I was flushed and shivering and scared that I'd survive all this only to get pneumonia, but the wolf's gashes closed, his fur sprouting in healthy tufts now that the collar was gone.

Buoyed by those results, I tugged on the leash, my teeth chattering. "Up. The pain you feel walking should go away soon because your healing magic has kicked in." I surveyed the ground, trying to determine which direction took us downhill. That had to be the way off the mountain, right?

Gideon didn't move, so I tramped through the snow

ahead of him until I'd dragged him onto all fours, and he understood what I was trying to do. He didn't fight me, but I saw no sign of human awareness either.

We plodded over slippery compressed snow. Correction, the wolf plodded, I slid, buffeted by wind and thinking fondly of the crampons in my daypack that Gideon had included as part of our gear.

I was freezing and numb and starting to fall asleep on my feet, which would be lethal. The leash had fallen apart under the encroaching darkness, but I didn't have it in me to care.

Yawning, I lowered myself to the ground.

The wolf growled, and grabbed the hem of my fleece hoodie, yanking me backward.

My heart flew into my throat.

Instead of attacking, the wolf tugged me sharply to the left. Another few feet in the direction I'd been headed and I'd have fallen down a crevasse.

Overwhelmed, I froze, shaking.

The wolf growled softly and nudged my leg.

I went on autopilot, allowing him to take the lead, because I was falling asleep more and more often. Every time I felt consciousness leave me, he'd growl, tug me farther, and keep us going.

Eventually, nature won, as I knew it would. You can't be a scientist and not be willing to admit the facts to yourself. The woods were lovely, dark, and deep, and I had walked so many miles.

It was finally, finally, time to sleep.

I died.

But even that was okay. I've heard people who came back from near-death experiences and say that it was nice, and I was pleased to see that they'd been right. The afterlife was toasty warm, like a parent wrapping a child in a blanket and carrying them into a quiet room after a long party.

I wriggled my toes, not wanting to open my eyes yet, but kind of worried that I'd ended up in Gehenna, the Jewish Hell, for having made the assist on a murder.

Anxiety aside, it felt good to move, so I tried with my arms and legs, but I didn't go anywhere. I was bound.

My eyes snapped open. I thrashed viciously until I processed that I wasn't held captive. I was wrapped in mismatched blankets, my clothes drying on a chair in front of a cast-iron stove similar to the one in Gideon's cabin.

I struggled up with a gasp, letting out a relieved sigh at the sight of him collapsed facedown and twitching slightly on the narrow cot in an alcove at the back of this single room.

He'd shifted back into human form, for which I was profoundly grateful, but that meant he was naked.

As was I.

Suddenly, the flush on my skin had nothing to do with the heat pouring out of the stove.

Gideon had found us this hut, gotten me out of my wet clothes, set me in front of the heat, and saved me from hypothermia. So, he'd seen me naked. It was hardly a sexual moment. Just like now wasn't.

I tore my gaze away from his sculpted back muscles, secured one of the blankets around me like a bath towel, and walked over to his cot.

He was breathing, and his skin was a healthy color. I laid a hand on his forehead. There was no fever either. The poor guy was simply exhausted. Honestly, he was better off than I was because he had his innate shifter healing magic to rely on, whereas I didn't have the strength to weave what little infrared light I had into my cells yet.

His face rippled and I jumped. Fur sprouted over his cheeks, and his ears crawled up the side of his head, turning into fuzzy triangles.

My hand flew to my mouth. I stood there, fascinated,

terrified, and completely helpless against Gideon shifting in bits and pieces from human to wolf and back again to a cacophony of tearing and breaking.

He gave a low groan then seized up.

I was thrown back to those last nights by Robyn's side, unable to do anything to stem the pain from her burns, watching her blurry, pained gaze seeking me out through the protective mask I wore, and unable to hold her hand in mine—skin to skin—because of the gloves.

Gideon's left leg and right arm shifted; the toes on his left leg became claws. One eye narrowed to a wolf's tracking gaze, but the other remained foggy.

His breathing grew raspier, the sounds coming out of his mouth not animal and not quite human.

All I could do was stand over him as if my presence would eventually ward these changes off, because I was short-circuiting in a high-voltage live wire of fear. Even without a frame of reference, there was no way this was part of his healing process. It had to be some continued effect of whatever magic had been in that damn collar.

I was seized with worry that I'd made things more dangerous for Gideon. If he'd remained collared in the forest, only I would have died. This way, both of us might, him from these ongoing shifts and me because I wasn't getting out of here without him.

Gideon, fully human, shuddered violently, a harsh cry tearing from his lips, then fell still.

My hand shook as I placed it on his back, waiting for his spine to elongate or fur to sprout, but he remained human, although his skin was clammy. I couldn't get him off this cot and over to the stove, so I tucked a couple of blankets around him, resolutely not admiring his tight glutes because this was *not* a sexual moment.

Bracing a hand on the wall, I took a few deep breaths, which turned into a coughing fit, but I wasn't experiencing any rattling in my chest, nor did I have a fever, chest pain, or produce phlegm. Hopefully I'd avoid pneumonia.

My belly rumbled, so I rummaged around the stone and wood hut. Gideon had broken the door to get in and used a bucket filled with water to secure it closed. Despite the gravity of the situation, I smiled. His first B&E. I was so proud.

There was no sink in here so either the bucket had been filled with snow, or he'd managed to get to a well or pump of some sort.

Three lonely tins of food sat in the cupboard and some chopped wood was scattered by the stove. Through one of the windows, I saw a small pile of kindling stacked against the hut. We were in a press of trees, and I couldn't see the sky. It was dark, but this was the time of year when daylight was at its shortest, so that didn't mean much.

I found a wool sweater with holes in the elbows and a pair of waterproof pants, the kind you'd wear over trousers, and put them on the bed in case Gideon wanted them when he woke up. I wasn't sure what this place was used for—hikers seeking shelter or shepherds? Were there shepherds here? Either way, I was profoundly grateful for these provisions and for a clean place to rest.

Provided Anna didn't track us here, we had a fighting shot of surviving this. Then I'd come back for her with a small army and take that betraying psycho snake down for good.

There wasn't a can opener, so I took my feelings out on a can of beets with the sole kitchen knife until I'd punctured it, then sniffed it. Since it smelled okay, I shook the contents into my mouth until I'd polished it off. It would have tasted better if I'd warmed it up in a pot, but that was beyond me right now.

I drank some clean cold water from the bucket, then checked my clothes. My bra, underwear, and T-shirt were nice and warm, so I threw those back on, then wrapped myself in my blanket pile again and slept.

I awoke, shivering, to the wind making the thin panes of glass groan. "Gideon?" I said in a raspy voice.

He didn't answer.

I waddled over in my blanket burrito and touched his back. He wasn't too cold, he was still human, or as much as I could determine without moving the blanket, and his breathing was even. So why hadn't he woken up yet?

I tucked his foot back under the cover and called his name, but he didn't respond. Frowning, I went to the stove to deal with the chill.

The fire in the stove was almost out, so I threw in a couple more logs, careful not to extinguish the glowing embers, since there were only two matches left in the box on the nearby shelf. Hopefully I wouldn't have to use them because "don't snuff out the flames" was the extent of my knowledge on keeping a fire alive.

I was a city girl through and through. Right now, I wasn't exactly proud of that fact, but I couldn't change it either.

I waited hours for Gideon to wake up, eating half of the two remaining cans of food: peas and some tinned meat product that was pink yet didn't taste like pork. Every little sound outside the windows made me jump. I was certain that Anna had found us, but we remained undisturbed.

Stuck here.

When I was thirsty, I drank the water in the bucket, but my one attempt to give Gideon a couple sips using a small glass I found ended with the water going down his front, so I resorted to placing drops on his lips.

He didn't have any bathroom needs, but I did, gingerly making my way outside to do my business as quickly as possible, since my clothes, though dry and warm, were still no match for the weather.

Once Gideon was up and could lead us out of here, I planned to wrap my torso in blankets to stay warm enough to get back to civilization.

Meantime, I talked to Gideon. Just like I had with Robyn. It was as much to keep my own terror that he'd never wake up at bay as it was to encourage him to find his way back to me.

I reminisced about how one time at the beach Robyn saw these nuns walking along the promenade with ice cream and wondered if nuns could wear bathing suits. This turned into a running joke about a nun who was exceptionally pious except for her deep love of thong bikinis that no amount of prayer and guidance could break her of, leading to her new name, Sister Badonkadonk. (We were fifteen and this was the height of hilarity.)

I shared pranks I'd played in the lab as a grad student and the box of screws and dowels left over from putting together my different pieces of IKEA furniture that I'd "rake" with an Allen key as if it was a Zen sand garden because the sound was soothing in a weird way.

When my funny stories didn't work, I annoyed him with facts. Not science facts, since those wouldn't bug him enough to make him wake up and give me an earful.

"I'm going to share all the werewolf knowledge I researched when I got back to Toronto from Marrakesh," I said. "You can either open your eyes or be forced to lie there and listen to me because you're my captive audience." I added a villainous laugh, but he didn't react.

I sat on his cot with my knees tucked into my chest. "I bet you didn't know that the guy credited with making up a lot of the traits we associate with werewolves nowadays was a Jewish screenwriter who fled Nazi Germany. Werewolves obviously existed in myths way before him. They're even in the Torah with the story of Benjamin, and there's this whole Yiddish tale about one that was written in the 1920s, but this screenwriter gave the wolf man an origin story and the whole shifting during a full moon deal. This was in the early 1940s." I propped my chin on my knees. "I thought about you when I was reading all this because the screenwriter's version of the werewolf struggled a lot with his identity."

Gideon made a soft snuffling sound.

I patted his foot. The first few times he'd made noises during my monologues I'd gotten really excited, but he hadn't progressed past that. "Yeah, I figured you'd relate. Through no fault of his own, the wolf man was othered. No, it went further than that. He was cursed, not because of anything he'd done, but people viewed him as a threat. They were terrified because on the surface, he looked like them."

I gazed off into the distance. "You know how many times I heard 'you don't look Jewish' when I was growing up? Apparently, our people aren't supposed to be blonde with blue eyes, and we wouldn't want to challenge those negative stereotypes." I bit off a cuticle. "Robyn and I probably could have passed for Aryan if we'd lived during the Holocaust. I'm Jewish but I don't look it according to some prescribed view. I'm also a twin without my sibling, and I don't talk about it because I hate the pitying looks I get. Both those connections really matter to me, but it's hard not to let people's assumptions get to me, and it's exhausting to hear them. So, I keep my mouth shut, but denying a part of myself is horrible. It's hard to live in that skin."

Shaking off those musings, I lightened my tone. "Apparently in that *Wolf Man* movie back in the '40s, a pentagram would appear on his victims. That seems like a super Christian ethos, but if you look at it historically, it was people bearing a star who were marked for death. Same as the Jews were. Okay, this is staying dark. Maybe I should sing to you? I can sing 'Bohemian Rhapsody.' Phonetically, because I'm not sure of all the words, but you'd love that, right?"

Nothing. Nothing. And nothing.

I sighed and slid off the bed. "I need some water." I crouched over the bucket and scooped out liquid in my cupped hands.

"You should have offered to sing 'Werewolf In London,'" said a hoarse voice. "Way to stay thematic."

I jerked my head up. While Gideon had faint purple bags under his eyes, they were clear, and their hazel color had returned in full force.

I leapt across the room and crushed him in a hug.

He grunted, then hugged me back tightly—as if I'd disappear if he let me go.

Our embrace felt electric. My heart pounded against my chest as we clung to each other. His scent flooded my senses, and I breathed him in deeply.

As the moment lingered, we both pulled back, looking each other in the eyes.

"This isn't just adrenaline," he said. "Not for me."

"Me neither," I whispered.

Gideon reached out and brushed a strand of hair from my face, his touch sending shivers down my spine. "Can I kiss you?"

Chapter 22

Our mouths met. The exquisite dance of his hands, tracing a trail from the nape of my neck down my bare arms, sent shivers of delight skipping through my blood.

I leaned into Gideon, wanting to absorb everything he made me feel—strong and secure, like nothing could touch us here. His firm muscles were velvet beneath my fingertips; it was hard to resist the urge to run them all over his body.

Gideon moved his hands down to my hips and pulled me closer on top of the blanket, his lips again claiming mine and his erection pressing against me.

My heart raced and my body tingled. I felt like I was in a trance, swept out along tides of happiness that rose higher with every heartbeat. I rested my hands against his chest, exploring the contours of his body, and an electrifying surge coursed through every fiber of my being.

I broke the kiss, my thoughts scattered as I looked into his eyes, which held mine captive like a gravitational force.

The room seemed to shrink, collapsing into the space between us as if the walls themselves were drawn toward our magnetic connection. The air grew dense with an unspoken anticipation, and in that moment, it was as if time held its breath, freezing around us.

Gideon pulled back, breaking the spell. His chest heaved raggedly, and the intensity of his darkened gaze confirmed that he wanted to keep going as much as I did. He nuzzled his nose against mine, then sighed. "The timing sucks."

We didn't have Anna to deliver to the Queen of Hearts, my fake friend would be coming for my data, and until she was neutralized as a threat, there was no way I could start my job on January 4 in… I worried my bottom lip. I didn't even know how many days I had left.

"Yeah." I allowed myself one last nuzzle in the crook of his neck before heading back to the bucket to splash icy water on my face. It did nothing to quell my throbbing need for him.

"Now would be a good time for some dry, boring facts." Gideon sat up, the blanket sliding down to his hip. He caught it, then stared at his hand, transfixed. He flexed his fingers, even touched them with his other hand as if checking they were really there, but when he caught me watching him, he clenched them into a fist, which he dropped in his lap.

"I'm sorry," I blurted out.

"For what?"

"If I hadn't insisted on tracking Anna down, you never would have suffered…" I shrugged helplessly because I couldn't imagine the particular hell he'd experienced. "Whatever they did to you."

"That wasn't your fault," he said insistently. He tucked the blanket around himself like some kind of stoic Roman senator, not meeting my eyes. "Is there any food?"

Was he embarrassed that I'd seen him in that tortured state? He shouldn't be, but protesting he had nothing to be ashamed of would only make things worse.

"There was only a bit of food, but I saved you half." I

gave him the tins, expecting him to wolf down the contents, pun only sort of intended, but he ate with deliberate care like he expected to be judged. "I owe you dinner for saving my life," I said.

"Forget about it."

"Come on," I said weakly. "My life is worth at least a large poutine. I do have a doctorate after all."

"You don't owe me, okay?" he said harshly.

I flinched but nodded.

Gideon ran a hand over his hair that had matted up into golden curls. "It was luck more than anything that we were lower down on the mountain range. We only had a short hike before I found this place."

"It didn't feel short."

"Short enough. Can we table questions for later?"

I nodded again, feeling my heart sink deeper into my stomach. That closeness of a moment ago was gone, the lack of Gideon's touch making me shiver and wrap my arms around myself. Coming on the heels of that kiss, the coldness of his retreat was brutal.

Especially since I should have seen it coming. So much for smart.

Fabric rustled behind me.

When I turned back, Gideon was dressed in the sweater and waterproof pants, both of which were too short and tight. He didn't look comfortable, but it beat wearing a blanket.

"What's the plan?" I said briskly. "You shift, lead us to some village, and we call in reinforcements to go after them?"

"Fuck that." His eyes hardened to a deep amber. "I'm going back and finishing this."

"That's a brilliant idea. I'll hang out here and wait around for them to bring me your corpse before they kill me, shall I? Or perhaps I should try and get off the mountain myself with no jacket or mountaineering skills? Or wait." I snapped my fingers. "I'll go back and accept Ella's offer to cure disease and create more shifters using my serum. I mean, I always planned on having my own lab someday. This one is subterranean and evil, but it'll have the best toys."

"Who's Ella?"

That was the relevant part? I threw up my hands, seething.

His eyes bore holes into me while he waited for an answer.

"Ella," I said. "The woman you saved at Perrault Biotech."

"Your friend?"

I snorted, a dull ache twisting in my chest. "More like the opposite of friend. Try the big bad witch living in a hut on chicken legs."

"She's Anna? I saved the woman who made our lives hell?" His chest rose in a ragged breath, the wool sweater looking like it was hanging on for dear life. He strode across the room, picked up the metal collar that had fallen out of my jeans pocket, and shook it like he wished he could kill the inanimate object. "It was bad enough that she made me lose everything. This fucking device was designed to strip me of my humanity and turn me into a killing machine." He clenched his fists, his face twisting in pain. "Mission accomplished, right? I murdered that man?"

"Jeremy was going to kill me."

Gideon laughed bitterly. "I almost tore your throat out as well."

"Yet once again, when you had me at your mercy," I said, "you didn't hurt me."

"Because you hit me with a rock then broke my leg."

I shrugged unrepentantly. "Not a very top-quality killing machine if I could take you down so easily."

"Ah yes, another of your risk-averse life choices," he said dryly. "For the record, I was badly wounded, and my mind was somewhat broken. Cut me a freaking break."

"Jeremy wasn't a good person. You are."

He sighed heavily, slumping in defeat. "I've tried to be. I don't think I would ever lose all sense of myself when I'm my wolf under normal circumstances, but those scientists broke me."

"Gideon." I clapped my hands. "That's the first time you've called it 'my wolf.'"

"Yeah, well." He flexed his fingers. "There was a point when the scientists were forcing me to—" He sucked in a breath through his teeth. "I remember thinking that I couldn't hold on. I have no memories of anything after that, not even blurry flashes until this really clear moment where you were standing in front of me. It was like I'd been pulled up from drowning and could breathe. Then I saw that man with his throat torn out, and suddenly I felt thrown under again."

"When I first dented the latch, it must have loosened the hold of the magic in the collar just enough for your human consciousness to resurface."

"You stood there, armed with a rock." He shook his head, an incredulous expression on his face. "You told me off for being a bad wolf and quoted poetry at me. You were absolutely fearless. Glorious."

I blushed. "Thank you."

"Then the magic kicked in again, but you'd brought me out of the darkness, and I refused to be lost again. I took a chapter from the Dr. Montefiore playbook and threw myself back into the fight with everything I had. I could be fearless too, especially because I wasn't alone."

My blush deepened at all his compliments, but then my eyes went wide. "When you were chasing me out of the tunnels, it wasn't to hunt me?"

"Nope. I was trying to keep up, despite the leg you'd broken."

"Whoops."

"You've always been able to connect with me, whether I was man or wolf."

"I mean, the best versions of Red Riding Hood are the ones where she vanquishes the wolf."

"Hardly vanquished."

"Tamed."

"Like a *puppy*?"

I smothered my laugh at his grimace.

"Be that as it may," he said in an even voice, "if you were mistaken about my intentions, they will be as well. If they see me wearing the collar, they'll assume I'm still under their control and that I killed you. No one will expect me to turn on them and finish this."

"You can't put that collar back on."

"No shit, since I won't have opposable thumbs. You'll put it on right before we enter the underground forest. The latch is broken, so you'll have to make sure it stays on my neck."

"I hate everything about this plan. What if they capture us again?"

"Right now we have the element of surprise on our side." He dropped his gaze and ran his hand over his jaw. "I don't know about you," he said softly, "but I don't want to give this to someone else to finish, even if that's the smart thing to do. You don't have to come," he said more decisively. "I can take you to safety first and then go back. But I *am* going back to win this fight."

Not once in all these years had I had the element of surprise on my side. Anna had monitored me every step of the way, the facts of my life at her disposal. She'd known who my preschool teacher was to pull me into that first experiment, she'd known about Robyn's death, my grad advisor's name to pass on the job posting to, the details of my research at Perrault Biotech. She'd know about Levi too, and she'd happily use those facts to determine my next move.

All this time, she'd predicted every single step I took, because I was predictable. Even if I followed the trajectory of myths, I'd escaped the woods and now I should get to safety.

So no, going back wasn't smart, but it was my choice, and in the end, it might be the one move to save me.

"Red and the wolf go into the woods, but on our terms?" I said.

"Exactly!"

"Which are what, Gideon? We kill Anna and destroy the lab? We capture her and give her to the Queen to carry out her brand of vengeance?" I shook my head sadly and sat down on the cot. "My life has been shaped by some truly awful events. My family was gone, Dad and Robyn literally, and Mom checked out in all the ways that mattered. In searching for that connection, I trusted some parental figures that I shouldn't have."

With my own parents effectively taken from me at seventeen, I'd sought others to believe in me and validate my choices.

"I get that you've felt guilty all these years for your decision to let Robyn impersonate you," Gideon said, "but trusting Woody wasn't a mistake. Much as I hate to cut the guy any slack, because he fucked up badly and should face justice, he tried to protect you and your work from his mess. My dad never cared about protecting his marks' reputations or saving the things that meant the most to them. Real con artists don't have that instinct. Not even with the people they claim to care about most." He gave a bitter laugh. "Living with my dad made me believe that there were very few things, if any, worth risking yourself for. Woody knew your work and your dreams had merit. He believed in you.

So much that he risked all his plans being undone to ensure they'd come to fruition."

I watched a drop of water race another down the windowpane. I was doing it again, focusing on the horrible blip at the end of a relationship instead of the wonderful entirety of it. I'd cherished my mentor. Rightfully so.

Woody had spent hours patiently talking through my research with me, his unwavering belief in me had propped me up when things felt bleakest moving forward with my work, and in the end, even though he felt cornered, he protected me and my data.

True, he'd gone down a dark path in his single-minded quest for knowledge. It wasn't nearly as far as Anna had gone, but hadn't I stepped on that path as well, sacrificing everything for the serum? It was time to accept Woody as flawed without discounting everything we'd built together.

And without beating myself up for trusting him.

Did the same hold true for my friendship with Ella? Anna had lost her way and, in the process, lost her humanity. Not entirely; there remained a sliver of it in Ella. She'd memorized the scientists' drink orders and favorite treats, slipping them to us as a pick-me-up when we pulled an all-nighter. She ordered pizza for her office staff once a month, hovering protectively over them if any of the scientists tried to bug them during their dinner party. Those weren't evil manipulations; they were gestures from the heart from a woman searching for a familial connection as much as I was.

My life was definitely shaped by Anna, but it was shaped by Ella as well. Maybe the same was true for her where I was concerned.

It threw into question everything I'd assumed about the person I'd become—and the one I meant to be from here on out.

I didn't need a clean break from the past, because I believed in my serum for more reasons than my promise.

Also, because there were a lot of great memories in my life that I cherished and intended to revisit. I didn't want to lock them away any longer.

Having survived the woods once, I wasn't going to stray onto the wrong path now.

Inflicting vengeance on Anna was possible; the Queen would give us as many guards as necessary. It would likely come with strings, but if that was the path I intended to pursue, I'd deal with it. I didn't have to always go it alone and expect everything on my own terms. There were times that I'd have to compromise or become beholden to someone, and if my goal mattered enough, so be it.

However, in this case, I didn't have to be ruthless to get what I wanted.

I glanced at Gideon.

Especially since what I wanted had changed.

"I'll stop beating myself up for trusting the wrong people," I said, "but if I'm going to truly move forward, I have to trust myself above all else. So no, I won't kill Anna or give her to the Queen. We do either of those things and we've lost our humanity. I want to be better than that. I *need* to be better than that."

"You think Levi can make Anna face justice?" Gideon protested hotly. "She'll disappear again, and the Queen will have your head. Sula tried to kidnap Her Majesty's daughter when she was a baby. The Queen of Hearts has never forgiven that, nor will she forgive you for this." He grabbed my shoulders. "You're trading your life for Anna's."

"She won't disappear because I've got something she wants." For Anna to have achieved her extreme—albeit horrendous—goals, she had to possess incredible focus and be task driven. As our lab manager, Ella was one of the most organized people I'd known, deftly steering the company toward success, even when one of us went overbudget (cough, Woody) on a project. Plus, when Ella started a job, she had to finish it. She was a stickler for crossing things off her list, with all the T's crossed and I's dotted.

If I didn't count as unfinished business in her head, I don't know what did. I smiled coldly. She'd meet with me, all right, especially since I had the perfect invitation.

"I'm going to make Anna an offer she can't refuse, then I'll deal with Her Majesty. Besides, she'll have to get me into Hedon to entomb me, right?" I gave Gideon a cheeky grin. "It's a big world out there. I'm sure I can manage to steer clear of one measly alternate reality."

"Even if that's where I am?" he said. "I made a deal with the Queen of Hearts. I serve her. She'll come after me if she can't have you. Is Anna worth more than me?"

"Now you want answers about the two of us? Is that how it's going to be? You decide what you're comfortable discussing, and if it's too hard, you wall up? Or worse, ghost me again?"

"That's not going to happen."

"Based on previous experience, I beg to differ." I smoothed out the blankets on the cot. "May I remind you that the reason I showed up in the first place was because your ex-fiancée asked you to contact her? You remember, Janna, right? The woman who hoped to get back together with you, but you decided otherwise because you didn't want to tell her you'd become a shifter?"

"I remember Janna perfectly well, thanks. I also remember how much you love facts, and the fact is she's not relevant to my question. I told you we were over."

"She *is* relevant because ten minutes ago, I wasn't allowed to buy you dinner for saving me, and you certainly didn't want to talk about it. Your first instinct is to shut down instead of communicating. And this time you did it right after we kissed. Do you remember that part, or did you leave that memory outside your fortress walls, along with me?"

"I haven't forgotten a single second of a single minute that we've spent together." Gideon's eyes glinted dangerously. "And I sure as hell didn't shut down in that kiss or hold any part of myself back. You're turning this into something it's not. Why? Are you feeling guilty? That's *your* specialty, right?"

Asshole. I shoved him backward. "Then prove me wrong and tell me why you got weird about the dinner thing."

He scrubbed a hand over his face. "I didn't want us to be about who owed who and who saved who," he snarled. "What kind of life is that?"

I blinked, taken aback, because that wasn't in the top hundred reasons I expected from him.

Gideon was as smart, logical, and focused as I was. Like me, he struggled with emotion. I'd been telling myself that we were so different because he avoided the tough stuff, but hadn't I done the same? With my mom, with Levi? I'd avoided the hard but necessary conversations with my mother and ghosted my cousin, keeping my focus on the serum as the only thing that mattered.

I'd been so wrong. Gideon was the first person I'd trusted with my emotional wounds, but I should have reached out to Mom and Levi so we could share our pain and grieve together.

I think I was the first person who Gideon had trusted as well.

He watched me, his expression tight and his hands on his hips looking like they were digging painfully into his flesh while he waited for me to answer.

Gideon wasn't running from me now, he simply wanted any future between us to start as equals.

My anger left me in a rush. "You're right," I said simply. "Keeping score isn't any kind of life. But Gideon, what kind of life is it if we can't look ourselves in the mirror?"

"I'll look myself in the mirror just fine if we go back for them," he said.

"Will you? Really?"

He looked away.

I placed my hand on his sleeve. "We're not Anna and we're not the Queen. We aren't going to live in darkness, and we aren't going to stay lost in the woods. We're going to get out, make our stand, fight for what's right, and keep our humanity. There can't be anything else if there isn't that. Those are the terms."

I held out my hand—and held my breath.

Chapter 23

"You did say we should have New Year's brunch." I motioned for Anna to take the seat across from me at our favorite restaurant in Toronto. "Well, Ella did."

"I also said you should come work with me," Anna said. She unwound her familiar thick scarf and draped it over her winter jacket before sitting down. "Yet, you went for the least interesting option."

"I mean, it is the one with the fabulous eggs Benedict."

Our regular server came by with the pot of tea that I'd already ordered, and yes, we both got the eggs Benny. He chatted with us, and while I usually enjoyed seeing him, it was painful watching Anna fall back into being Ella in front of him.

"You need to up your cryptic clue game," she said once he'd left. Her Canadian voice reverted to her Slovakian accent. "Yours was far too basic and clunky. I figured out the answer was data in about a second."

The animated chatter and soft clank of cutlery covered our conversation, but I checked that there wasn't anyone at the next table before speaking. It might be freezing outside, but the sun was shining brightly, and people were out in droves kicking off the new year.

"It got you here, didn't it?" I lifted the pot of tea that I'd ordered. "Darjeeling?"

"Please." She scanned the restaurant while I poured. "I don't see the wolf. Did you bring House operatives? Some of the Queen's guards?"

"His name is Gideon," I said, topping up my own mug. "I have no idea where he is, but I kept my promise about this meeting. No operatives. No representatives of the Queen. Just me."

"Without the data, I imagine."

I smiled and added milk to my cup.

"Since I doubt you've changed your mind about coming to work for me, what's the point of this little get-together?"

As I watched my nemesis unfold her napkin and remove her cutlery, it occurred to me that truly risk-averse people did not invite the Big Bad to brunch.

I really wasn't risk averse; I never had been.

You're only getting this now? Gideon's wry voice said in my head.

Yeah, okay, Mr. Smarty-Pants, but I was finally ready to stop telling that story. To lose that skin. It had never fit properly anyway.

I was intelligent enough to know which risks were worth gambling on. Besides, I liked being the woman who ran with the wolves. Or one wolf. Wherever he was.

However, meeting with Anna was the smartest course of action—and if I got a rush from the possible danger of it, well, I wasn't lying to myself about it. Once I'd determined my plan, a feeling of peace had descended over me. It hadn't been without its bumps. Neither Levi nor the Queen had been happy about my text saying I was fine and further information was to come, but this was my way forward.

My way out of the woods once and for all.

The server deposited our plates.

"The point," I said, cutting into the delicious runny mess to get egg, sauce, and English muffin in my first forkful, "is that I'm done with you running my life from the shadows."

"If that were the case," Anna said, "you'd have handed over your research. Your stubbornness was charming once, but I'm finding it less and less cute." She shrugged. "My people are in place. You'll hand over the data before this meal is over."

Thus far, Anna had followed normal brunch etiquette, however, she wasn't eating or even pushing the food around on her plate. Had our shared love of this dish been a lie or was something else up?

My stomach clenched in a knot. I wiped my mouth with the linen napkin while covertly studying the restaurant. She'd admitted her operatives were coming for me, yet I didn't see anyone who obviously fit the bill.

Wait. She hadn't specifically said they were here, just that they were in place. That could mean anything. She'd shown no hesitation in torturing Gideon and sending him after me. Did she plan to harm someone else I cared about?

Anna was watching me, so I dug into my food again, even though my appetite was gone.

I chewed a mouthful that tasted like cardboard and rejected my impulse to warn her away from any of my loved ones. This called for fearless mode.

"Once you have the data, you'll use your stolen gold token to vanish yet again." I scooped up some hash browns. "Will you be changing your name once more? Your face?"

Anna, refilling her mug with tea, peered suspiciously at me. "Why are you so calm? I've accounted for all the outcomes of this meeting and none of them end in your favor."

There was a high probability that she was right on that score.

I pressed my hands between my thighs until I was certain their shaking wouldn't betray my brave façade, then I forced myself to keep eating. Damn. Being consciously fearless was tough. "That's very Doctor Strange of you."

Anna grimaced at the reference in such an Ella-like way that my heart twinged. "I hate Marvel," she said. "You know I'm a DC fan from way back."

"Yeah." It was something we'd bugged each other about. I'd figured it was an act, but I guess there had been some truth between us after all. I tightened my hold on my fork and knife. It had been a good friendship. Time to send it off in style. "Did I ever tell you about my dad's love of mob movies?"

Anna squinted at me, her brows wrinkled, then settled back in her chair with her tea. "No. Is this a warning that I'm going to find a horse head in my bed?"

"Well, he did pass on his love of *The Godfather* to me and Robyn. With all the mob films we watched with him, all that violence, the scene that always stuck in my head was an opening scene where a saloon owner refuses to buy beer from some guy. A little girl has gone in to get something, and as she's leaving, she realizes he left his briefcase behind and runs after him, calling out for him."

"I assume it explodes and everyone dies. What does that have to do with me?" She scratched her jaw. An itch or a signal?

I peered into the teapot, then flipped the lid over.

"Raisa?" A blonde woman in really nice soft-looking leisure pants and a brightly patterned blouse did a double take as she passed by our table with her friend. "I haven't seen you in ages. Are you coming to the Italian club's New Year's open house?"

Anna knew I didn't have a lot of friends. She also knew I attended club functions sometimes out of some weird sense of obligation to my dad, who'd been a member.

"Not sure yet." I stood up to speak with her. "Anna, this is Jan. Jan, Anna."

Janna Favreau, House Ontario legal counsel, and definitely not a member of any Italian club. "Nice to meet you."

"You too," Anna said.

The "friend" had been lingering shyly behind Janna, but she stepped forward, standing next to Anna. "Vanessa. Hi."

"Hi," I said. "Would you like to join us?"

Anna arched an eyebrow at me. "We aren't finish—" She blinked at the soft click.

Vanessa had pulled a pair of magic-nulling cuffs out of her pocket and slapped them on Anna's left wrist. Before Anna could jerk away, the woman grabbed her free hand and slapped the other cuff on. "Anna Sula, you're under arrest by the authority of House Ontario."

Not only was Anna's magic nulled, so was the gold token. I'd learned that fact from Gideon.

Anna laughed incredulously. "On what charges? I haven't done anything wrong."

"Oh." I clapped my hands together. "This is where that movie gets relevant. See, the title of that film was *The Untouchables*, and it was all about Eliot Ness's attempts to catch Al Capone. After everything that mob boss did, you know what tripped him up? Tax evasion."

"Which I am also innocent of," Anna said, snapping her wrists against the cuffs.

"True, but you lived in House Ontario territory under an assumed name as a Mundane for years." Shark Janna was back. "Failure to register as Nefesh with our House is, in fact, a criminal offense."

"Uncuff me," Anna said to me, "or in about five minutes, you're going to deeply regret it."

Right. Those people she had in place. Mom had come back here to Toronto and was waiting at our House HQ until she got the all-clear from me. Anna might touch Dr.

Nakahara, but after thinking long and hard, I'd decided that the high-profile Mundane was safe.

Everyone else who mattered could take care of themselves, and if they weren't safe? It wasn't on me to save everyone or be terrified that if I didn't, I'd failed them.

"Take her away," I said to Janna.

She jerked Anna out of her chair.

Other patrons had stopped their conversations to stare. I did too, because the look on Anna's face was priceless. Her expression twisted and she snarled at me.

I held up a hand, cutting off any villainous threat she was about to level. "I contacted House authorities in Bratislava and gave them the location of your lab. They're raiding it now, and they'll have a lot of material to sift through. I'm sure Dr. Eggers and your other staff will deeply regret not having you able to write them reference letters for their new positions, but," I said with a sigh, "as someone who's survived similar career upheavals, I assure you they'll land on their feet. In prison, obviously, but still."

"You could have made a real difference to the lives of so many people." Anna sneered.

Like Robyn, Gideon, Miss Toby, the hybrid shifter who'd killed himself after he attacked us, and, yes, myself. "I have. And I'll continue to, except on my terms."

Janna and Vanessa led Anna off, though Janna glanced around the restaurant once more with a hopeful look before she left. Gideon still hadn't contacted her? Idiot.

After our mad dash down the mountain where he'd made me ride him wolfy-back to stay warm (which was neither sexy nor comfortable, but way cool), he'd shifted to human, put the clothes from the hut back on, and called his bank to free up funds to get us to Toronto by plane since he no longer had a gold token.

We'd landed yesterday, on the afternoon of January 1.

Gideon stuck around long enough to make sure I got home safely, then said he had things to take care of and left.

I was certain he'd be back. There was a high probability anyway. Okay, it was a reasonable assumption.

Sighing, I called back the server for some more hot water, then texted Mom that she was good to leave House HQ. I was about to add that she might want to join me here, but she replied that she'd already left and was with a friend. I shook my head.

I also texted Dr. Nakahara Happy New Year and that I'd see her bright and early the day after tomorrow. She replied that she was looking forward to it.

I leaned back in my chair with a relieved sigh. I wasn't sure if I'd ever get over the shock of Ella being Anna and the length that her shadow had cast over my life, but I'd meant everything I said to Gideon. Ever since I lost Robyn and my dad—and Levi and Mom in different ways—I'd wrapped myself up in science as a coping mechanism to keep going.

Just like Anna had.

But I wasn't alone anymore. I had my cousin back, along with Ash and their friends. Plus, I had new colleagues to befriend, and I intended to find Woody. I'd help him remain in hiding, but I wanted him in my life, however he was comfortable with.

I also had Gideon. We hadn't discussed what we were or even if we intended to pursue anything between us and that was okay by me. Gideon had to figure out his life, though as far as I was concerned, it shouldn't involve him playing servant to the Queen. He was meant for justice, not vengeance.

As was I.

So, I had no regrets about handing Anna over to House Ontario instead of to Her Majesty. I didn't want revenge. Not anymore.

I fell upon my delicious eggs Benedict and hash browns,

and was soaking up the last of the sauce with a piece of bread when there was a commotion at the restaurant's entrance.

The Queen of Hearts pushed past the hostess, her furious gaze zeroed in on me like a laser scope. Moran followed her, his expression grim, then Ash, who held tightly to the arm of a very tense Levi, her body slightly in front of his like she was keeping him from attacking the other two.

Blue eyes that were twins of my own met mine, filled with worry. Levi hadn't left me in the caves of his own volition.

I let out a relieved sigh and motioned to the server. "You better move me to a—"

Four servers were already falling over themselves to attend to the Queen, setting up a table in a private dining room that despite all my previous visits, I had no idea existed.

Moran and the Queen ended up across from me, while I was flanked by Ash and Levi.

I ordered tea for everyone and a couple of the restaurant's dessert samplers.

"We're not here to eat," Moran said in his nasal voice.

"You stormed a local business and now you will sit down and enjoy their excellent selection of cheesecakes." Honestly, after the past few days, I didn't have the energy to be scared. All my fear had been completely exhausted. What remained wasn't necessarily fearlessness, but more a breathless, heady version of que será será.

Also, I was mostly convinced that the Queen couldn't nab me and statue me up.

"Mouthy." Hedon's ruler frowned. "I see why you're fond of her," she said to Ash.

Levi draped his arm over my chair. "I'm fond of Raisa too. Since she's my cousin and all."

"Okay, before we get into a pissing contest over me…" I

248

grimaced. "Not the best phrasing, but you get my point. How did you know I was here?"

"Gideon texted all of us saying Anna was at this restaurant with you right now. Guess he got the timing off." Ash popped a forkful of chocolate cheesecake in her mouth, swallowed, and smiled. "You're right. This is excellent."

"Anna Sula has been taken into custody by House Ontario for not registering as Nefesh," I said.

"*The Untouchables*." Levi nodded. "Nice."

I grinned—he'd watched his share of mob movies with us on family vacations—and put a square of cake on a plate. "For that you get the entire piece of key lime."

"Sweet!" He grabbed a fork and dug in.

I returned to my portion of classic New York style cheesecake, but Moran pulled my plate away before my fork hit the dessert and the tines bounced off the tablecloth.

"You and Stern promised to deliver that woman to the Queen. You cannot break promises to Her Majesty and expect to get off consequence-free."

Even the slightest delay in reporting to Her Majesty was life-threatening, but Gideon had agreed with me that this was the best outcome. He'd made sure Anna was arrested and taken away, but I had no idea he planned to send this group in.

"Is Gideon okay?" I said sharply. "He's not in a dungeon or anything?"

"Since he contacted us from Toronto," Moran said, "he's fine."

"Which is how he will remain," I said. "Even if he returns to Hedon and does a little dance in front of you, you will not touch him."

The Queen smiled. It wasn't soft or pretty. "Why are you so certain of this, chica?"

"Because we didn't come to this decision lightly, but in the end, Sula's fate was not yours to decide." I pulled my dessert closer with a warning look at Moran but didn't eat yet. "Did Anna actually kidnap your daughter, Your Highness, or did you foil the attempt?"

Ash choked on her dessert, and Levi reached past me to pat her back with a shake of his head.

"What do you think?" she said contemptuously.

"I think that your daughter is lucky she had you. My sister and I were lucky to have our parents too, but they couldn't keep us safe, and…" My voice faltered.

Levi took my hand.

"They didn't even know what had happened to us until after Robyn's death," I said. "The shock killed my father, and it made my mother run away from me out of guilt. I didn't understand that because the entire thing was so traumatic that I suppressed all memory of it. So, in the case of Anna Sula, yes, I broke my promise to you, but her impact on me trumps what happened to your daughter, and I made the call."

The Queen blinked her violet eyes and poured herself some tea. "It's a sad story, but what's the real reason?"

"Excuse me?" Levi said icily and leaned forward. "Are you saying my cousin lied or that she didn't suffer enough?"

Moran's eyes glittered. "Keep going with that tone of voice, Montefiore. It'll take you all kinds of interesting places."

Ash tutted him. "You're outside Hedon. No Black Heart Rule protection for you. Keep threatening my fiancé. It'll take *you* all kinds of interesting places."

"Stop it, all of you." I ate a forkful of cheesecake. Yum. Fan-freaking-tastic. "All of that really happened, but yes, I was still ready to hand Anna over to you. That wasn't a lie. Then I met her and discovered she'd been posing as my friend and former lab manager for the last three years."

Levi let out a soft whistle.

"She'd been watching me my entire life. Directing my

every move. She asked me to come work with her, and when I said no, she augmented Gideon somehow and sent him in to kill me."

"Yet you still let her go," the Queen said.

I swallowed my food before speaking. "I didn't 'let her go.'" I made the air quotes. "With everything the House in Bratislava has found by now in her labs, she'll be put away for a long time."

"Entombment lasts longer," Moran pointed out. He was actually pouting.

"Anna was once a good person with a family and a career," I said. "Then tragedy struck and she got all twisted up. There but for the grace of God and all that. I didn't keep her from becoming a statue for her sake, I did it for mine, because I was on that same road and I had to get off. I'm asking you to let me have that closure. As a woman who understands power, let me take mine back. But in terms of consequences, I talked Gideon into this plan. Blame me. Not him."

"Sula is with House Ontario and will likely be transported to Bratislava?" The Queen abruptly pushed back her chair and stood up. "Come, Moran."

She waltzed out of the private dining room, her henchman following her.

Moran stopped at the door. "I'll see Mrs. Hudson on Sunday." It wasn't a question.

Ash nodded. "Same as usual."

The second the door shut behind them, I sagged back against my chair. "She's totally going to kidnap Anna and take her to Hedon, isn't she?"

"Yeah," Ash said. "But your conscience can stay clear. Once Anna was in House Ontario's system, the Queen would have gotten that information regardless."

"You went for justice, not vengeance," Levi said. "That's what mattered."

"Is it?" I pushed away my plate, sickened by the thought of Anna joining those other statues. I told myself that she'd brought this on herself by attempting to kidnap the Queen's daughter, but this wasn't justice. It was a fate worse than death. Anna would be trapped there for all eternity. *Ella* would be trapped there. The fact that I'd played a role in that, despite my best efforts otherwise, would haunt me forever.

I sighed. "How come you didn't come looking for me? I was gone for days, and I'd told you where I was going."

"The Slovakian House were being dicks," Levi muttered.

"Next time you host a leader you think is a closed-minded asshole," Ash said, "maybe use your inside voice and you won't run into problems when it's urgent."

I punched my cousin and he flinched. "You're lucky I'm alive."

"I know," he said. "And to celebrate that fact, we're going out for drinks."

"I guess we're still on holiday time but it's only 11AM, and we're not exactly day drinkers."

"It's later where we're going."

Despite my curiosity, I shook my head. "Rain check? The past couple weeks have been a lot, and I need to get in the right mindset for my new job on Thursday."

He pointed at me. "That needs to be celebrated properly as well. What if I said drinks were in Rome? Not just drinks; dinner from one of Italy's top chefs."

Levi, his parents, and my dad had all been born there, but I'd never had a chance to visit. "You don't pull any punches, do you?"

"Nope." He smirked, then wrapped me in a hug. "I'm just proud of you, Red. You did it, on your own terms. That deserves something extraordinary."

"Then by all means. Token me away to the Eternal City for some dolce vita. Unless it's not safe to use the token for a while?" We'd have to jump via Hedon, and I didn't want any greeting parties.

"The Queen will leave us alone." Ash winked at me. "I'm not sure how Anna avoided detection using her gold token, but it sure would be nice to have that model and be able to go about my business, because I see far too much of Moran. Oh. Before I forget." She held out a velvet bag. "Your earrings. I figured you might want to put them in before we go since it's a fancy place."

"You bet I do." I took the bag, relieved to have that part of myself back. Yes, the familiar was good, but so, too, were new beginnings. "Before we go, I want to tell you both that I really was honored you asked me to be part of your wedding party, and my answer is yes."

Levi grinned. "Obviously you are and obviously it is."

"Imperious." Ash sighed.

"I'm simply right with statistically improbable frequency," he replied.

He insisted on paying the bill, leaving me and Ash to chat. After all these years, I had a family again. There was still a long, bumpy road to get my relationship with my mother back to where I'd like it, but I'd get there.

After all I'd survived, I was still standing, and more than ever, I liked the person I'd become. Scarred, wiser, more cynical, but also more ready to embrace emotion and not just facts.

The Baba Yaga World Tour was finally over, save for one final encore in Rome. Not bad, if I did say so myself.

Chapter 24

My cousin took one look at my wardrobe and declared it entirely unsuitable for our destination. I was lucky he didn't comment on the rest of my place, though given his eye twitch, it took a ton of willpower to keep his mouth shut.

I studied my starter apartment with its university furniture and dead plants and decided that I wouldn't be staying here much longer. This place had been cheap, but it hadn't been home. I hadn't been ready for that. Now I was. After I settled into my new job, I'd start looking for a nicer place that aligned better with my new station in life.

After our split-second transit through Hedon, Ash brought Levi and me to the front of a building made of dark sandstone blocks with narrow stone balconies staggered up the front. Discreet glass doors tinted black slid open, allowing us entrance into one of Rome's most opulent hotels.

Levi commandeered the penthouse suite like that was a perfectly normal thing to do.

It was crazy, but who was I to look a ridiculously-expensive-for-one-night-of-drinks gift horse in the mouth?

There was barely time to poke through the expansive

living room, the bedroom with a gold gild canopy bed, and the bathroom that was larger than my kitchen before the makeup, hair, and wardrobe stylists that Levi had arranged at a moment's notice (i.e. thrown obscene amounts of money at to make happen) arrived, their arms laden with supplies and garments.

Ash refused to let me wear black for our night out, insisting this was a party. She forced me to go with a floor-length royal blue satin gown that Cinderella could have worn to the ball. The full skirt actually billowed out when I spun—which I did until I got dizzy. The halter top didn't allow for a bra, not that my girls were huge, but the stylist did something with tape that made them perkily sit there as if defying gravity.

My blond hair was slicked back, and I was given a smoky eye with light lipstick. Combined with all my blingy ear piercings, I looked like an elegant stranger.

I also looked beautiful.

The princess transformation was complete with matching sparkly sandals.

"You clean up pretty good, Red," Levi teased. "But there's one more thing you need." He handed me a flat velvet necklace box.

I wrinkled my nose. "How did you have time to buy this?"

He simply looked smug.

I opened the box, gasped, and almost dropped it. A dainty ruby heart hung from a gold chain. Deep in its center was a crooked dark line. I'd recognized it at once because it had been our nonna's, passed down on her mother's side. Family legend was that when this ruby was originally given to a bride, it didn't have any flaw in it, but there was a terrible earthquake in her village, and she lost her family right before the wedding. Her sorrow was so vast that the ruby heart broke along with her own. The thing about the women in my family was that they didn't lie down and die; they persevered. When the heart was passed on to the bride's daughter, it was done so as a symbol of resilience.

Nonna used to call it "Big Red" in her broken English.

I fired off a torrent of Italian curse words at my cousin because I was crying, and I had no idea if my mascara was waterproof.

Levi clasped the chain around my neck and kissed the top of my head. "Now quit giving me heart attacks."

"No promises," I said shakily and went to find the makeup artist.

We were waiting for Ash to come out of the bedroom where the wardrobe stylist had whisked her away into when she called out for Levi, her voice thick with frustration.

"The damn zipper is stuck and I can't get out of this dress. I need help."

Levi rolled his eyes good-naturedly and said he was coming. He slid me a key card. "I got you a room for tonight, but for now, head up to the rooftop lounge and get yourself a drink. We'll be along momentarily." Ash cursed loudly from behind the closed door to her room, and he grimaced. "I hope."

"Uh, okay." It was a little weird to be kicking off my special celebration night alone, but whatever. I tucked the key card into the matching beaded handbag I'd been given and headed out.

I couldn't stop admiring myself in the reflective glass of the elevator to the top floor because I was so fancy. Honestly, this dress had set a pretty high bar; the place they'd chosen had a lot to live up to.

The doors opened on a restaurant with a sweeping panoramic view of Rome. The dome of St. Peter's Basilica rose above the jumble of softly illuminated apartment buildings, which ranged from ancient to merely pre-dating Canada newbs. I practically floated to the window in time with the soft piano music from the musician at the baby grand.

"What are you doing here?"

I jumped at Arkady's voice. "Levi and Ash brought me here for drinks. Why are you here?"

Arkady, clad in a dark suit that fit him like a second skin, narrowed his eyes, then put his two fingers into his mouth and whistled.

I flinched.

"Jesus, Ark." Miles was at his side in a second, also in a beautifully tailored suit. He frowned at me, a highball glass in hand. "Raisa? Why are you at our impromptu team thank-you dinner?"

"I'm not. They brought me here for drinks."

Priya, outfitted in a stunning green gown that matched her eyes and her bobbing emerald earrings, hurried up, clutching a wineglass. "Mummy and Krishan are here," she hissed.

She nodded none-too-subtly at a striking older woman in a dark gold sari, standing with a slender man a few years older than Priya. He had the rigid posture and conservative air of a banker.

"Dad couldn't make it because he's on a business trip," Priya said. "Ash told them I was getting some kind of promotion, and my dumb brother started in on me demanding to know about my upgraded benefits. What the actual hell?" She saw me, did a double take, and then planted her free hand on her hips. "Oooh. Those tricky bastards."

Arkady nodded. "Right?"

I laughed, the penny dropping. Drinks and team dinner, my ass. "Ash faked a zipper emergency to get me out of the room."

Miles looked between them in bewilderment. "Can someone please tell me what's going on?"

257

Rafael trundled up, unsurprisingly also in a bespoke suit. "I just ran into Levi's mother and..." His eyes widened comically. "Ooooh."

Miles pinched the bridge of his nose. "They're ditching the House wedding that we've spent months arranging security for and holding endless meetings of protocol regarding other Houses, and getting hitched now, aren't they?" He lifted his highball glass with an expression like he was a drowning man and shot it all back.

A woman in her early twenties in a deep purple gown with striking—and familiar—violet eyes hustled over to our group. She bore down on us like a woman with a mission, her fluffy hair floating around her adorable face like feathers. "So, Ash invites me out to dinner as a belated birthday present complete with this gorgeous dress," she said in a stage whisper. "In Rome, which is crazy enough." She leaned in, her eyes wide. "Then on my way out the door, Mom and Moran announce they're coming because Ash insisted on treating them to dinner to say thank you for behaving reasonably at some meeting today?"

"The Queen is here but not a single House Head?" Miles swayed, looking faintly green.

Arkady grabbed the highball glass before Miles lost hold of it and set it on a nearby table. "Did you bring a stress ball, babe?"

"Where are they?" Priya looked around the restaurant, but there was no sign of them.

No one was here other than our group and Priya's family. Levi must have bought the place out.

"They're on their way," the young woman said. "Moran was forbidden from wearing white, which a fun message to deliver, but because of it there were wardrobe issues." She stuck out her hand. "Hi, I'm Isabel. You must be Levi's cousin, Raisa." Her smile deepened, bringing out a dimple.

This was the Queen's daughter? But she was so sunny and cute.

"Everything you're thinking?" Arkady murmured into my ear. "Yes."

I shook her hand. "Nice to meet you."

A thin blonde woman in pale mauve entered the restaurant, looking around as if searching for someone, but her expression turned tentative when she spotted me.

My heart leapt into my throat, but I crossed over to her. "Zia Nicola."

I hadn't seen her since Dad's funeral, and the years of resentment that she hadn't reached out bubbled up.

"Raisa," she said, her Italian accent heavy with emotion, "you've grown into a lovely woman. Your father would be so proud." Tears filled her eyes. "Sam tried to get me to leave Isaac so many times, but I wasn't ready, and I'm so sorry I wasn't there for you."

I took a deep, slow breath. Seeing Zia Nicola after all these years brought back memories that I had buried deep within me. Good ones of my father, Robyn, and all the time we spent with Levi, Zia Nicola, and even Zio Isaac. However, there were also memories of the events that led to our estrangement.

As I held her hands, looking into her warm eyes with the familiar scent of her Chanel perfume wrapping around me, my anger melted away. She'd been Zio Isaac's victim, trapped under his thumb. He was the one who cut us off, after my dad, his only brother, died. Nicola had suffered enough.

I didn't want old baggage and outdated resentments in this new chapter of my life.

"I'm sorry too, Zia," I said. "I wish things could have been different before, but they will be now."

My aunt squeezed my hands. "Me too, bella, but we can't change the past. All we can do is make the most of the present."

I nodded. It was overwhelming to see her after so long, but a weight had been lifted off my shoulders. "Maybe we could have dinner the next time I visit Vancouver?"

Zia Nicola smiled. "I'd like that. I'd like to see your mother again too."

"I'm sure she'd like that as well," I lied. My smile faded when my aunt left.

Mom wasn't here, and there's no way Levi would have left her off his guest list. That meant, even though she didn't know this was a wedding, she wasn't ready to be in contact with him yet. He was still too much of a reminder of what she'd lost.

Despite the warm, lavish atmosphere, the fact that she wasn't here for this tinted everything in a melancholy gray. Would she feel regret when she heard that she'd missed the wedding, or would it be one more thing she'd use to keep her distance?

I walked over to the bar, intent on casting off my sorrows with a stiff drink. The bartender, a middle-aged man with a receding hairline, greeted me with a smile.

"Can I get something strong, please?" I said.

He nodded and poured me a generous amount of whiskey, a swirl of amber with a strong, almost sweet scent. I took a sip, feeling the liquid burn as it went down my throat, the fruity note that tasted kind of like apple pie catching me off guard.

I held the rest of the glass up to Ash and Levi in a silent toast.

Priya joined me with a flute of prosecco and a plate holding a mini potato latke drizzled in something that looked like crème fraîche. "Try this."

I'd popped the appetizer in my mouth with a happy moan when a ripple ran through the room. It started with the staff closest to the door, speared to Miles loudly grinding his teeth, and ended with Isabel facepalming as her mother held out her hand, expecting a glass of prosecco to be placed in it.

Which, to be fair, it was.

The Queen of Hearts wore red, as always, this time in a sumptuous silky gown that hugged all her curves.

"She's definitely on the bride's side," Rafael joked. "I can't believe Levi let Ash invite her."

Moran had traded all white for a black shirt and a black suit with a modern cut. He sported a red pocket square to match the Queen's dress.

"Is he wearing a bolero tie?" Arkady sputtered, gesturing with his glass. "Who does that?"

Miles elbowed him sharply, drawing one hand across his throat.

Priya grinned and waved at a woman with a sharp blond bob in a severely tailored pantsuit. "Talia!"

The woman smiled warmly and waved back, headed for my zia Nicola.

"Ash's mom," Priya explained.

Another blonde woman in a fantastic sheath dress entered behind Talia. I recognized her a second later: Levi's executive assistant, Veronica. She and I hadn't gotten on well at our first visit, and I decided to steer clear of her now.

Veronica openly gaped at our surroundings, then she wrinkled her brow, and shook her head with a laugh.

Priya smirked. "Levi pulled one over on the dragon."

"She's *not* an all-knowing oracle?" Rafael said. "What a relief."

A hotel employee in a suit clapped his hands to get everyone's attention. "Prego," he said in a loud voice. "If you'd all follow me to the terrace?"

We followed him around the curve of the restaurant and through tall wooden doors onto a terrace with more of that jaw-dropping view. On this side of the hotel, it featured the Colosseum, its arches lit up, the forum to one side, and an enormous white monument made up of many stairs and columns topped with two huge bronze statues of winged deities in a chariot pulled by horses. Ancient crumbling walls and colossal pillars stood side by side with former palazzos from the sixteenth century, and piazzas were dotted throughout the city with patches of tall sculpted trees providing clusters of green space.

If it weren't for the occasional siren and distant sound of traffic, it would be easy to forget we were in the twenty-first century.

Stiff white fabric panels hung overhead in the shape of an open fan. Chunky blue and green glass vases on high bistro tables held bouquets of wildflowers, each one surrounded by a cluster of tea lights, while the night air was transformed into a warm breeze courtesy of free-standing patio heaters.

Flower petals in every color of the rainbow were strewn in a path from the door to the Jewish wedding chuppah at one end. It had a billowy white top, and its four poles were wrapped in garlands of wildflowers and fairy lights.

Zia Nicola laughed aloud in pure delight when she saw the chuppah.

Her Majesty took up position across the flower-strewn pathway from me. It's not like sides had been delegated to all of us guests, but I decided that yes, she was on the bride's half.

I bobbed a nervous curtsy at her, which she calmly took as her due with a regal head nod.

Isabel rolled her eyes.

A string quartet launched into a light classical tune, and a silver-haired female rabbi in a black suit and a white tallis walked through the door and down the aisle to the chuppah, smiling and holding Mrs. Hudson's leash.

Ash's sandy-colored pug trotted along with tongue lolling out and a crooked flower garland around her neck.

"Dog sitter, huh?" Priya muttered.

Ash and Levi entered together. My cousin looked dapper in an elegantly cut black tux, his black satin kippah matching the trim on his lapels, and Ash was a vision in her off-the-shoulder white lace wedding dress with its long flowing train.

They could have been wearing sackcloth because the only thing that mattered were the serene, utterly certain smiles on their faces, the way their fingers were intertwined, and the look they shared before proceeding toward the chuppah.

The surroundings were beautiful, but their love for each other was mesmerizing.

We stood around informally while they were wed in a short Hebrew ceremony. I shivered in a good way under the sense of history, tradition, and the coming together of this new family. Everyone else was just as rapt, completely and joyously focused on the ritual. Miles even stopped grinding his teeth. Mostly.

When Levi stepped on the glass wrapped in a white cloth to break it, all of us burst into wild cheers and applause. He dipped Ash and kissed her.

Both of them looked dazed, flustered, and delirious with happiness when they broke apart and the rabbi whisked them away to sign documents.

Servers came out with trays of appetizers and more drinks.

I wouldn't say the small group of guests mingled exactly, since I kept my distance from the Queen and Moran, but it wasn't uncomfortable either. Zia Nicola happily chatted to the ruler, who seemed animate and engaged, instead of cynically amused, while Moran and Miles bonded over the lack of visible security in the restaurant.

I overheard Talia and Priya's family discussing legislation

designed to deepen Nefesh rights in Canada that Talia had written.

The happy couple, hands clasped, made their entrance to "You Shook Me All Night Long" by AC/DC, which seemed like a weird ass choice.

Priya spit out her prosecco in laughter, so there was clearly some inside joke there.

Mrs. Hudson trotted along beside them, her wreath gone and petals stuck to her fur.

Levi held up his free hand to silence our clapping. "I realize this is a bit of a shock to some of you, especially after all the trials and tribulations of arranging the wedding so far." He grinned wryly at Miles.

"All those security plans just scrapped." Miles sounded pained.

"I wasn't going to have my best friend working at my wedding," Levi said.

Miles opened his mouth to argue, but the entire friend group, including Levi and Ash, shot him incredulous looks, and he capitulated the point with a shrug.

"Besides," my cousin said, "if the combined force of the people here can't handle any threat that might arise, then no one can. That said, the hotel has excellent security." He put an arm around Ash and tugged her close. "Our wedding was turning into a circus, something for the public and not us." He shook his head. "We couldn't do it."

"We're sorry we pulled being in the wedding party out from under your feet," Ash added. "It meant the world to us that you'd stand by our side while we said our vows, but external pressures were driving things out of control. We wanted to simplify it down to the things that mattered, the *people* that mattered, not rituals for the sake of some tradition we didn't care about, or political appearance."

My cousin announced that he'd bought out the top three floors with rooms for everyone. This wasn't a huge hotel, but it was hardly chump change to have done that either. He'd even chartered a private plane to take everyone back to Vancouver the next day, though he paused and grinned cheekily, adding, "My wife and I won't be on it."

Everyone gave knowing oohs. Ash blushed and ducked her head, but Levi looked smug.

Ash swung their clasped hands. "Levi and I got to this point because we built something together—"

"After you drove us all crazy for years annoying the crap out of each other," Priya said, none too quietly.

Levi laughed. "Fair. Each of you are part of our foundation, and that's why we chose to start our marriage walking down the aisle together, surrounded by the people who shore us up and make us stronger. Sorry we couldn't give any of you more notice, but it was all in limbo until Raisa came back safe and sound."

I gave a loud sniff and drank some water to clear the thickness from my throat, but someone else had gotten loudly verklempt as well. I glanced over my shoulder, sure that it was my zia Nicola, but it was the Queen.

Moran pulled out his pocket square and handed it over.

Ash smiled fondly at Her Majesty, who dabbed her eyes, while the rest of us looked carefully away. Then Ash grinned. "Now let's party!"

Chapter 25

It was the bash of the century. One of Rome's top chefs prepared dish after dish of divine food, paired perfectly with wine. Not like I had any clue about that or even drank it, but Rafael kept nodding approvingly.

Better still was all the laughter and good-natured ribbing during the impromptu speeches.

Levi and Ash's first dance was "Come Rain or Come Shine" by Ray Charles, then everyone piled onto the floor to dance the night away.

Moran and the Queen went back to Hedon, the swordsman insisting on taking Mrs. Hudson with him. Priya and he had a bit of a tussle over that, since apparently, she had co-custody of the dog with Ash, but she capitulated.

I think it was mostly because Isabel and Priya's brother, Krishan, had been hanging out all night, and she wanted the Queen's attention off her sibling. The three moms, Geeta, Talia, and Nicola, meanwhile, banded together. They were getting happily hammered and dancing their asses off.

Somewhere around 1AM, I was sitting on the sidelines, eating a jelly doughnut from the tower of them that formed the wedding cake, and watching everyone: Levi and Ash swaying dreamily together despite it being a fast song, Arkady trying to embarrass Miles with more and more outlandish moves, and Priya and Rafael laughing and egging Arkady on.

It had been awesome being part of this. I wasn't the girl who had to be the center of attention anymore, but I didn't want to be as introverted and secluded as I had been since Robyn's death either. Tonight had shown me a happy medium.

Arkady beckoned me onto the floor, but I shook my head with a smile. The events—and emotions—of the last couple weeks had hit me hard. Combined with all my socializing this evening, well, I needed to get away and spend some time recharging.

I set my water glass down and said my goodbyes, claiming fatigue.

Everyone tried to get me to stay, but Levi simply took a good look at me, and bundled me into a huge hug. "Thank you for being here," he said.

"I wouldn't have missed it for the world." I hugged Ash next. "He picked a winner. Welcome to the family."

She squeezed me tight. "You and I are going to spend some one-on-one time soon. I want to hear all about your new job."

"I'd love that." After a final round of hugs from Priya and Arkady, I took the elevator down to my floor.

I toed off my heels with a sigh of relief, and let my feet sink into the plush carpet. Hooking the straps in one finger, I ambled to the far end of the hushed hallway, tipsy and full, past large vases in alcoves holding tasteful arrays of white flowers.

I flicked on the light to my suite—and dropped my heels. Did I need a room that was the size of my apartment?

No. Was I going to take advantage of every bath sample and minibar item in the place? Hell, yes.

I tossed my clutch on the wine-colored velvet sectional and plucked a chocolate-covered strawberry off the small platter of fruit and pastries on the coffee table. Popping it in my mouth, I peeked out the cream curtains, grinning at the same panoramic view that had captivated me upstairs on the terrace.

I danced my way into the bedroom, complete with a glass fireplace, and onward to the bathroom, where I had to brace a hand on the tiled wall and sigh at the choice of jacuzzi tub or huge shower with multiple jets, both facing tinted glass windows overlooking the city.

The artisanal bath products were laid out on an embossed silver platter, and the bath towels were the size of small area rugs. Squealing in delight, I hopped back to the bedroom and threw myself backward on the mattress.

Tonight had been a dream. I touched my ruby pendant, my arm brushing blue silk, and laughed. I'd even had a fairy godfather. I closed my fist around my nonna's jewel, my smile faltering at the heavy fizziness in my chest that was not quite sorrow and not quite excitement.

Being with Levi had healed a last fractured piece inside me. While it was impossible not to see how much he and Ash loved each other, I wasn't jealous.

I felt more like I was caught in unfinished business.

I found my phone and texted Gideon. *Fancy a drink in Rome?* I added the hotel's details and my room number.

Moran had mentioned that Gideon had been given a new gold token, which was a relief. Sort of. He was in Her Majesty's good graces and not a statue, but I guess he was also still working for her.

It's not like I sat around and waited for Gideon to reply, but by the time I'd smelled every bath product, tested the hand and face creams, poked through the minibar, and eaten another two strawberries, he hadn't shown up.

Well, the ball was in his court. He could be asleep, or being mauled by a fanged manta ray and unable to return a text like a polite human being.

Or, he might have freaked out that I'd seen too many of his self-perceived imperfections and run.

I dug inside my dress and ripped off the boob tape that had been lifting, separating, and keeping my nipples from poking anyone's eye out. I wadded it into a ball and tossed it in the trash, feeling fully anchored on my own for the first time that I could remember.

All I could do was trust Gideon to come back. And if he didn't?

Gideon had made a difference to my world and that alone was worth thanking him for. If he wasn't interested in more, I'd be sad, but I'd survive and keep thriving. People would come into my life, and sometimes even the important ones would leave far too soon, but I'd deal with it.

From now on, I chose to honor life, not death, and that included the fact that in giving someone a chance to live, I had to be okay with the choices they then made.

I rubbed my chest, brushing away the wistful pang. I'd be okay, but damn would I miss him.

Enough of that. Nothing was going to ruin the excellence of tonight for me. I gave a sassy double snap at my reflection in the mirror by the front closet.

There was a soft rap on the door, and I jumped a half foot.

Gideon was here? It was him, right? Who else could it be? I frowned. I hadn't ordered room service. It could be someone from the wedding party wanting to see if I was up, but I doubted it was some stranger since Levi had bought out this floor and—

"I got out of a warm bed to take you up on that drink."

Gideon's voice was low, raspy, and grumpy. "You better not be having second thoughts, Donatella."

I tamped down my grin, opened the door—and almost swallowed my tongue.

Gideon hadn't thrown on any old thing to come visit. He looked tough as nails and hot as hell in a dark formal suit.

I blinked at him. "You dressed up."

"So did you." He raked a slow gaze over me.

The one thing I had never ever doubted about myself was my intelligence, but right now I was feeling about twelve kinds of dumb. Had the obvious way to interpret a "come for a drink in the middle of the night at my hotel in a romantic city" occurred to me before I'd sent the text?

No. Nope. Not even a bit.

Obviously I was fine with it going in that direction, but I hadn't presumed that would be the main event.

Gideon gently cleared his throat. "I dressed up because I looked up the hotel and saw how posh it was. We can go out or stay in. It's your choice. I just came for a drink."

"Okay." I bounced on my bare toes. "The minibar is on Levi's tab, and we are totally raiding it. Also, there is nothing mini about it. It's literally made out of a vintage steamer trunk."

"Have you never stayed in a hotel?" he asked, shutting the door behind him.

"You've seen my place," I said. "You think the kind of hotel I can afford has gourmet chocolates, handmade taralli, or a house brand amaretto?" I waved at the sectional. "Make yourself at home. I'll get the amaretto."

When I returned with two crystal cordial glasses and the bottle of amber liqueur, Gideon had settled in a corner of the sofa. I poured us both a drink and handed his over. "Salut," I said, clinking my glass to his.

"L'chaim." He sipped it, then nodded approvingly. "Smooth."

"It's the vanilla beans."

"There's notes of apricot too."

"I did not know that."

He nodded. "I can taste it."

Hello, awkward silence.

"Why are you in Rome?" he asked.

"Levi and Ash got married."

"Nice wedding?"

"It was perfect."

"Good for them."

We smiled politely at each other. Small talk: the eighth level of hell. Somebody throw me in a brimstone-stinky fire and be done with it.

I sipped my amaretto, tasting none of the rich flavor that I had before. That silence a moment ago hadn't been awkward. That was a precursor. The two of us had survived more dangerous situations than any normal person should, and yet, this oppressive hush that was so thick you could cut it with a knife was going to be the death of us. House-keeping would find our beautifully outfitted corpses in the morning. I ran a finger around the rim of my glass, really wishing I'd formulated what to say before I'd invited Gideon here.

"Raisa?"

I jerked my head up. "Yes?"

"While you're sorting through the tangle of thoughts running rampant in your head like weeds—"

"You're not funny." I glowered at him.

He spread his finger and thumb a little bit apart. "I have something for you."

I sat up straight and narrowed my eyes. "A present? Why?"

Reaching into his suit, he paused. "Most people say 'yes, please,' not appraise the giver like a security threat."

"Well, you know, after everything I've put you through." I shrugged one shoulder. "None of it was a traditional gift-giving occasion. Unless the gift involves a hit squad and you being free of me forever."

He pulled out a small, flat-ish package and gave it to me. "Just open it."

Curious at what this squishy thing was, I tore off the wrapping, and shook out the item.

It was a black V-neck T-shirt in my size. Emblazoned across the top was "Baba Yaga World Tour." Tour stops of Toronto, Hedon, Vancouver, Bratislava, and the High Tatras were listed on the back, while the front was dominated by a silkscreen of a Red Riding Hood figure riding on a wolf's back, her body bent close to his and the wind streaming her cape out behind them as they careened out of a forest.

I opened and closed my mouth several times, but when words failed me, I felt the soft fabric, feeling the smoothness of the design under my fingers. It was a touchstone of our adventures, a reminder that despite everything that had happened or how this story had started, there was this bond between us.

Gideon's frown grew deeper and deeper. "Okay, I guess I'm not totally fluent in your expressions, because I can't tell if you hate it or if you're at a loss for words at what an amazing gift giver I am."

What other man would have done this for the woman who'd blown up his life?

"Do you like it?" he asked, a hint of nervousness in his tone.

Like was too paltry an answer. I could use the scientific method to parse out every emotion swelling up inside me, quantify and label them, write a scholarly publication on my findings, and still not have captured the entirety of my response.

Though, perhaps in the end, all I needed was one word. I mean, if it was good enough for the Tenth Doctor?

Cool silk rustled around my legs as I leaned in close.

Gideon held himself warily, his eyes tracking my movements as I laid my hand on his freshly shaven cheek.

"Geronimo," I said—and kissed him.

Chapter 26

The kiss was a tingle on my lips, a slow, gentle exploration that filled my blood with honey. My eyes fluttered shut with a sigh, and I splayed my hands over his chest, falling into the sweet lingering alcohol taste of him.

Suddenly, Gideon nipped on my bottom lip and pulled away sharply.

I snapped my eyes open because that wasn't the start of a sexy fun game. It was the full stop end of the kiss.

"If this is some kind of damn thank-you for the shirt," he said tersely, "you don't owe me."

He was so prickly, holding himself carefully away from me, but his eyes burned, drowning me in a hungry light, and his fingers twitched like he'd been presented with a toy he'd been waiting a long time for. Like the only thing that kept him from pouncing were his manners—and those were being severely tested.

My insatiable curiosity poked its head up. *Pouncing, hmmm?*

"I want you," I said simply. I paused. "Though we should probably talk about—"

He laid his finger against my mouth. "Dear God, no."

I arched a brow imperiously. "I shall not be silenced."

A wild and dangerous grin split his features, his eyes glinting in amusement. "Challenge accepted," he murmured, cupped the back of my head, and slanted his mouth over mine.

The world melted around me. His touch sparked an electric charge that ran down to my toes, and I was gripped by a wild exhilaration like the rush of going over a waterfall.

So this is pouncing. I clutched the front of his shirt.

Gideon kissed me hungrily, his tongue tangling with mine. He gripped my waist with one hand and hauled me onto his lap, snaking his arm around my back to lock me against him.

My sensitive nipples were two stiff peaks, and every brush of our bodies sent chills through me. I greedily pushed his jacket off his shoulders, wriggling against his hard length.

Gideon sucked in a breath. "Slow down." He trailed his lips along the column of my throat, running his hands up my thighs.

My nerve endings flared up like he'd hit full tilt on a pinball machine, and I arched up against him. "Want. This. Shirt. Off," I panted, fumbling at the buttons.

"Not yet," he said evenly.

"We've been on multiple death-defying adventures," I snapped. "How much more foreplay do you need?"

I was being tossed in the ebbs and swells of desire, already far from any familiar shore. My skin was hot and tight and I rubbed against him, because even this with Gideon was better than I'd ever felt with anyone else. Was it not the same for him? Was that why his control didn't appear tattered?

Gideon sighed heavily. "You're thinking again." He rested his forehead against mine. "You've got a fearsome intellect, sweetheart, but we are really going to have to work on shutting the damn thing down."

I squirmed, half turned on beyond belief at the compliment and the endearment, and half wanting to challenge the shutting-it-down part, but he lowered his head and sucked my breast into his mouth, the fabric becoming hot and damp, and my mind went blank. He laved my nipple with his tongue, and I groaned lustily.

"Better," he murmured, and turned his attention back to using his mouth on my heavy, tingling breasts.

My bones liquified, my brain was mush, and I had only enough motor function to clasp his shoulders and hold on for this ride. I writhed against him, my body throbbing, and my underwear soaked.

He groaned harshly and stood up, swinging me into his arms.

"Is it naked time?" I said hopefully, my arms clasped around his neck.

He shook his head sadly. "You're still capable of speech. I haven't done my job well enough."

I smacked him and he winked, diving in for another hungry kiss without breaking his stride to the bedroom.

He deposited me on the mattress, his body stretched on top of me and his lips never leaving mine. The air between us grew hotter with every passing second. His hands roamed over my body, exploring every curve and contour, sending shivers of pleasure through me.

I wrapped a leg around his waist, pressing myself closer to him, the blue silk puddling to one side.

His hard length pressed against my thigh.

My heart pounded in anticipation, and I deepened the kiss.

Gideon let out a low growl of desire, his nostrils flaring. "You have no idea how sweet you smell, as aroused as you are."

I flushed and covered my face with my arm, but he gently moved it.

"Don't ever be embarrassed by being turned on." He scrubbed a hand over his face like he was overwhelmed for a moment. "Fuck. I've got to taste you." He moved away.

My fingers closed on cold air, but I chose to not be embarrassed and happily embrace whatever came next. Hopefully me.

Nothing happened.

I cracked an eye open.

Gideon stood at the edge of the bed, bathed in moonlight, looking down at me with a reverent expression. The front of his shirt was wrinkled and half-untucked, and his erection tented the front of his trousers. "You aren't Red Riding Hood," he said. "You're fucking Cinderella." He shook his head. "But I'm no prince, baby."

I propped myself up on my elbow, my breathing ragged. "No, you're my wolf, and it's time for one of us to get eaten. And by one of us, I mean me."

He threw back his head and laughed. He was magnificent, teasing and arousing me in equal measure, both in and out of bed. He was also far too dressed, but one thing at a time.

Gideon sank to his knees. "As you wish."

I pressed a hand to my heart. "A pop culture quote? I *am* rubbing off on you."

"Yeah," he said softly. "I watched it the other night. Inconceivable, right?"

The no doubt brilliant teasing I was formulating fled, because he slid my underwear off with one swift motion and licked my clit.

"This would be a good place to employ the scientific method," he said.

I fell onto my back. "You are seriously fucking with me."

"Not yet, but I will be. Back to this scientific method though. You once told me step one was to make an observation that describes a problem. You need to get off. Now I ask a question, right?"

Smiling, I closed my eyes. "Right."

He slid a finger into me. "Why are you already soaking? Want to know my hypothesis?"

I wriggled against his hand. "Does it involve short-circuiting my vibrator in an unfortunate dishwasher mishap?"

He gave a shocked chuckle. "No. I was thinking more of a lack of competent human partners. Until now."

"You plan to test that, do you?" I asked.

"I do." His voice was full of smug satisfaction, but it was hard to get mad at the guy when I was riding his hand and he'd gone back to using his tongue in such an exquisite manner.

I fisted the sheets, my hips rolling in tighter and tighter spirals, lost to a tsunami of lust. Every atom in my body fizzed higher and higher, until I crested and cried out his name, shattered. Once I'd returned to reality, I opened my eyes. "You need to run another test."

Gideon sat back on his haunches. "Well, you are the scientist. Far be it from me to question your wisdom."

"Good. Stick with that line of thinking." I sat up and crooked a finger at him.

He lunged for me, the two of us falling back against the mattress in a tangle of lips, limbs, and laughter.

I finally got that damn shirt off and ran my hands over the hard planes of his sculpted chest, following their path with my lips and teeth.

Gideon, working down the zipper of my dress, hissed and pushed me onto my back. He wriggled the fabric off me and pitched it onto a chair.

I reached for the ruby pendant, but he stopped me.

"Leave it. It glows against your skin."

I whisked his belt from its loops, the glossy leather supple in my hands.

Gideon plucked it away from me. His hair stuck up in tiny, disarrayed spikes. "Thanks. I have plans for that."

I tilted my head, my eyes narrowed, and my tongue poking into the corner of my mouth.

He grinned crookedly. "I am going to enjoy finding all the ways to put that fascinated expression on your face."

"I don't want to be spanked."

"Not in the plan, but good to know." He stood up. "Anything you don't like, don't want, *ever*, say the word and I stop. Okay?"

I nodded. "What are you going to do with the belt?"

He caught my wrists, wound the belt around them, and pressed the length of leather into my hands. "Don't let go." He positioned my arms above my head, then reached for the button on his pants.

I let my knees fall open. There was something heady about lying there naked and exposed, bound in his belt, while he undressed.

Gideon rocked back on his heels and shucked off his trousers in record time. His cock sprang free, and he fisted it a couple of times in his hand.

I tracked the movement, sucking my bottom lip into my mouth. I had a hypothesis of my own. This was going to be a tight fit.

Gideon went down on me again until all I heard was my harsh panting. I would take a tight fit so long as it got him inside me now. He positioned himself over me and licked a stripe up my body. Then his mouth was on mine. Capturing my wrists in one of his huge hands, he drove himself inside me.

I tensed and he immediately stilled.

"It's okay," I assured him. "I just need a second to adjust."

"We don't have to—"

"I swear to God, Gideon, if you use more of that preter-natural Canadian politeness on me right now, I will punch you."

He pressed his lips together, his shoulders shaking.

I squirmed underneath him, wishing I had a free hand to smack him. "Shut up and fuck me. This is in the interests of science, remember?"

It was like I'd given him the permission he required for his control to snap because he drove into me, pounding me into the mattress, each thrust harder and deeper than the last. With his free hand, he played with my clit, his mouth capturing every single one of my moans.

I licked salty moisture off his sweat-soaked skin, my fingers flexing on the belt in time to his thrusts. The scent of leather and his natural aroma of rich earth and cool air teth-ered me and kept me from floating away.

Gideon growled. A wild sheen covered his drugged-out hazel eyes, and his kiss was as carnal as our fucking. He'd unleashed himself on me.

I came hard.

He followed seconds later, calling my name in a ragged moan. A moment later he rolled onto his back next to me. "I love science."

I burst out laughing and Gideon joined. I lay there in a puddle of mushy happiness, my body aching in all the most delicious ways.

"What are you humming?" he said.

I chuckled softly. "I didn't even realize I was. It's this old R&B song called 'Lovely Day' that was one of Mom's favorites. Whenever she heard it, she'd grab whoever of us was nearest and dance around. Robyn learned it and would sing along." I pulled a snarky face. "But my asshole sister only let me sing backup because my voice sucked."

Gideon rolled onto his side, his head propped in his

hand. "That's the first time I've ever heard you say something normal and bitchy about your sibling."

"Come on. I said plenty about her when…"

"When she was alive?"

I winced. "Robyn would have haaaaated being canonized. I'm amazed she hasn't come back and haunted me for it. Oh wait. I did the haunting for both of us." I stared up at the ceiling.

"What are you thinking?"

I traced my thumb along the edge of my ruby pendant. "Now that I'll have a steady paycheck, I'm going to fund a scholarship in her name at WONDER, the arts organization where she did all her singing and drawing lessons."

He kissed my shoulder. "Can you spend the day with me here in Rome or do you have to go back and get ready for your job on Thursday?"

I smiled because he'd remembered my start date. "I think I can probably hang around provided someone uses their gold token to take me back." My fevered skin had cooled. I shivered and nudged him. "Gideon."

He pulled the blanket over me. "For the record, I resolved things with Janna."

My body still throbbed, every single place that he'd kissed me tingled like a neon map, and I was still bushwhacked from the two orgasms he'd given me. Gideon was not a douchebag. There was no way he'd have fucked me if he'd gone back to her. Plus, he'd made it clear that it was over between them.

"We scientists like to be very, very careful with our definitions," I said, gripping the blanket like a weapon. "What exactly do you mean by resolved?"

"Huh?" He sat up, his eyes going comically wide. "No. I didn't—not like that—I wouldn't—" He raked one hand through his hair, flapping the other like he was trying to get liftoff.

I pushed him back down onto the bed and draped myself half-over him. "I know."

He sighed and nodded. "I meant that I spoke to her. She deserved to know why I left the force and that I was honestly okay now." He went quiet again.

"Is she working with Slovakian authorities to sort everything out? If the Queen has Anna, is there still a case?"

"I think so. Everything is tangled up under at least two countries' laws, and it's a mess."

I poked his side. "Don't make me beg for scraps of your thoughts. How did it go with her?"

"Sorry. It went fine." He pressed a kiss to the corner of my mouth. "We're on the same page about us being a thing of the past. I even told her..." He took a deep breath. "Okay, here's the thing. I've been struggling with an identity, a skin that didn't fit right for a while, but I wasn't ready to admit that to myself."

"A lot easier to focus on becoming a shifter," I said, wondering where this was going.

"Exactly. You keep saying you blew up my life, and yeah, you did, but it was the best thing that could have happened to me. Being a cop was great, but I don't miss all the bureaucracy and bad policies and red tape. I want to keep working for the Queen."

My heart sank and I sighed, clutching the ruby heart, and reminding myself that above all else, Montefiore women were resilient. "You're a man of justice, not vengeance."

I hoped.

"I made my moral line clear. I'll only take on assignments that make the world a better place, but it's time to stop letting my dad dictate who I am."

"You realize stunt car driving is the infinitely safer choice, right?" I said, but my words had no heat to them.

"I can live with this version of myself, shifter and all.

No, more than that. I'm excited for it, but are you okay with me working for Her Majesty?"

Gideon hadn't gotten stuck honoring a death like I had. His rut had been in honoring a life, or more precisely, putting his mom's well-being above his own. Now he'd found a way to make his skin fit, and I didn't begrudge it.

This was his choice, and I would honor it.

I nodded. "I'm more than okay. Besides, it's not like I've been Little Miss Prudent where Her Majesty is concerned, and if push comes to shove, I'll get tips from Levi on how to deal with her. He learned to live with the Queen for Ash's sake, and I will too."

We could form the Montefiore "Help, My Partner Is in Deep with Hedon" Support Club. Huh. I wondered if Levi would make biscotti?

Gideon traced a finger along the curve of my hip. "I told her that arresting Anna was my decision, but she didn't believe me."

I laughed. "I said the same thing."

"Great minds." He rubbed my back. "Moran sent guards to Toronto to keep me company while she determined the truth for herself. I was able to call Ash and Levi, but I couldn't be there with you. I'm sorry."

"It's okay. I needed to handle them on my own. By which I mean, sandwiched between Ash and Levi and their combined resources and force. Is everything truly copacetic with you and Her Majesty?"

"Yes. We squared everything away between us. I'm going to also keep investigating concerns outside Hedon on her behalf that she can't be seen to be a part of." He grinned wickedly. "No red tape. It'll be fun."

"Concerns like Golden Radial. Will you be working with Janna?"

"I'm not sure, but maybe. I wasn't sure how you'd react."

I shrugged with a lightness I didn't feel. "It's your life."

"Don't." He clasped my shoulders, preventing me from moving off him. "I want it to be our life. I've spent years believing that very little was worth risking myself for and that being vulnerable was to be avoided at all costs."

"That's understandable given your dad."

"Understandable but wrong. Living behind these walls was cold and lonely. It wasn't fair to Janna, and it wasn't fair to myself. But you tore them down." He threw his arms wide. "I am all yours. I can't promise I won't fall back into bad habits and run if I can't handle the emotional stuff." He took my hands in his. "I'm asking for grace when I mess up because I'm not as fearless as you. In return, I swear that the second I realize I'm doing that again, I'll turn around and come straight back because you're worth risking everything for."

A dopey smile spread across my face, and I leaned in to kiss him. It was a soft, sweet kiss, a promise that I was his as well, but my heart pounded in my chest, and I felt a newfound freedom and excitement. Being with my wolf would be a wild ride, but I couldn't wait to see where it led us.

"I foresee more commemorative T-shirts in our future," I said.

He grimaced, then winked. "I don't know how any of this is going to work," he said. "There's no precedence or previous data set for a Hedon-based wolf and a Toronto scientist, but maybe we can come up with a hypothesis and test it for the next eighty years or so?"

His tone was teasing, but his expression was dead serious.

I held up a fist. "Go, science."

"Go, science." Gideon knocked his fist against mine. "So, you wanna do some more testing?"

"You better believe it."

"Good." He gazed up at me with heat and affection.

My world was no longer grief, regret, and a constant unease like the dark woods were pressing in, but there was no such thing as a storybook ending either. Bad things would happen, but the difference now was all the good people I had in my life.

So no, I didn't believe in happily ever after. But once upon a time? I smiled at my wolf. Yeah. That had just begun.

∾

THANK you for reading LOST IN THE WOODS.

If you enjoyed this book and want to be first in the know about bonus content, reveals, and exclusive giveaways, become a Wilde One by joining my newsletter: http://www.deborahwilde.com/subscribe

You'll immediately receive short stories set in my various worlds and available FREE only to my newsletter subscribers.

Now, are you ready for more funny, sexy urban fantasy storytelling, but with a smart librarian in her forties?

It's a truth universally acknowledged that angry women get shit done. Miriam Feldman is ditching her shapewear and letting her magic fly free.

Turn the page for a sneak peek from THROWING SHADE (Magic After Midlife #1).

Sneak Peek of Throwing
Shade

A man kneeled next to Alex's body. He seemed a few years younger than me, probably in his late thirties, and was about six inches taller, putting the shifter at about six-foot-two. His hair was a riot of dark curls.

The man's jaw was firm, his lips full, but right now, they were set in a severe line. Moonlight kissed the olive skin of his broad shoulders and leanly muscled torso, a trail of hair leading down to—

Jeans. I gusted out a breath.

The man huffed softly. "You came back," he said dryly, with a slight accent I couldn't place. "You've got balls, I'll give you that."

I gave a weak laugh and he locked his brilliant emerald gaze onto mine. Thickly lashed, his eyes were what I would have called beautiful in his human form, but there was a hardness to them—like he'd seen too much and all innocence was long gone.

Eli had looked that way after his first year in homicide. Fuuuuck! This guy had to be a Lonestar. Okay, looking on the bright side, he could help me find Jude—if he didn't destroy me. I'd been so bent on getting answers from Alex that I'd thrown away every single safety procedure that I'd lived by and shown a stranger my magic. I could have left when the shifter took off with Alex but no, I had to play detective.

I reached behind me, clutching the railing because my legs felt rubbery.

The Ohrist reached into a duffel bag, revealing a nasty silver jagged scar that ran halfway up the left side of his back, and pulled on a faded blue T-shirt that said "Bite Me." This wasn't a gym rat with a six-pack for show; he was a warrior and his body was his well-honed weapon, in or out of wolf form.

Ohrist magic was based in light and life, while Banim Shovavim powers were rooted in death and darkness. Historically, they'd taken that as clear-cut signs of good and evil. They pitied Sapiens but had hunted my kind into near extinction.

There was even a skipping game sung by Ohrist kids: "Clap for the light, 'cause light is right. All other magic is a blight. How many shadow freaks will we smite?" At which point they'd jump as fast as they could while counting.

I eyed the wolf shifter with a sinking feeling that he'd probably counted pretty damn high.

Maybe he didn't remember the exact details of his time in his wolf form? Could I bluff my way out of here?

"Did you want something?" he said, impatiently.

My brain short-circuited. "I'm guessing that light magic allowed you to cut through his breastbone and rib cage only using your claws," I said, "but why isn't there blood all over the place?"

I could have smacked myself. This was not the time for curiosity or further questions like "How do you have more than one magic ability?" It was the time for well-crafted lies.

"The magic cauterized the blood vessels." The man rolled his "r's." He grabbed a box of table salt from the duffel bag.

"Regular sodium," I said thickly. "How bland. I prefer Pink Himalayan to balance the delicate flavor of human flesh."

"I'm not eating him." He dumped the salt over the corpse. "It interferes with the scent so animals don't show up before Ohrists get here to retrieve the body."

"That's good, because cannibalism can make you sick. You get this brain disease called kuru and—"

"Like mad cow?" He tapped the last of the salt onto the body with a contemplative expression.

I blinked. People didn't generally come back with follow-up questions to my random facts. "Not quite. People can't get mad cow disease, but in rare cases they get a form called…" I shook my head because cows, mad or otherwise, were not the issue. "Was Alex human?"

Or was he some other species entirely and did that make a difference to the answer? He had looked human, even if what was inside of him wasn't.

My moral compass was having trouble finding true north.

"Not anymore," the wolfman said.

I knelt down beside Alex to close his lids because his lifeless stare felt accusatory, but the man batted my arm away.

He lay a hand on the deceased's forehead and stared into his eyes as if committing him to memory. There was both a gravitas and a resignation in the shifter's expression, and I couldn't tell if he did this to honor the dead or torment himself with a parade of his kills. Maybe it was one and the same.

When he was done, I checked Alex's back pockets for his wallet.

"The man's body isn't even cold and you're robbing him?" Wolf Dude said.

"I'm looking for identification," I said through ground teeth. There was a cracked phone but no wallet. It must have fallen out at some point during the fight. A vise tightened around my chest and I shoved the Ohrist, banking on the fact that if he'd intended to hurt me, he'd have done it already. "You ruined my chance to get information about—"

"I saved you." The man stuffed his bare feet into motorcycle boots, which also came out of the duffel bag. "I don't know what interrogation skills you think you have, but I can assure you that dybbuk wouldn't have given up shit."

"Dybbuk?"

"Merde," he said in perfect French. Ah. "You went after him without knowing what you were dealing with?" His full lips twisted. "Fucking BS."

He remembered.

I took two wobbly steps back, Delilah by my side, but he didn't come after me.

He laced up his boots. Okay, he was a derisive son of a bitch, but he lacked the horror others of his ilk displayed upon meeting my kind, nor did he seem inclined to kill me.

I'd take the win.

"Alex had attacked me once already," I said, "and if he did something to my friend—"

The shifter pulled out a beaten-up brown leather jacket and shrugged into it, his shoulders bunching. "Then she's gone. Sorry for your loss."

My eyebrows shot up. Yes, this guy was an ass, but surely he was connected to an infrastructure that could help me find Jude. "Sorry for your loss? How about you help me find her? Aren't you a Lonestar?"

He laughed without an ounce of humor. "Hardly."

Then what was he? He'd already killed one person, and yes, that dybbuk thing seemed to justify Alex's death, but I was alone out here. If he was working on his own vigilante moral code, how safe was I?

I eyed the stairs. How many were there? Thirty? Then perhaps another fifty feet to lose myself in the crowds in

Terence Poole Plaza? He'd be faster than me, even as a human. I bit my lip. If I screamed for help, would anyone come?

Screw that. I had magic and could cloak and get away at any point, but his rudeness was grating. I threw my hands up. "That's all you have to say?"

"No." The man raked a shrewd glance over me. "Should we ever have the misfortune to meet again, get out of my way."

"Or what? You'll huff and you'll puff and you'll blow my house down?"

He bared his lips, briefly shifting his canines to wolf form. *My, what big teeth you have.* A strangled laugh burbled out of me. My epistemological crisis involved a hell of a Freudian undertone.

"I'll do whatever the fuck is necessary," he said.

"Is that your action hero catchphrase or something? Because it's a little on the nose."

He zipped up the duffel bag. "My reputation doesn't precede me? Shocking." His voice was laced with bitterness.

"Wow. Someone is full of themselves. I've got no idea who you are."

He peered at me suspiciously. "Are you new in town?"

"No."

He shrugged. "Then you know who I am."

"Hate to disappoint you, but you're just some rando who crashed my party and ruined my plan—"

"To get answers from someone who wouldn't tell you anything you actually wanted to know. Brilliant strategy. You've the mind of a tactician. Even if you did get something out of him, did you think he'd let you walk away after?" His accent thickened when he got annoyed.

"I had my shadow."

"I wouldn't brag about that if I were you."

"For your information, I'm doing an admirable job.

Before yesterday, the only monsters I had to worry about were of the human variety." I shot him a pointed look.

"There's no way you didn't know about dybbuks. You're too—" He snapped his mouth shut.

Delilah pulled up behind me. "Oh, no," I said "Finish that sentence."

The man crossed his arms, rustling the leather. "Old," he said levelly.

My shadow bopped Wolfman in the nose with a swift jab. Ha!

The man pinched his nostrils together to staunch the bleeding, his emerald eyes glinting dangerously.

My amusement drained away, my magic swirling around my feet, ready to cloak me, but I'd hit the wall and I was out of fucks to give.

"Should we ever have the misfortune to meet again, get out of my way," I said.

"Vraiment? Why?"

"I'm a woman in my forties who's remembered how powerful she can be. Don't fuck with me, Huff 'n' Puff." Head held high, Delilah and I sailed past him into the night.

Acknowledgments

Thank you to Italy for an incredible trip that refilled my creative fuel, and to my editor, Dr. Alex Yuschik, for helping me turn a first draft that I was ready to set fire to, into this fantastic story.

Writing this book happened while recovering from ankle surgery, a bout of Covid, and facing some serious personal challenges. I definitely felt lost in the woods more than once. To all my family and friends who kept pulling me back onto the path, I love you and thank you.

About the Author

Former screenwriter, global wanderer, and total cynic with a broken edit button, Deborah Wilde writes funny, sexy urban fantasy books and paranormal women's fiction.

Smart, sassy women who can solve a mystery, kick supernatural butt, banter with hot men, and still make time for their best female friend are the cornerstones of Deborah's stories. Her books are beloved by readers craving magic adventures, swoon worthy steamy romances, hilarity, and happily ever after.

"Magic, sparks, and snark!"

www.deborahwilde.com

facebook.com/DeborahWildeAuthor

Made in the USA
Coppell, TX
09 April 2024

31109446R00173